Samantha—she wa[...]
naive as a chil[...]
passions of a woman. . . .

Captain Abdul stared at Samantha in disbelief and then threw back his great head and roared like a bull. "*You* are going to make a deal with *me*? Didn't you forget something, my fine lady? *I* am captain of this ship—*I*!" he shouted. "*I* give the commands. *I* say how each man—and each woman —will earn his way, and *I* have other plans for *you*!"

He grabbed Samantha roughly, pulled her head back viciously by her long tawny hair, and punished her lips with his. She tried to scratch and claw at his face, but he pinned her arms behind her back easily with one huge hand. Then, letting go of her arms, he quickly grabbed at each side of her shirt and ripped it off. Samantha gasped in horror as she stood before him in nothing but Freddie's knickers.

Captain Abdul could not suppress his astonishment and delight as he gazed at her high, firm breasts, surprisingly full and as white as pearls. He picked her up easily and carried her to the bed. It was the first real bed she had lain on since leaving China. The satin sheets felt cool and inviting against her bare back and, for an instant, she sank sensually into the downy mattress. Then, catching herself, she tried to roll off the bed, but she was no match for Captain Abdul.

His voice thick with lust, he said, "I want to drink from your white fountains, Samantha, and I will, whatever you do. . . ."

SAMANTHA

Angelica Aimes

PINNACLE BOOKS   LOS ANGELES

This is a work of fiction. All the characters and events portrayed in this book are fictional, and any resemblance to real people or incidents is purely coincidental.

SAMANTHA

Copyright © 1978 by Angelica Aimes

An original Pinnacle Books edition, published for the first time anywhere.

First printing, June 1978

ISBN: 0-523-40351-8

Cover illustration by Bill Maughan

Printed in the United States of America

PINNACLE BOOKS, INC.
One Century Plaza
2029 Century Park East
Los Angeles, California 90067

SAMANTHA

Prologue

Scorching fingers of flames like crimson spears leaped out in his path. Suffocating clouds of black smoke engulfed him. The shouts of men calling him back in many languages echoed like Babel in his ears. Still he fought his way through the rampaging inferno, battling the furious fire as if his only entry into paradise lay through the fatal blaze.

His tall, lean frame was bent almost double, his arms raised across his face in a futile effort to protect himself from the raging fire. Flames licked at his blond hair and singed his eyebrows and lashes. But he struggled on, hurling himself into the living hell that threatened to consume him, only to be driven back by a wall of intense heat as impenetrable as a sheet of iron. Crying out in desperation and despair, he rushed into the fiery furnace again.

He woke up trembling, his body cold and clammy with sweat. He rubbed his eyes, trying to wipe away the memory of the terrible inferno that haunted his sleeping and waking hours, and instinctively touched the thin purple scar that ran from his left temple to his ear. Exhausted in body, tormented in soul, he stumbled into the night. Walking—walking the hills and winding roads of Macao—was the only release he had from the frightening nightmare which allowed him no rest, no peace of mind.

It was midnight. The streets and byways were deserted when the man began his desperate walk. He strode on for miles, unaware of his surroundings, of the steepness of the climb or the fragrance of the summer air—driven by demons he could not exorcise, by memories he could not escape, by passions he thought he would never know again. A faint ripple of far-off music added to the strangeness of the night and to his dangerous, feverish mood. He paused to catch the melody that seemed to waft in off the river. Lost in the eerie moment, he did not notice the figure coming toward him until she was kneeling in his path, like a gift heaven-sent to deliver him from his torment.

He stared in amazement at the apparition on her knees in front of him, bathed in moonlight. She was dressed in an exquisite raspberry satin robe. Silver dragons danced in its graceful folds, and silver thread outlined its mandarin collar and long, full sleeves. Her jet black hair hung thick

3

and straight to her shoulders. Her forehead was powdered a lily white, her mouth painted in a ruby bow. A satin mask, the same raspberry shade as her robe, hid the rest of her features. He held out his hand to help her up and the sweet scent of jasmine drifted over him. It was, he suddenly realized, the evening of Colonel Blackstone's masked ball, the highlight of the summer season in Macao, and the old soldier must have imported boatloads of the willing girls from the flower boats of Canton to pleasure his guests.

Released from his searing memories by this unexpected encounter, the man laughed aloud. *I don't have to suffer the boredom of the Colonel and his guests*, he thought, *to savor the delights he provides*. Pulling the girl to her feet, he pressed his mouth firmly against her crimson lips. She stood motionless, frozen in his arms. "I hope you're not on land because your rivers have run dry," he said in perfect Chinese as he kissed her again, lightly, curiously this time. Without further ceremony, he picked her up into his arms, and then deposited her beneath the wide spread of a pomegranate tree.

The tree's heavy boughs blocked out the moonlight. Darkness closed in on them. He could no longer see the girl distinctly, could barely discern the outline of her figure. The suddenness, the mysteriousness of their meeting excited him and he fell on top of her, his eager hands searching her rigid body. Suddenly, like a volcano long dormant, she erupted, tossing and rolling, biting

4

and clawing like a tiger. The more she struggled, the more aroused he became. He had been on the flower boats many times and knew that a world of immeasurable pleasure floated on the Pearl River, exotic sex with beautiful women skilled in the fine art of arousal. Anything a man desired he could have from these girls, as well as some things he never dreamed of. "If you like to be hurt, I will hurt you. If you like to be forced, I will force you," he whispered savagely as she struggled with him on the shadowy hillside.

The passionate tussle with the silent, masked girl who had appeared from nowhere drove him wild with desire. He flung one strong arm across her heaving chest, pinning her beneath him. With the other, he lifted her dragon robe to her waist and ripped away her linen bloomers.

If there had been enough moonlight to see the girl clearly, he would have been shocked by what he had uncovered. For, instead of the wispy black hair of the Oriental flower girls, there was a luxurious crown of tawny-colored curls.

In the shadow of the tree, though, all he could see was the curve of her hip. His nostrils filled with the womanly aroma of her body. The sound of her labored breath beat in his ears, and he entered her roughly, his ardor driving him deeper and deeper.

CHAPTER ONE

To China

The *Carol Anne* faced the open sea alone. The escort of small boats that had guided the square-rigger out of Boston Harbor, past Marblehead to Baker's Island, was turning back. Samantha Shaw stood in the stern and waved vigorously until the last sail sank below the horizon and the sea stretched flat and empty as far as the eye could see. All that was familiar lay behind her now. Ahead was a perilous voyage across open seas.

In one hundred thirty days or so, if all went well, Samantha would disembark in the mysterious Orient. Shivering with excitement and trepidation, she stared out at the infinity of blue-green water, dreaming of a rainbow of Chinese silks.

Fifty years before, while the ink was still drying on the Treaty of Versailles, the first Yankee ship sailed from America for Canton. She was the *Empress of China*. At her helm was Samantha's cousin, Major Samuel Shaw, who had received his commission fighting under General Washington in the War of Independence. The round-trip voyage to the Orient and back took two years. The *Empress of China* carried a cargo of silver and ginseng, a forked root that grew in the forests of New England. Ginseng was a highly prized herb in the Orient. Because of its odd, human shape, the Chinese believed it possessed magical powers to heighten male potency and called it "dose for immortality."

On her return voyage, the *Empress of China*

carried home teas and silks and romantic tales of the exotic East. Ships from Boston and Salem, from Providence and Philadelphia followed in her wake, often making roundabout trips to pick up cargo along the way—otter pelts from the Northwest coast, sandalwood, and *beche de mer* from the South Seas, and from Turkey the poisonous but highly profitable opium.

Many ships never returned. Pirates preyed on trading vessels passing through the Sundra Straits. Typhoons and tropical storms threatened all who dared the dangerous passage around the Cape of Good Hope. The China trade posed great risks, but it brought even greater rewards. It returned the highest profits of any branch of foreign commerce. It attracted the best ships and the most daring seamen. And it made the China merchants the wealthiest men in the New World.

Soon the young country was in the grip of a China fever. Along the Eastern seaboard, the best families vied to outdo each other in Oriental opulence. They dressed in Chinese silks, dined off Chinese porcelain, and decorated their homes with Chinese landscapes, teakwood tables, and japanned screens. The Yankees clamored for fine furnishings, delicately carved ivory accessories, even ordinary household goods. To them, "Made in China" spelled an exotic, manicured world of pagodas and impeccable ivory-skinned women in pastel robes. If it was Chinese, they wanted it.

Nowhere was the China fever more intense than in Boston and no one was caught up in its spell more than Jonathan Shaw. Samantha's earliest memory was of her father sitting in his study, listening avidly to Major Sam's stories of the Far East. The room would grow dim as the afternoon faded into evening, but her father never seemed to notice. Drawing deeply on his cigar, the tip glowing eerily in the half-light, he would ply his cousin with question after question about life in the distant land. But Jonathan Shaw never made the voyage to Canton. Destiny had steered him along a very different path, and now Samantha was taking the trip for both of them.

"Well, young lady, have you found your sea legs yet?" Captain Stevens' booming voice broke Samantha's reverie sharply. She turned to him smiling, one hand raised, clasping her bonnet to secure it from the ocean breeze now blowing in her face.

"I still can't believe we are really on our way, Captain," she said, "and I can't imagine that much harm could come to Aunt Maude and myself from an ocean as calm as this one. Why, I've seen rougher waters in my bath at home."

Captain Stevens laughed heartily. Samantha had been a spirited tyke and he was glad to hear she had not lost any of her old sassiness at the fancy French schools her father had sent her to.

"Maybe you will bring the *Carol Anne* luck and she will have smooth sailing all the way to China," he chuckled. "But I'm not going to count on it."

Samantha turned away from the captain and

stared out to sea again. "We cannot count on anything really," she said wistfully. "I just learned that a few months ago."

"Now, now, Samantha, there will be no brooding aboard my ship."

"Aye, aye, sir." Samantha mustered up a mock salute. "But," she hesitated, "I do, I do wish Father were with us."

Captain Stevens looked fondly at the girl silhouetted before him. Her bonnet framed her lovely face—deep green eyes flecked with gold and set far apart; a delicate, straight nose; generous, sensual lips that curled up at the corners invitingly. Her waist, so slim a man's hands could encircle it with ease, enhanced the slope of her small, high breasts and the gentle curve of her hips. She was a willowy, long-legged beauty. But a hint of something indefinable seemed to smolder beneath the cool, graceful exterior, making Samantha not just a pretty girl but a startling woman.

Captain Stevens sighed deeply, "So do I, my dear. So do I." The responsibility for the girl weighed heavily on his shoulders. *She is much too lovely, too young and too innocent, to make a trip like this without a man to protect her,* he thought to himself. *Jonathan Shaw would never have allowed it, and I shouldn't have either.*

Clearing his throat, the captain said gruffly, "I had best look in on your aunt now. Make sure she has found everything she needs."

It was only with the greatest reluctance that

Stevens had given the Shaw women passage. He had pleaded with them to stay at home; regaled them with ghastly stories of shipwrecks and storms; warned them darkly that the Orient was no place for women alone. Samantha had listened to the captain attentively. But her bags were packed. Her house shuttered. Her mind made up.

"Captain Stevens," she said simply when he had finished speaking, "we are making the voyage for my father. It was his last wish." A tear escaped from her wide green eyes and rolled slowly down her smooth cheek.

Captain Stevens assigned the best quarters on the *Carol Anne* to Samantha and Maude Shaw. But now, as he made his way down to their cabin, he deeply regretted his momentary weakness.

"It was good of you to take us aboard, Edward," Maude said as the captain made himself comfortable in the small cabin. "I know women are a frightful inconvenience on a voyage like this."

"I did it for Jonathan, you understand. Nothing else could make me do it. We were boys together; even so, I made him give me his word as a gentleman that you and Samantha would be his responsibility. If I gave you passage, your safety and health would be in his hands alone."

"And now, Edward," Maude said in her customary blunt way, "you are thinking how irresponsible I am to make this voyage without him."

"Well," he hemmed, "frankly, after Jonathan's death I just figured you would cancel the trip."

"So did I," she laughed. "But Samantha would have none of it. I begged her. I pleaded with her, but I could not budge her. As you recently discovered, my niece can be as stubborn and willful as her father. She threatened to make the voyage alone if I would not accompany her, and she meant it, too. Samantha is so young, she does not realize what could happen to a girl as beautiful as she is. She insisted no harm would come to us, because we would be in the hands of her father's dear friends. You would be escorting us out, and Mallory Jones and Peter Thomson would look after us once we arrived. Mallory had written to Jonathan promising us his villa in Macao for the season and Peter had offered to be our official guide." Maude paused, uncertainly. "I only hope Samantha is right," she said.

"She's a beauty all right, like her mother," Captain Stevens said thoughtfully, "but a tragic one, it looks to me, what with never knowing her mother and then losing her father so suddenly like that."

"Yes, and so soon after she had finally come home to him. It was a great loss . . . for all of us," Maude's voice broke and she swallowed hard. "Samantha is much stronger than she appears, though. She is a very independent young lady."

Captain Stevens sighed deeply. "I don't have to tell you, Maude, that the China trade has taken

13

some of the best sailors in all of New England. But it is not just the danger of stormy seas and shipwrecks that worries me. The waters we will be navigating are dotted with tiny islands—primitive places with customs far different from our own. Why, I've heard tell of an island where the natives paint their bodies blue and the men line up at a great feast to take their turn with a virgin girl. It makes my blood run cold to think what they would do if they got their hands on a beauty like Samantha. A voyage like this is no place for a woman, Maude," he said shaking his head ominously, "no place for a woman."

The captain lumbered to the door. He was a big, burly, red-faced man. "It is a relief to know that Jones and Thomson will be looking out for you in Macao. There are no more trusted men in China than those two. Still and all," he added, "I won't get a wink of easy sleep until I deliver both of you safely in their hands."

Captain Stevens was following a direct course to China—across the Atlantic Ocean to the Cape Verde islands, around the Cape of Good Hope, through the torrid Indian Ocean into the China Sea. The weather held and the *Carol Anne* made the Atlantic crossing in good time. After weeks of endless ocean, they sighted the northernmost Canary island. Although it was their first glimpse of land since leaving Boston, Captain Stevens sailed by.

At St. Jago, the largest of the Cape Verde

islands, he made the first stop for fresh supplies. St. Jago was a walled city that squatted at the foot of a hill, with the sea lapping at its feet. Within the walls was a cluster of stone buildings covered with brick tiles, and beyond were mountains and fertile valleys where pineapples, tamarinds, figs, and bananas grew in abundance and small green monkeys with black faces ran wild.

Although Captain Stevens refused to permit Samantha to bring a monkey aboard to be the *Carol Anne*'s mascot, she was so pleased to feel land beneath her feet once more that she barely protested. The respite on land was all too brief, however, and two days later they were heading toward the Equator.

Crossing the great dividing line between the Northern and Southern Hemispheres was the mark of a seasoned seaman, and always an occasion of celebration aboard ship. Young sailors who had never been as far as the Equator before were initiated into the band of salty, weathered adventurers in a day of bawdy fun and practical jokes. Although the hijinks aboard the sturdy *Carol Anne* were more restrained than usual in deference to the ladies, Samantha and Maude joined in the festivities gaily, even daring to toast their first Equatorial crossing with a taste of Captain Stevens' rum grog.

It was the last easy time for the crew of the *Carol Anne*, because no sooner had they crossed the Equator than the balmy weather they'd been enjoying ceased. The worst gales of the voyage swept their rolling, wind-torn home as they ploughed down the southwest coast of Africa. Once they rounded the Cape of Good Hope they left the terrible tropical storms behind them and entered the Indian Ocean in full sail.

More than three months out of Boston, the watch sighted the first boobies, gray birds the size of ducks with long beaks and wings, that signaled they were approaching Java. Samantha and Maude gazed in amazement as the *Carol Anne* anchored in the Straits of Sundra and a canoe of natives—brown-skinned and black-toothed from chewing betel nuts—rowed out to the ship with fresh fish and fowl, cocoa nuts, and an incredible fifty-pound turtle. But, before the men could take on the new supplies, a great thundering resounded across the water and Samantha saw off the starboard side two of the most awesome sea creatures engaged in a contest that pitted strength against cunning.

A swordfish and a whale were locked in mortal combat. Swimming in ever smaller circles, the whale plunged through the waves, pounding the water with its mighty tail until the sea roared and sprayed like a geyser. But the swordfish never quaked. Shrewdly, tirelessly, it swam around its victim, slicing the whale's big belly first on the left side, then on the right, never even threatened by the pounding tail. All hands watched aghast as the seasoned killer slowly slashed its helpless victim to death. The swordfish cut, not with the point of its beak, but with the toothed edges, until the sea was red for miles around and the great behemoth was too weak to raise its powerful tail again.

And so it was that the *Carol Anne* made its way through a red sea to China. If it was an omen of what lay ahead, Samantha never suspected it, so great was her excitement at reaching the end of the long voyage.

From Java Head, it was just ten days to the Gaspar Islands, then ten more to Macao, the island at the mouth of the Pearl River that opened Canton to the South China Sea and the West, and would be home to Samantha and Maude Shaw as long as they stayed in China. Although the ship stopped briefly in Macao for a permit to enter Chinese territory and obtain a pilot boat to guide her the thirty miles up the Pearl River to the anchorage at Whampoa, no one was allowed to disembark. Escorted by the pilot boat, the *Carol Anne* sailed up the bay to Tiger's Mouth, the opening into the Pearl River. Samantha stood in the prow, drinking in her first view of the exotic Orient. Nothing escaped her hungry eyes.

To the left of the narrow mouth was the Bogue Fort, a forbidding sandstone eminence that was supposed to guard the mainland from foreign attack, but actually provided dubious protection against invasion, since the guns, firmly planted in stone sockets, could shoot in only one direction. Beyond, a wasteland slowly gave way to a sweeping spread of rice paddies, and then, rounding a band in the river, Samantha caught her first glimpse of Whampoa.

In the winter months when the tea and silk trade was at its peak and the foreign fleet was in, Whampoa was an imposing sight. Rounding a narrow bend in the river, a long line of great ships, sometimes stretching for three miles, came suddenly in view. But Whampoa was just an introduction.

Twelve miles upriver at Canton, great, ungainly salt junks and six-hundred-ton vessels for the Java trade—their high sterns fantastically decorated, their sharp prows painted with huge eyes to spy out the devils of the sea—lined the banks or made their way slowly downstream. Chop boats carrying chests of tea to Whampoa, their peculiar circular decks and sides making them look like floating watermelons, passed river junks manned by gangs of naked coolies who treaded paddle wheels or pulled on long sweeps. Mandarin boats, with red sashes tied to the muzzles of their cannons and white and vermillion flags flying from their masts, patrolled the shores, while the mandarins themselves lounged in gaily decorated flower boats, surrendering willingly to the girls who handled them so expertly.

Threading in and out among the larger boats were thousands of tiny sampans: sampans to load and unload cargoes of sea-going junks; sampans that served as shops for barbers, vendors, and fortune-tellers, or a stage for theatrical performers; sampans that housed the great floating population of the Chinese city, pots and pans cluttering their decks, wicker baskets of hens and ducks slung over their sides, and children, wooden buoys tied to their backs, paddling happily alongside.

By day, the river was a blaring, congested city. By night, a sleepy town—silent except for the haunting music that wafted from the flower boats and clung to the cool night air, dark except for the small fires that flickered in the sterns of the sampans as the women prepared the meager evening meal.

But Samantha would never see Canton, for the Son of Heaven decreed that "Neither women, guns, spears, nor arms of any kind" could be brought there by the foreign merchants.

CHAPTER TWO

Samantha Shaw

Peter Thomson was the charming, cosmopolitan, highly influential head of the British East India Company, the largest trading house in China. But he felt like a schoolboy as he watched Samantha being strapped in the bosun's chair and lowered over the side of the *Carol Anne* to the yacht he had hired to ferry the Shaw women back to Macao. Although he rarely admitted it to himself, Thomson had loved Samantha ever since she was in pigtails—and he had loved her mother before her.

Thirty years ago, when the Countess Marie de Beauport fled to London to escape the violent revolutionaries in Paris who were sending every aristocrat they could find to the guillotine, he had been her constant companion. She was the most beautiful, the most desirable woman he had ever known and, when the Directory came to power and Marie returned to France, he followed her. Just when he was sure he had won her hand,

22

Jonathan Shaw, his American friend, came to Paris.

Even as a very young man, Peter Thomson was the perfect British gentleman—reserved, impeccably mannered, always correct. But Jonathan Shaw was a daring, adventurous Yankee. He was a hero in the War of Independence, who had fought beside Rochambeau when he was only seventeen. Too restless to settle down again in Boston after the war, he went West and grew rich trapping and selling furs.

When his Yankee friend visited him in Paris that summer, Thomson did not mention the special girl who had stolen his heart. He wanted to introduce them first and gauge his friend's impressions before revealing his deepest feelings. But by then it was too late.

From the moment Jonathan Shaw met the Countess Marie de Beauport, Thomson knew he had lost his love. He could see in Marie's radiant face that his suit was lost. Jonathan was a rugged, brawny, fiercely independent man, unlike anyone Marie had ever met, and she fell in love with him at first sight.

Later, drunk with desire and anticipation, Jonathan threw his arm across his friend's shoulder. "Peter, you are a man like no other," he said. "Who else would introduce his friend to the most beautiful girl in Europe, and look on without ever trying to win her for himself? I don't know if I would have done the same,

23

even for you. Certainly if the girl were Marie, I would not. I could not. I am insanely jealous of every man who even looks at her."

Although his heart was breaking, Thomson forced himself to answer jokingly. "Hold on a minute, Jonathan. Listen to yourself. You sound like a fifteen-year-old with his first glimpse of an ankle. You have hardly met the girl and already you are giving your heart away."

"It is true. I have given it, completely and forever," Jonathan responded. "In that first instant when I touched her tapering fingers through her white kid gloves, I felt her take my heart, my life. In that moment, I became hers completely, forever. I can't explain it. I know it must sound ridiculous to you. After all, we have had some fairly scandalous times together, but this is different, Peter. It is sacred—and exciting."

Jonathan and Marie whirled through Parisian society in a cloud of happiness. It seemed like only weeks later that their marriage was the social event of the season, and the young couple was sailing away to Boston.

Thomson never told Jonathan how he felt— there was no point in it. And he suspected that Marie never said anything either. He only saw her once again after she went to America as Jonathan's bride. She was carrying her first child and that special condition, he thought, made her more beautiful than ever, more lovely, more desirable. No one would have imagined that the devastating girl who took such pains to maintain her slim figure would take so perfectly to the awkward condition of motherhood. But Marie had. She glowed with the life in her—and with love for her husband.

Although she talked nostalgically of Paris and the gay times they had there together and treated him tenderly, Thomson did not fool himself. He left Boston sure of Marie's deep and very special affection, but equally sure that she reserved the love that united a man and a woman into eternity completely for Jonathan.

Thirteen years later, Peter Thomson was still unmarried. He had never found a woman who could make him yearn as Marie had. Of course, he squired his share of glamorous ladies, enjoyed his share of good times, and built up a store of memories to fall back on. But no one ever touched his heart again. Then, after years of silence, he received a letter from Jonathan.

"Dear Peter," the letter read. "I am writing to you, a grieving, heart-sick man in the hope that, out of the friendship you once had for Marie and myself, you will lighten the burden of my repentance. Although it has been many years since I have enjoyed your good counsel, you have never been far from my thoughts. As I commit these lines to you, I look for inspiration at the portrait of my dearest Marie which hangs in front of me, over the library mantel. Although I built this house for her, her lovely figure has never graced its rooms, for the month before it was complete, Marie died in childbirth.

"Even now as I write these words thirteen years later, my lonely heart cries out for my dearest wife, but time has dulled the pain and made me see the folly and the selfishness of my sorrow. My fondest hope is that Marie will forgive me for what I have done to our child.

"Peter, the terrible truth is that I wanted the child to die and Marie to live. When the doctor told me he could not save both mother and child, I said, 'We will have another, many more children, as long as my wife is well.' 'Mr. Shaw,' he said, 'I don't think you understand. You are the father of a healthy girl.' I stopped cold at his words, and then I struck him blindly, cursing him and calling wildly to Marie.

"My grief was boundless. I would not even look at the child. I gave her to my sister, Maude, and went West. I joined up with a couple of men, Lewis and Clark their names were, who were leading an expedition to explore the territory of Louisiana that Jefferson purchased from the French. We traveled up the Missouri, across a treacherous mountain range, and down a river, which we named the Columbia. We were almost to the Pacific Ocean by then.

"The expedition kept me away from Boston for three years, and still my grieving heart would permit no rest. I saw my daughter, Samantha, for the first time, and then I left again. I became a long hunter—living in the wilderness for a year at a time, trading furs as I had done before I met Marie, and returning to Boston for no more than two or three months at a time.

"Finally, last year, I went home to Boston to stay. I expected to find a quiet, demure little daughter. Instead, I found a wild, untamed injun. She rode like the wind and shot an arrow with uncanny accuracy. She was as independent as any boy and had a temper as fearsome as my own. In short, Peter, my daughter, Samantha, was a spirited, high-bred filly who needed training, and so I took her to Paris to enroll her in the convent school that Marie had attended before the revolution.

"During the ocean passage, I discovered my little girl for the first time. In all those years of my selfish grief, I blamed Samantha for her mother's death, and I made the innocent child pay dearly for my loss. It was not enough that she was robbed of a mother's love. I deprived her, as well, of a father's guiding hand.

"When we arrived in Paris, I could hardly bear to leave the child after finding her so late, and ever since returning to Boston I have been tormented with grief over the way I neglected her. I pray that my darling Marie will forgive me for mistreating her daughter so heartlessly and I assure you, dear Peter, that she would join with me in begging you this kindness. If business takes you to Paris, would you in the name of our old friendship relieve my torment by visiting the child? Knowing that a dear friend would look in on her from time to time would be a source of immense consolation to me."

The letter was signed, "Yours with the deepest gratitude, Jonathan Shaw."

Peter Thomson read the letter over several times. Marie had died for him when he visited her in Boston and then died for Jonathan just a few short months later. He wondered if either of them would ever get over their loss. He doubted it. Yet Jonathan was right. Marie would want him to be kind to her daughter.

As he waited in the convent parlour the first time, the heavy oak furniture polished to a high luster, the thick damask drapes drawn to keep the sunlight from fading the wall hangings, Thomson wondered if the girl would look like her mother, the young Marie he had loved so dearly.

He expected a young lady, but Samantha was still a little girl in a blue serge uniform, black stockings, and pigtails. *What does one say to a small girl?* he wondered nervously as she shook his hand and curtsied politely. Still, he asked the mother superior for permission to take her out for the afternoon. They rode in his carriage to the pastry shop for lemon ice and raspberry tarts. She was shy and perfectly mannered, not at all the hellion whom her father had described in his letter, and, while she concentrated on her ice,

28

served in a deep, frosted silver dish, with a straw-berry on the top and a generous dollop of whipped cream, he studied her face for a glimpse of Marie. The only hint of her mother he could see then was in her eyes—the same deep green, the same unusual flecks of gold that flickered mischievously in the sunlight and glowed invitingly by candlelight. After the first visit, Peter Thomson always made a point of calling on Samantha whenever business brought him to Paris. At first he visited her for old times sake, for Marie and Jonathan, and because he felt sorry for the motherless, reserved little girl so far away from home. But gradually, as he broke through her aloofness and discovered her sassy, independent spirit, he began visiting because he enjoyed her company.

She became "Sammy" and he became "Uncle Peter." An easy camaraderie developed between them and they were soon the best of friends. She often asked him about her mother and never seemed to tire of his stories about the beautiful young Countess Marie de Beaufort sweeping across London and Paris, turning the heads of every man as she went by.

One year, he invited her to come to London and spend the holidays with him. Although she had just turned sixteen, he still thought of her as the little pigtailed child who had curtsied to him in the convent parlor. In her convent uniform, he hadn't noticed her body ripening. But when

29

he went to the dock to meet her and her maid, he was taken aback. Samantha was no longer a little convent girl. The bud was beginning to blossom into not just another pretty young lady, but into Marie's daughter. There was no mistaking the big, wide eyes or the erect way she held her head.

"No more lemon ice and raspberry tarts on this visit," Samantha laughed, pleased with the obvious impression she had made on her Uncle Peter. "You may not have noticed it before, but I'm not a devilish little child anymore and this holiday I want to do all the grown-up things you would normally do."

She smiled wickedly and he realized that, whether she understood it or not, Samantha was testing her new self on the safest person she knew. He laughed warmly at how young she still was in spite of the miracle of nature taking place in her adolescent body.

"All right, Sammy," he said, "we will begin this very evening, by attending the Queen's Christmas Ball."

"Do you mean it, Uncle Peter?" she cried gleefully.

"I most certainly do, if you will allow an old man the pleasure of escorting the prettiest girl in London."

"Oh, I love you, Uncle Peter." She kissed him impulsively on the cheek. "My very first ball!"

"There's just one thing, Sammy. Do you have a suitable gown to wear?"

Samantha's face dropped immediately. That was reply enough.

"Good. Then I will have the additional pleasure of helping you to choose the perfect dress. I know a wonderful shop and a wonderful seamstress who, even at this late date, will not fail us. Miss Charlotte will know exactly what you need, my dear. We'll go around to her shop as soon as you freshen up, and see what she suggests."

The Christmas holidays flew by. Peter Thomson had not enjoyed himself as much in years. He could not remember when he had laughed more, he told Samantha. But it was a white lie. He had not had such a wonderful time since he had been with her mother. He was an old fool, he knew, but he was falling in love all over again with this reincarnation of Marie.

Was it the memory that was captivating him, or the girl herself? No matter. He knew it was impossible and so he disguised it, taking pleasure in Samantha's company as he had always done, only more often now. He no longer needed the excuse of business to go to Paris. Samantha was reason enough. But he was always careful not to let the depths of his feelings show through, even when she graduated from her convent school and he put her on the ship that would take her back to Boston and out of his life, perhaps forever.

Now she had come to China, just a year after he had resumed control of the powerful East India Company. He was proud of the courage she displayed by taking the long, dangerous voyage with only her Aunt Maude to accompany her, and overwhelmed by her beauty.

"Sammy, I do not understand how it is possible," he smiled when he finally had her beside him again, "but you look more beautiful now than you did when you left Paris two years ago."

"Uncle Peter," she laughed gaily, "no one can be beautiful after four and one half months at sea. And no more Sammy. I am too old for nicknames now. You must call me Samantha and pretend, at least, that I am a very proper young lady."

She gave him a warm hug. "Now, you must tell me everything you know about China and show me every inch of the place I can see without having my head chopped off by the Emperor himself."

It was Thomson's turn to laugh at her gloriously youthful exuberance. "Very well, Sammy —I beg your pardon, Samantha—I will take you at your word." He was escorting them back down the Pearl River to Macao.

"As soon as we dock," he said, "we will take sedan chairs to Mallory Jones's villa high in the hills overlooking the harbor. I received word from him yesterday morning that his servants were awaiting your arrival. When you are settled there, I will leave you to rest and refresh yourself. Then, if you have gotten accustomed to the feel of land beneath your feet again by this evening, I would like nothing more than to have you and your aunt be my guests at the most elegant ball of the season. Will that be enough for your first day in China?" he smiled at Marie/ Samantha, Samantha/Marie. What pleasure it gave him just to know she was close by.

CHAPTER THREE

A Rude Awakening

The air felt cool and refreshing after the crowded ballroom. Tired and dazed from the long trip and from the excitement of arriving at last in the exotic Orient, Samantha left the gala and walked through the formal gardens. Her mind was swirling with her first impressions of China.

She wished that she had worn a simple face mask to the ball instead of dressing up like an Oriental girl. But it was her first night in Macao. She had felt daring and adventuresome, and had fallen in love with the elegant native dress her Uncle Peter had bought her. The color was so rich, the silver embroidery so delicate, even the name itself she found enchanting. It was called *chi-fu*, or dragon robe. Now the black wig pressed uncomfortably at her temples, and the jasmine scent that she had dabbed behind her ears to provide the final touch of authenticity seemed cloyingly sweet.

Samantha was feeling strange and light-headed

when she realized with a pang of fear that she had drifted far from Colonel Blackstone's gardens. She turned back and tried to follow the strain of the music, but instead of drawing closer, the music seemed to be fading away from her. Weak and lost in an unknown land, Samantha stumbled on until, overcome with exhaustion, she sank to her knees and could go no further.

When she opened her eyes again, a strange figure, cloaked in the satin robes of an Oriental mandarin, was bending over her and a pair of depthless eyes were staring into her own. She had never seen such compelling eyes. She felt hypnotized by them, unable to move. Even when he took her hands and, murmuring strange foreign words, drew her up toward him, she was still unable to act. She wanted to scream but she couldn't find her voice. She wanted to fight him when he kissed her mouth hungrily, but she had no strength to resist, and he scooped her up as if she was a porcelain doll and tossed her under a tree.

Terrified by what she feared would happen next, Samantha lay motionless in the shadows hoping he would disappear in the darkness. But in the next instant, he was on top of her, his hands searching her most intimate parts. As she felt his fingers on her heaving bosom, she summoned hidden reservoirs of strength and battled fiercely against her mysterious aggressor. But his passion was too great to be denied.

Violently, cruelly, he thrust himself in her. She

felt the first sharp, agonizing pain as he shattered her innocence and then, thinking bitterly, *This truly is a country of barbarians*, the night closed in mercifully.

When Samantha regained consciousness, she was being carried through the woods. For a moment, the strong arms that held her felt reassuring and she relaxed in their safety. Then, she remembered with horror what had happened and she began screaming, fighting desperately, crying out against her unknown captor. But he walked on as if she were lying peacefully in his arms, instead of fighting like a cobra. His eyes never faltered. His pace never changed, until he arrived at a small house completely hidden in a wooded copse. Kicking the door open, he carried her inside and put her down in the middle of the single room. Her wig had fallen off and her lustrous, tawny hair cascaded to her shoulders.

"I am sorry," he said softly, his voice deep and gentle. "I did not know you were a virgin. I did not know . . . " His voice broke and trailed off, and he closed his extraordinary eyes and covered his face in his hands as if he were the one who had suffered grievously.

He looked like no one Samantha had ever seen before. His features were as finely etched as a Chinese landscape: a long, straight nose, high cheekbones, finely chiseled lips. His deep-blue satin mandarin robe, now stained with her blood, was tied loosely at the waist with a narrow cord. Yet he was at least six feet tall and angular, with blond hair that curled at his ears and eyes as clear and blue as a summer sky.

He was a strange merging of East and West, Samantha thought, a mountain water picture in a Western frame. As she stared at his anguished figure, all the anger washed out of her. "It's all right," she said soothingly. "It is over."

His spirit seemed to revive at her words and he turned to look at her hesitatingly, questioningly. She nodded her head in encouragement.

"Yes, it's over," she repeated, "finished." Overcome by an irrational compulsion to ease this strange man's torment, she did not understand the full meaning of her words.

His eyes looked intently into hers, mesmerizing her again. His voice caressed her warmly. "Let me at least clean away the blood I have spilt," he said.

He clapped his hands twice and an Oriental boy appeared with a basin of water and a linen towel. The man placed the basin on the floor beside Samantha. "Here, I will help you," he said.

With expert fingers he unfastened the diagonal closing, opened her dragon robe, and let it slip to the floor. Samantha submitted without protest, afraid of what this erratic man would do if she angered him again, but when he tried to raise her camisole, she shivered uncontrollably and covered her bosom with her hands. No man had ever looked on her bare flesh.

"Don't be frightened. I won't hurt you again," he said. His voice was low and warm. His fathomless blue eyes pierced her heart. "I promise you."

He raised her limp arms and stripped off her camisole, petticoat, stockings and torn bloomers, and she stood utterly naked except for the raspberry silk mask which still covered her eyes.

Although the mask made Samantha feel oddly protected, her body still burned beneath his scrutiny and she tried to cover herself with her hands.

"Don't," he commanded, stepping back so that he could see her more clearly. "I want to look at you, savor you."

He walked around her in a full circle.

"You are beautiful," he whispered in a hushed, awed voice, "so beautiful. I have never seen a white woman before."

He took her face in both his hands and raised it toward him, kissing her hair and her forehead. Then gently removing the raspberry mask, he kissed her eyes and her creamy cheeks and, ever so softly, he kissed her ruby lips. As he did, he ran his hands over her full breasts, down across her smooth stomach, and back over her round buttocks.

Samantha felt a flood of warmth surge through her tired body. Her skin flushed and tingled at his touch, and she experienced a thrilling, tantalizing sensation she had never known before. Gazing into her wide eyes, he murmured, "Let me wash away the evidence of my crime," and he knelt in front of her and began to gently wipe the dried blood, the last trace of her purity, from her legs.

The warm water soothed her bruised thighs. Slowly, he worked his way up until he reached her luxurious, tawny-colored crown. He squeezed the warm water into her matted hair and she felt it trickle down between her legs. In the next instant, the towel was gone and his damp fingers were parting her other lips, following the trickle of water into her secret enclave.

Samantha felt a powerful stirring within her. Unconsciously, she moved her legs apart, opening her legs wider for his magical fingers. She was surprised and confused by what she was feeling. Yet she wanted it to go on—whatever it was, whatever he was doing.

By the time he lifted her in his arms and carried her to the bare cot in the corner, she was trembling like an aspen. In one quick motion he undid his satin robe and was standing over her naked, his body bare, his manhood looming immense and frightening above her. As Samantha looked on a man for the first time, all her terror returned. She became again like a slab of marble, frozen and inflexible. She opened her mouth to scream, "No, no," but it was too late.

Unaware of her innocent fear, he fell on top of her, stifling her cry with his mouth and, penetrating her in one swift, sure stroke, he rode her fiercely, heedless of her struggles to free herself. Then he rolled off of her and lay silent and spent beside her, his blue eyes icy, staring blankly into the ceiling. Exhausted, Samantha fell into a merciful sleep.

When Samantha woke up, she saw a spartan room, furnished with a straight chair and simple wood table, on top of which was an alabaster bust of a beautiful Chinese girl. Otherwise the room was bare. She lay perfectly still, trying to remember where she was and what she was doing in the strange room. There was a terrible aching between her legs, and suddenly the evening swept before her. At first she felt mortified, then ruined, then furious. The touch of tenderness she felt remembering his sadness and her momentary pleasure turned to fury when she realized the brutal stranger had vanished without a trace. Embarrassed by her nakedness, Samantha reached for her clothes, which lay clean and mended at the foot of the bed. She dressed quickly and ran out into the still dark night. She had no idea where she was or how to find her way back. As she hesitated in the doorway, uncertain of which direction to take, a small Chinese stepped out of the shadows and, bowing deeply, said, "I will show you the way. Please follow."

Samantha recognized the boy who had brought the basin of water. "Where is your master? Who is he?" she asked angrily. But the boy looked at her, his round face imperturbable. "Please follow," he repeated, and started walking into the darkness. He led her surely to the outskirts of Colonel Blackstone's gardens. "I leave you here, missy," he said and, bowing deeply again, he disappeared into the night without another word.

Samantha had no idea how much time had passed. It seemed like a lifetime ago that she had walked through these very gardens, along these very paths, with nothing in mind but a breath of fresh air to clear her head, and a brief respite from the crowded dance floor. Remembering how innocent she had been, and how enthusiastic to taste life in the romantic Orient, she laughed to herself mirthlessly, bitterly.

But Samantha was not a Shaw for nothing. Her grandfather had cleared the woodlands, fought the Indians, and built a home for his family with his own hands. He had died fighting back the Redcoats at the Battle of Saratoga. Her own father, then just a boy of fourteen, picked up the smoking musket and took her grandfather's place in the line. He fought so gallantly that by the time the War of Independence was won, he was the youngest colonel in George Washington's army.

Although Samantha rarely saw her father in the first nineteen years of her life, when she returned from Paris they began to know each other and to love each other. Jonathan Shaw still had enough spirit in him to dream of one last adventure with the daughter he had discovered at last at his side. He wrote to his old friends in the China trade and, when both Peter Thomson and Mallory Jones replied, urging him to visit the Orient, he and Samantha began planning their

43

trip in earnest. For months they pored over maps, studied the routes of the square-riggers, and read everything they could find on the Far East.

Jonathan booked passage for them on the *Carol Anne*. Samantha ordered a stunning new wardrobe. All the arrangements were set. But a month before departure, as he sat in his study reading beneath the portrait of Marie, Jonathan Shaw's heart stopped beating. The shock of his death stunned Samantha, yet even in the depths of her grief, she knew that her father would want her to continue the journey just as they had planned it.

"Miss Shaw, I have been searching for you for hours. Why did you abandon me to the arms of others so much less beautiful than yourself?" Jean Levoir's gay words brought Samantha back to Macao abruptly. The dark, charming Frenchman she had danced with earlier that evening was standing at her side, his pearly teeth flashing in the darkness.

Samantha took a deep breath, squared her shoulders and lowered the raspberry silk mask over her eyes. She was determined to behave as if nothing had happened at all. "I was just testing you to see how many pretty faces you would succumb to," she replied lightly.

"When you have looked at beauty, you no longer have eyes for a pretty face. Allow me," he said gallantly and offered her his arm.

Samantha danced every dance for the rest of

the evening. The names and faces blurred, but she forced herself to keep on dancing and by the end of the night all the young merchants in Macao were enthralled by the graceful, effervescent American, but none more so than the cunning Jean Levoir.

CHAPTER FOUR

Love's Fatal Fire

Samantha woke up with a fever. She stayed in bed all day with the curtains drawn while her solicitous aunt brought her tea and cooled her warm brow with cold compresses. Samantha wished she could stay in the darkened room forever and never be forced to face the awful memories of the night before. But the ache in her thighs was a constant, painful reminder of her humiliation. She tried once to tell her aunt what had happened.

"Aunt Maude," she began tentatively, "last night . . . "

"Yes, darling, it was a lovely party. But the excitement was just too much for you so soon after the long voyage." Maude was bending over her bed, her staunch face creased with concern, and Samantha knew then that she could never confess her shame.

"Yes, too much excitement," she murmured, closing her eyes. Her aunt touched her cheek lightly, then tiptoed out of the room. The tears Samantha had been holding back for so long welled up behind her closed lids and she wept inconsolably. She wept for her father and the horror that this trip, which he had planned so lovingly, had brought her. And she wept for herself, degraded by a strange, brutal man in an alien country.

The torrent of tears seemed to wash away her feelings of guilt, and hours later she awoke refreshed, the same strong, independent Shaw she had been when she sailed out of Boston Harbor.

Dispassionately, Samantha went over each step of the night before in her mind as if it had happened to someone else. She reviewed each point with clinical coolness, facing every detail, no matter how disgusting it was to her, until she came to the place where he carried her into his house. Then she faltered. She wanted to sleep again, to block out the rest of the night, but she forced herself to go on.

You are the same Samantha Shaw today as you were yesterday, she told herself. *Nothing in your heart is different. You have to face what happened squarely or you will never be able to put your life back together again.*

Even as she reassured herself, Samantha knew her words were false. Something was different, very different. She began to remember the anguished way he looked at her and the tormented way he said, "I am sorry." She remembered how tenderly he undressed her and the awe in his eyes

49

as he gazed at her nakedness for the first time. She began to tremble all over as she remembered how it felt when he washed her thighs and parted her lips with his cool, gentle fingers. Almost unconsciously, her fingers followed the path his had taken. Samantha had never touched herself like that before and, as she did, she knew that she must find him again. She did not know who he was or where he had taken her, and she couldn't ask. But somehow she had to find him—no matter how dangerous or insane it might be.

In the next days, Samantha tried to put him out of her mind entirely. Escorted by her devoted Uncle Peter or by the attentive Jean Levoir, she explored the lovely island of Macao. It was the only part of China that a foreign woman was permitted to set foot on.

When Samantha sailed up the Pearl River on the *Carol Anne*, she had reached the center of the world. She had arrived at the Celestial Empire of China, ruled over by an Emperor who called himself the Son of Heaven, bound by customs and ideas she would never understand.

Perhaps because of their central location on the globe, the Chinese considered themselves a superior race. Everyone who was not Chinese was a barbarian. To prevent these inferior people from sullying the Celestial Empire, no foreigners were allowed in mainland China.

The "Fan-kwae"—the foreign devils—who came across the western oceans to buy the silks and teas of China were restricted to one small parcel of land, one quarter mile long by three quarter miles deep, between the banks of the Pearl River and the walls of Canton. And, even there, their lives were carefully prescribed.

No Chinese were allowed to conduct any business with the visitors except the Cohong, a group of thirteen merchants who monopolized the foreign trade. In their warehouses on the creeks east of the river, they received goods from the interior and shipped them to Whampoa in watermelon boats that could carry five hundred chests of tea in one trip.

As long as they remained in their miniature Canton, the foreign merchants were bound by strict rules of behavior, known as the "Eight Regulations." Each ordinance was enforced firmly, including the rule that banned women from Canton. As a result, from October on, when the favorable southwest monsoons brought the trading fleets to Whampoa and the fresh teas began arriving in Canton from the interior, the Fan-kwae lived in the atmosphere of an elegant men's club. But in late spring, when the northwest wind dropped and all the ships were loaded, they made the exodus to Macao, the beautiful island at the mouth of the Pearl River where the Western women waited.

Jointly administered by the Chinese and the Portugese, Macao pyramided from the sea like a tiered wedding cake. Elegant bayfront shops wound around the lowest tier, protected by the Práya Grande, a broad esplanade with a low parapet supported by a sea wall. An old Portugese cathedral occupied the highest tier, and on the levels in between were white stone villas, each with its own gardens.

The Mallory Jones villa, which the Shaws were occupying, was one of the biggest and most beautiful in Macao. Nestled high in the hills by the old cathedral, it contained a private observatory that commanded a breathtaking view of the harbor and was surrounded by lush gardens, planted with brilliant flowers, fragrant pomegranate trees, and wide-leafed pines for shade. Tiny, colorful birds as exquisite as fine gems perched in the pomegranates, but they were always silent. They had no song to sing.

During the tea season, Macao was almost entirely women and servants. But now, in the middle of summer, it was a bustle of activity and Samantha was caught up in the rush of balls, dinner parties, quadrilles, amateur theatrics, and fireworks displays.

Every day was full, and yet the mysterious stranger was never out of her mind. Try as she would, Samantha could not forget. She was so consumed with him that she began to deliberately formulate a plan to deceive her aunt and steal away unnoticed for an afternoon. George Chinnery provided the perfect alibi.

Uncle Peter had commissioned Chinnery to paint Samantha's portrait for him. The artist, who claimed quite cheerfully that he was the ugliest man in the Orient, was a fixture in Macao, renowned as well for his clever puns, the prodigious quantities of cold tea he drank, and his considerable talent with brush and oils.

Samantha hated herself for lying to Maude, but she had to resolve the strange passion that absorbed her—one way or another. She dressed carefully, choosing a simple, pale peach, cotton frock with a high neck and tucked bodice that subtly accentuated the roundness of her breasts. Under the pretense of sitting for Mr. Chinnery, she slipped away.

Samantha began to walk in the same direction she had taken that fatal night, trying not to think, just letting fate lead her. In the bright afternoon light, the path looked unfamiliar. She was beginning to fear that she was utterly lost, when she came to the spot where she had tripped. Samantha shuddered involuntarily and quickened her pace. Just walking by the spot where she had been ravished made her angry again. But then a deeper, more powerful emotion transformed her fury into a searing fire that frightened and excited her. Recklessly, she rushed on, driven by an unquenchable desire. Her bosom heaved tumultuously and she began to run as if she knew the way as surely as the hallways of her father's home, never faltering or hesitating until she reached the secret copse.

Only when Samantha stood at his door did the danger she was courting impress itself upon her. But by then it was too late. She was a hostage of her heart. She knocked, not a tentative, demure rap, but a hard, repeated pounding that echoed the pounding of her heart, and threw the door open.

The bare room was empty. There was no trace of life anywhere. *He's gone*, Samantha thought, *gone forever*. She walked around the room, blinded by her tears, and unconsciously picked up the beautiful alabaster head from the table. She ran her fingers over it as great sobs wracked her body.

"What are you doing?" The sudden angry voice frightened Samantha. "Put that down. Never touch it." A rough hand grabbed the statue from her.

He was standing in front of her, a furious golden god. His naked body was brown and glistening. Long fluid muscles rippled across his broad smooth chest. His lean, graceful body was poised as if might strike out at her. A thin purple scar that ran from his left temple to his ear pulsated rapidly.

He placed the statue on the table carefully. She had caught him unaware and touched his most sensitive spot. He thought the wound was healing but, in that instant, when he walked in and saw her handling the statue, all the grief, all the despair, all the bitterness and heartache that had been consuming him for two years, exploded. He regretted his outburst immediately. Looking at the beautiful girl before him, her green eyes wide with fear, he wanted to make up to her for his sharpness.

"Don't be afraid," he said quietly. "I didn't mean to frighten you." He smiled at Samantha, a sudden, dazzling, boyish smile that lit and warmed his cold blue eyes like a light going on in an empty room.

"I am sorry I startled you," he said, drawing her to him. "Some things cannot be violated, and you took me by surprise."

He held her tightly against his wet body. The touch of his skin reassured her, as did the murmur of his voice against her hair. "I hope you will forgive my appearance," he said laughingly. "I was bathing in the river. I . . . I . . . " he hesitated, his face hidden in her tawny locks. "I didn't think you would ever come back, though I hoped you would. I wanted you to come. I want you." His low, gentle voice caressed her lovingly.

He kissed her hair and with the tip of his tongue he licked the salty tears that were drying on her cheeks. Then he kissed her mouth, a long, searching kiss that made Samantha forget her fear and his fury. This time she didn't need any help. She drew away from him and slipped quickly out of her clothes, letting them drop randomly to the bare floor. Samantha stood boldly in a pile of petticoats and stockings, and let his admiring eyes linger over her lush form.

He walked toward her slowly and stood in front of her. With only the palms of his hands touching hers, he traced her generous lips with the tip of his tongue. She touched his tongue with hers, tentatively at first. A tingle of anticipation swept through her as their tongues met and he drew her against him. Moving her body sensually against him, she felt his rough hair entangle in hers and she felt him growing huge and hard between her legs. Then they walked hand in hand to the bed and lay down together.

Unashamed by her nakedness, she pressed her body against the length of his and he answered her with his lips, kissing her neck and breasts. Although he was throbbing wildly with desire, he didn't force himself on her. He lay beside her, caressing her body gently, exploring her most intimate secrets, until she was hungry to receive him.

He ran his tongue around her soft pink aureole and took her nipple in his mouth, biting it gently. Wherever his lips touched, they kindled a mighty fire. He kissed her stomach and her thighs, and then he kissed her other lips. When her breasts were firm with desire and her thighs were moist and creamy, he took her hand tenderly and placed it between his legs.

"Don't be afraid," he said softly, as she began to draw away, reluctant to touch him there. "I won't hurt you again."

Bashfully, her fingers closed around his manhood and she felt it pulsate feverishly at her touch. At his gentle urging, she stroked him slowly.

"You see, there is nothing to be afraid of," he

said and, slipping his fingers beneath her buttocks, he raised her to him.

Samantha felt his fingers sink deliciously into the soft flesh of her cheeks as he drew her to him and entered her. This time, she was ready to receive him. Crying out in surprise and delight, she arched her back to take him fully.

"Kiss me," she whispered urgently, and he responded with steamy desire. Opening her lips with his tongue, he thrust deeply into both her mouths, driving slowly at first, than harder, faster, until he had unleashed the searing passions that lay dormant in the innocent girl.

He lay contented and spent beside her, but now Samantha was even hungrier than before. Every part of her body was ablaze with a passion she had never dreamed of. Boldly, avidly, she pressed her mouth against his, slipping her tongue seductively between his parted lips. Her curious fingers reached down shyly to touch and caress him. He came to life in her hands, responding quickly to her touch.

"My beautiful vixen," he groaned with pleasure, "you are like a diamond, cool and sharp on the outside but hot and fiery within."

Samantha could feel him throbbing in her fingers. Then he mounted her again and rode her swiftly, powerfully, satisfying her deepest hungers until her legs ached with sweet exhaustion, and then exploding with her in a wild paroxysm of joy, bringing her to an ecstasy so intense it was almost more than she could bear.

This is madness. I still don't know his name, Samantha thought drowsily, as she fell asleep in his arms, her hair clinging to his moist chest. *Heavenly madness!*

She dreamed they were lying by a river, the clear water lapping at their bare feet. The river was rising slowly, creeping up around them until they were immersed in the icy waters. The coldness soothed and numbed their tired bodies and they floated with the current as effortlessly as lily pads. But when she awoke, happy and glowing, she was alone.

At first Samantha thought she was still dreaming. Then, as her head cleared and she wiped the cobwebs from her eyes, she saw that even the alabaster bust was gone from the table. She woke up abruptly to the bitter truth. This time he was gone for good. She didn't weep. She didn't even want to. A cold fury worse than any tears overwhelmed her. Samantha felt nothing but contempt for herself and hatred for the blue-eyed stranger she had given herself to so completely, so trustingly.

What kind of a woman are you, she asked herself angrily, *throwing yourself at the man who raped you, a man whose name you still don't know? How ashamed your father would be to see his treasure giving herself away like a slut.*

Samantha vowed she would never again be humiliated by any man. From now on, she would hold the upper hand. She would become invulnerable. She would never give her heart so freely, so trustingly, again, and if she ever discovered the identity of her abuser, she would even the score—somehow.

CHAPTER FIVE

Forgetting

Samantha forced herself to put the mysterious stranger out of her mind. Her days in Macao were filled with Spanish lessons, spirited games of whist and loo, and the unflagging attentions of Jean Levoir. Chaperoned by Aunt Maude, she and Jean sailed to the little islands off Macao, picnicked at Casilla's Bay, and promenaded the Prãya Grande. Although Maude urged her niece to spend more time with the other young men in Macao, Jean, with his impeccable continental manners, reminded Samantha of her happy schooldays in Paris and she allowed him to monopolize her attentions.

Samantha sensed that Jean Levoir was not popular with the other merchants in Macao, but she credited their coolness to jealousy. All the women swooned at his feet, but he had eyes only for her, and everyone on the island agreed they made a handsome couple. Jean had dark, suave good looks, a trim, pointed black beard, and soft brown eyes—and was always tailored to perfection.

He was easy to be with, ever gallant and attentive, never threatening. Samantha enjoyed his company and was flattered by his affection. The only thing that troubled her was Jean Levoir's friendship with Pierre Bonner.

Samantha knew the two Frenchmen were business partners and close associates, but she never suspected the heart of their lucrative trading business was opium. Although it was illegal, many of the foreign traders were making fortunes bringing the dangerous drug into China. But there were no more successful opium smugglers than Levoir and Bonner.

Two years before, when ships carrying opium were banned from the anchorage at Whampoa, the Frenchmen made Lintin the center of their illicit operations. The small island, just twenty miles from Macao, was perfectly suited to their needs. When their ships arrived with chests of opium, the cargo was transferred to big storage vessels, permanently anchored at Lintin like floating warehouses.

The Chinese opium buyers came to Lintin in long, swift galleys with as many as thirty oars on each side and made their purchases aboard the storage ships. Their galleys looked like centipedes, but they were fast enough to outrun the government patrol boats and smuggle the illegal poppy juice into the Celestial Empire.

Instinctively Samantha feared the dark, secretive Bonner. Where ever she and Jean went, he seemed to be there waiting for them, watching them from a distance. At every quadrille, he lurked in the shadows, and each time she noticed him, she would find his black, beady eyes staring slyly at her.

But Samantha never mentioned her aversion to Jean. She only hoped that tonight the slippery little man would be nowhere in sight. It was the last big ball of the season in Macao and Jean had intimated that he might have something important to ask her.

Although he never touched her lips, contenting himself with a kiss on her hand or, in a rare display of emotion, a chaste kiss on her cheek, Samantha knew what his question would be and so she wanted to look very special tonight. She chose a white organdy gown with a green velvet sash at the empire waist that matched her eyes perfectly. The low, square neck revealed her milky throat and shoulders and suggested the high arc of her bosom.

Just enough to entice Jean, she thought naughtily, as she twirled in front of the full-length mirror, pleased with the reflection she saw. *What answer should I give? Yes or no or maybe?*

"Madame Jean Levoir," she said aloud to herself in the mirror, "Samantha Levoir."

It has a certain ring to it, she thought excitedly, as she picked up a satin rosebud to put in her tawny hair, *but I don't think I shall give*

Jean an answer tonight. I will make up my mind before I leave Macao, but not until then, she decided. The memory of her humiliation still ached in her heart, but she refused to let herself brood over it. "Jean and Samantha Levoir," she whispered dreamily, as she looked for a clasp to fasten the satin rose. "Samantha et Jean."

Soon every drawer in her dresser was open in her search for the elusive clasp, and still Samantha could not remember where she had put it. There was only one place left to look, the desk, and so she began a hurried search.

How did it get there? she wondered as she opened the narrow corner drawer and saw the glimmer of gold. Reaching in, she felt something soft and luxurious and saw that her clasp was resting on a dark brown velvet box.

Samantha lifted the box out of the drawer curiously. It was wide and flat and closed with a gold latch. She knew that it must belong to Mallory Jones. Although he had opened his villa to them and placed his servants at their disposal, Mr. Jones had never come to call. Strolling through his lush gardens or exploring the house he had furnished with a subtle blend of Oriental formality and easy American grace, Samantha often wondered about her unknown host. His taste was exquisite, his servants well-treated and devoted, but beyond that she knew little about the man and could find out even less. She knew from her Aunt Maude that he had been a fine boy, almost a son to Jonathan Shaw, and when she pressed Uncle Peter he would always say, "He's a fine man, Samantha, a fine man. You must meet him before you leave China." But Uncle Peter would say nothing more, and when she mentioned him to Jean, he always became uncharacteristically cold and sharp. "Mr. Jones prefers to select his own company. He does not deign to honor us with his."

Now, unable to contain her curiosity, Samantha opened the velvet box. In the center, resting on a blue satin pillow, was a beautiful ring. It was a wedding band, but a wedding band unlike any she had ever seen before. Two strands, one of platinum, the other of vermilion, were wound together so intricately it was impossible to tell where one began and the other ended. A row of perfect rubies ran through the center of the platinum strand and a row of flawless diamonds ran through the vermilion. But the ring, for all of its detail, was tiny, too small even for her little finger, Samantha guessed. Not daring to try it on, she closed the box and slipped it back in the drawer.

Fastening the satin rose in her hair, Samantha gave one final glance in the mirror. *Who is Mallory Jones*, she wondered as she swept down the stairs to meet Jean Levoir, *and why does he have a wedding band that would only fit a child —or an Oriental woman?*

CHAPTER SIX

Mallory Jones

Mallory Jones was a legend in Canton. He had come to China at fifteen, adopted the ways of the Orient, and established a trading house that soon outdistanced all others, even the prosperous British East India Company. Now, at thirty, he was the most successful merchant in Canton, and the richest, with a personal fortune comparable to Houqua's own. Yet, for the past two years he had lived like a counting house monk, avoiding the society of the foreign community and shunning the dinners and quadrilles held in Macao in the summer season. He had become a recluse, an eccentric. Few knew him intimately, but everyone knew about him.

When Jones first arrived in China, the Americans did not have their own factory in Canton. As he sailed up the Pearl River past the Chinese forts known as Dutch Folly and French Folly, he could make out the long row of foreign factories set some three hundred feet back from the river, each two or three stories high with arched windows, sloping roofs, and white-washed walls. The flags of each nation flew in front—Portugese, Dutch, Swedish, Parsee, French, English—but there was no stars and stripes.

The Union Jack still dominated in Canton. It waved supreme over the East India Company hong, the grandest and most elaborate of all the foreign factories. The Chinese called it "the factory that ensures tranquility." Located at the extreme west end of the row, the British hong had a wide veranda, which stretched to the river-front, and an Anglican chapel with a high steeple tower, containing a large, ostentatious clock. It was the only public timepiece in Canton and everyone set his watch by it.

In front of the factories was a public square where vendors would congregate during the trading season, hoping to profit from the foreign devils. The square was bounded by Hog Lane and Old China Street, and behind it ran Factory Street.

Samshu, a fiery local wine, was the greatest attraction on Hog Lane, which thronged with sailors of every nationality whenever the ships were in port. But on Factory Street innumerable small shops offered a wide variety of native ware. The usual ivory, silks, silver, and gold might be exchanged, but you could also buy bird cages, fireworks, insects, medicinal herbs, cats, and dogs.

69

The Chinese communicated with the foreigners through a pidgin English derived from Portugese, because they were the first foreigners to trade with China; Indian, because the Parsees and Chinese carried on a mutual trade; English, because the British dominated the foreign trade; and Chinese. In this unique language all merchants were Fan-kwae, foreign devils, but the nationalities were differentiated. Since the first English trader had red hair, the British were "Red-haired Devils" and, once Mallory Jones arrived in China, the Americans became known as "Hwa-kwae," "Flowery Flag Devils," because he soon had the stars and stripes flying over his own American hong.

Built on the corner of Old China Street, it was three stories tall. The first floor was reserved for business, the second contained living and dining areas, the third was the sleeping quarter. Here Jones lived and worked and grew to manhood.

By the time he came of age, he had not only outstripped the awesome British East India Company, his firm of Porter and Company had gained control of half of the foreign trade in Canton. Although it was a fortified city, he enjoyed a nabob's life of luxury. He had wealth, servants, beautiful furnishings, and access to the most skillful women in China. For, although most of the foreign merchants were banned from the flower boats, Mallory Jones was a frequent and welcome guest. On these floating paradises, the scented, painted girls who fluttered behind their fans introduced the young Yankee to every pleasure of the flesh. The flower-boat girls possessed centuries of erotic skills and they practiced them often on the handsome and willing young American.

The Yankee merchants got a late start in the China trade. The British did not permit their colonies to trade with foreign nations, and so it was not until after they had thrown off the English yoke that the Americans entered the world market. When Mallory Jones arrived in Canton, twenty-five years after the War of Independence, the Yankees still lagged well behind the other major world traders, but he bridged the gap swiftly.

He did it with brilliance, daring, and the help of Houqua, the chief of the Cohong. While many of the foreigners disdained the Chinese merchants, the young American deferred to the older man's wisdom and acumen. He placed himself in Houqua's able hands and was amply rewarded for his trust and good judgment.

Although millions of dollars changed hands between them, Mallory Jones never had a written contract with Houqua, and never had a dispute in fifteen years of business dealings. Houqua's word was his bond and his honesty was beyond reproach. His teas, silks, porcelain, and cassia were shipped to every corner of the world. His chop or seal on a chest of tea in London or

Amsterdam, Boston, or Philadelphia was a certain guarantee of its excellence.

While several members of the Cohong failed and were forced into bankruptcy, Houqua's wealth increased steadily. His fortune was matched only by his generosity, and no man knew this better than Mallory Jones.

The elderly Chinese merchant and the young American made a striking contrast. Mallory Jones was tall and lean with blond curly hair and the bluest of blue eyes. Houqua was a small frail man with a broad bald dome and a wispy white goatee. His cheek bones were high, his cheeks hollow, his eyes large and dark. He resembled an aesthetic or philospher more than a businessman. Yet Houqua was the shrewdest trader in China.

Although he possessed the largest mercantile fortune in the world, the elderly man had simple tastes and frugal habits. Only his clothes and his five-acre estate on Honam Island across the river from Canton revealed his fabulous wealth.

He dressed in brocade robes, topped with a dark gown lined in white silk, and on his feet he always wore white-soled slippers turned up at the toes. A blue button on his cap served as a symbol of his rank and a barometer of the Fan-kwaes' behavior. If any of the merchants he sponsored was involved in serious trouble, he would be unbuttoned and disgraced.

Houqua dressed richly because his position as chief of the Cohong demanded it. His island estate, however, was the source of his greatest pleasure. The lavish mansion and gardens bordered the riverfront and were encircled by a brick wall. The river water was channeled to wander through the gardens in streams and waterfalls and ponds paved with lilies before it came to rest in a tidal pool in front of the main house where ducks and swans and ibises swam.

The house itself was an elegant showcase. Silk and velvet carpets covered marble floors; columns of marble and the light gray native granite extended as far as the eye could see. The furniture was of the finest japanned work. Shelves of precious scrolls filled the library and the finest paintings and porcelains were everywhere on display.

An invitation to Houqua's estate was a rare honor, coveted by every foreign merchant. Only Mallory Jones was a regular guest. In the years since he had come to Canton so young and eager to learn, he had forged a deep bond of trust and affection with the elderly Chinese.

Houqua was like a father to the young Yankee. He guided him through his youthful years, taught him everything he knew about the trading business, helped him to amass a fortune second only to his own, and welcomed him into his home.

Mallory liked nothing better than to roam through the famous gardens, following the intricate mosaic of waterways over the light bamboo bridges, past marble benches and parapets holding potted flowers and shrubs. The garden paths were paved with small colored stones forming patterns of fish, flowers, and birds. Gazebos and pavillions, grottos and shrines, all connected by bridges and pools, studded the vast gardens.

But one day, Mallory Jones wandered so far, he could never turn back again.

CHAPTER SEVEN

The Fire

The ball was the last of the season in Macao and the most spectacular. In a few days the foreign merchants would return to Canton for the start of the fall trading season, and Samantha and Maude would sail for home. There was a hint of devil-may-care in the room and Samantha caught the mood.

She felt romantic and impetuous. But Jean seemed preoccupied. Several times he excused himself to talk urgently, secretively with Pierre Bonner. There was something about the dark, shadowy man that Samantha didn't trust. But she had no time to think of that now, because Signor Montegard was bowing deeply before her.

"You are the most ravishing princess that China has ever seen, Miss Shaw, and I would trade all its tea for one waltz with you," he said as he swept her into a spirited dance.

Samantha was laughing gaily at this merry

Spaniard who always seemed to be brimming over with good humor, when she sensed a subtle change in the room. At first a hush, and then a low excited murmur spread across the floor.

Still with his arm around her waist, Montegard bent close to her ear. "Look discreetly, Miss Shaw. The tall, fair man who has just entered is the rich, enigmatic Mallory Jones. The tall, fair one, my dear," he repeated, nodding toward the door, "who is introducing himself to your aunt. In over a year I do not think that he has appeared at one social gathering."

Samantha turned slightly to catch a glimpse of her elusive host, who had opened his villa to her and her aunt but had never come to call—and turned suddenly ashen. Only Montegard's arm at her waist kept her from fainting.

"Miss Shaw, what is wrong?" he asked anxiously. "You are whiter than your dress."

"Please, Signor," she could barely manage a whisper, "help me to the garden."

"My dear, I am so sorry. We must have danced too fast. Please forgive me. I was carried away by your exquisite beauty."

While Montegard was apologizing profusely, the tall, blond stranger was walking toward Samantha.

"Samantha, dear," Maude called, "here is Mr. Mallory Jones, the man we've been so anxious to meet." Samantha turned slowly. "Mr. Jones, my niece."

The man bowed deeply and took her hand. "I

have been looking forward to this moment with the keenest pleasure," he said, raising her fingers to his lips. If Samantha had any doubts, his cool blue eyes removed them forever.

"We are most grateful to you, Mr. Jones, for the use of your villa," she said, meeting his gaze evenly.

"It is I who am grateful to you," he responded smoothly, "for now I will have the pleasure of picturing you there."

Mercifully, Maude interrupted their duel. "Samantha, you look so pale. Are you feeling quite well?" she asked.

"It is nothing, Aunt Maude, too much dancing and not enough air. Signor Montegard was about to escort me to the garden, so if you will excuse us."

"Montegard, I hope you will permit me the honor of escorting Miss Shaw in your place," Mallory Jones interrupted.

"It is a pleasure I would not think of relinquishing to anyone but you, Jones," the Spaniard replied.

Trying not to betray the turmoil that churned in her breast, Samantha turned to her conqueror, "Thank you, Mr. Jones, for your kind offer, but it is not necessary. Signor, shall we?" she said as she held out her arm to Montegard.

But in a motion so smooth it almost escaped the eye, Jones took her outstretched hand and placed it on his arm. "I insist, Miss Shaw. After all, your father commended you to my care."

Samantha scanned the room desperately, looking for an avenue of escape. But all eyes were focused on them. She had to go into the garden with Mallory Jones or create an ugly scene.

Arm in arm, they moved toward the French doors. Samantha walked at her most erect, her head held high and haughty. There was a smile glued to her face, but there was murder in her heart. Mallory Jones walked slowly, smiling warmly and greeting guests to their right and left while steering her expertly through the throng to the garden.

"You are the loveliest lady at the ball, Miss Shaw. No one even compares to you," he said charmingly as he closed the glass doors behind them and led her to a flowery arbor.

Samantha could barely recognize the troubled, brooding man she had known in this disarming man at her side. If they had been meeting for the first time, she would have been charmed by his golden good looks, his laughing blue eyes, his easy, flirtatious manner. But this was the violent, passionate man—the strange, haunted figure—who had ravished her and humiliated her, and the fury rose in her bosom.

"And you, Mr. Jones," she retorted coldly, "are not listed on my dance card. As you can see, every dance is taken—including the one that is being played now."

"I see you have wasted no time in spreading your favors," he laughed.

Although his intent was obviously good-humored, Samantha could think only of her lost virginity.

"What do you mean to imply by that remark, Mr. Jones?" she blushed angrily.

"Absolutely nothing that would offend you. I meant it simply as a joking comment on your popularity in Macao, although I suppose I could try to assert my right of eminent domain."

His voice was light, his words playful. "Have you heard of eminent domain, Miss Shaw? I believe that in America it is the newest idea in the Westward expansion. It means, if I understand the concept correctly, that once you have taken a territory, it becomes yours by right of possession. Or is that homesteading? No matter; I can't think of any lovelier territory to lay claim to than yours, and, although I am profoundly sorry for the way it happened, I can't in truth say I regret being the first man to get there."

Mallory Jones spoke tongue-in-cheek, hoping to thaw Samantha a little. He had to believe that she desired him; after all she had come to his retreat alone and hungry to receive him. Yet he needed to be absolutely sure, and so he was teasing her playfully, trying to take a measure of her feelings.

But Samantha turned on him furiously, slapping him across the face and spitting through clenched teeth, "You have no claim on me, Mallory Jones—no claim at all."

In her white gown she looked like a fierce

avenging angel and her anger excited him, made him impetuous with desire.

His face burned where she slapped him, but it was nothing compared to the fire within him. "You are beautiful, Samantha, more beautiful than the evening," Mallory marveled, "and haughtier than the Empress of China." He seized the hand that struck him and twisted it behind her back, pulling her toward him. Samantha struggled in his arms. When he forced her mouth open with his, she bit down hard on his tongue and tasted his blood. But her anger drove him wilder, and he pressed her harder against him until she could feel him throbbing.

"You wouldn't, not here," she gasped. His blood tasted warm in her mouth.

Mallory Jones looked down at her, his incredible blue eyes ablaze with desire. Then suddenly they turned cold. The inscrutable Oriental mask dropped. The rougish young American was gone.

"No," he said quietly, drawing away from her. "Forgive me—again."

But, in the instant that Mallory let her go, Samantha suddenly, irrationally, wanted his arms around her again. She clung to him urgently and in her recklessness sought his lips. But he turned his face from her, and pushed her gently away. Still, Samantha could not let go. She didn't care that they might be interrupted at any moment. She didn't care where they were or what he had done. She wanted only to be enveloped by this tempestuous, mercurial man—by him and no other.

Mallory Jones could feel Samantha's body trembling with the enormity of her desire, but still, he pushed her away.

"No, Samantha," he said, "not here, nor anywhere again. I should not have interrupted your party. Go back to your dancing beaus."

Samantha was stunned by his reply. Nothing he had done before seemed as harsh as these words. She was passionate. But she was proud. She would not beg for this man—she would not beg for any man—no matter how much she longed for him.

"And you to your cowardly evening activities on garden paths," she retorted fiercely.

Mallory accepted her insult silently, his unflinching eyes fixed intently on something behind her.

"Do you know Jean Levoir?" he asked sharply.

"I not only know Jean Levoir, Mr. Jones, I plan to announce our engagement this very night."

"Samantha," Mallory grabbed her arm so tightly that it hurt, "have nothing to do with that French fop, do you hear me?" He shook her slightly. "Have nothing to do with him."

"That French fop," Samantha said triumphantly, "is going to be my husband."

It was not exactly accurate. But she was sure Jean was going to propose to her that night and just then, more than anything, she wanted to hurt Mallory Jones. Earlier she could not decide whether or not she would accept Jean's proposal, but now her mind was made up.

"You don't know what you are doing or saying, Samantha." Jones was pleading with her now. "Your father entrusted you to my care. I cannot let you do this."

"How dare you mention my father or even speak his name? What can Jean Levoir do to me that is worse than what you have already done?"

"Believe me, Samantha, I never meant to hurt you. I would never have touched you if I had known you were Jonathan's daughter. It was only this morning that I discovered the spinster I had been imagining in my villa was you," Mallory Jones's voice was low and troubled, as if each word he spoke was being wrenched from his soul. "As a gentleman I should offer myself to you, humbly and apologetically. But I cannot— not now—I am not man enough now. The least I can do is keep you from Levoir. You do not know what you are doing. I cannot allow this marriage."

Too crushed, too humiliated from his earlier words to realize the full meaning of Mallory Jones' apology, Samantha hissed angrily, "You cannot allow this! What rights do you think you have over me? Well, let me tell you Mallory Jones, you have none—no rights at all."

Jean Levoir reached Samantha's side just in time to catch her last words. "I hope I am not interrupting anything important," he said suavely, "but, Samantha, you did promise me this dance."

"Levoir, what are you doing here?" Jones demanded.

"I am Miss Shaw's escort, or didn't you know? You so rarely allow us the pleasure of your company these days."

"You are not escorting her anywhere, Levoir. Is that clear? From this moment until the moment she leaves China, I am Miss Shaw's escort."

"Samantha, shall we?" Levoir said, holding out his arm to escort her back into the ballroom. "Everyone in Macao knows Mallory Jones only likes slanted eyes," he sneered cruelly.

Jones's eyes flashed with fury. Fast as lightning his fist struck out and caught Levoir squarely in the jaw. Blood gushed from the Frenchman's mouth and he fell unconscious on the stone walk.

Samantha ran at Mallory like a frenzied tiger, but he pushed her away disgustedly. His fury was icy, like a glacier that freezes everything, traps everything, withers everything in its glare.

"If that is what you want, I must have mistaken you for someone else, Miss Shaw." He bowed in mock courtesy and turned on his heel along the same path she had taken that first night when love's fatal fire was kindled in her breast.

Samantha was kneeling over the unconscious Levoir, cradling his head in her arms, when she looked up and saw that Mallory Jones had stopped on the path and was watching her silently. But when her eyes met his, he turned abruptly and vanished into the night.

Levoir was beginning to come to. He was dazed and angry, but otherwise would survive. Wiping the blood from his mouth with her handkerchief, Samantha helped him up.

"What were you doing out here with that man? I don't want you to have anything to do with him," Levoir said, and there was a curious note in his voice that Samantha had never heard before.

But before she could question or respond, Peter Thomson came into the garden and sized up the situation quickly.

"Go back to the ball, Samantha, and leave everything to me," he urged her. "I will patch up Levoir and no one will be the wiser."

Samantha did as her Uncle Peter bid her. She was angry and confused. This was the night she had been looking forward to with such excitement. Her mind was whirling. How could her father have spoken so highly of Mallory Jones? What did Jean mean about the slanted eyes? Why had Mallory been so cruel? She could not think clearly, and she had no time to anyway, because the moment she re-entered the ballroom, she was caught up in the dance.

The ingratiating Portugese minister whisked her into a waltz before she could protest, and for the next hour she moved in a trance, floating from partner to partner. She felt as though she was outside her body. She heard herself murmuring the appropriate pleasantries and smiling graciously at every extravagant compliment, but she was not consciously speaking. Her feet were carrying out the familiar dance steps, but she felt as if she was standing still, frozen in a moment of violence. Her mind was locked on the fury of those glacial blue eyes, and that picture merged with a red blur—with the blood as it spurted from Jean Levoir's mouth.

At last, Samantha floated into the protective arms of Peter Thomson.

"Where is Jean? Is he all right?" she asked anxiously as he waltzed her to a quiet corner.

"Sit down on the settee here with me for a moment, my dear," he said soothingly.

"But I should be with Jean now. I shouldn't have left him."

"Calm yourself now, Samantha. Jean was just shaken up a bit. No great damage done. Though, I must say, Jones certainly has a nasty left hook."

"Where is Jean now, Uncle Peter?"

"I sent him home in my carriage. Thought that would cause the least stir. Macao is really like a small town, you know. Any little bit of gossip can turn into a full-blown scandal overnight, and I wouldn't want you or Maude to be involved." Thomson chuckled. "I probably should mind my own business, Samantha, but I've always wanted to give Levoir his comeuppance. Understand exactly how Jones felt."

"Uncle Peter, how can you say such a thing?

Mallory Jones is one of the most arrogant, the most violent men I have ever had the misfortune to meet. He is nothing but a brute, and Jean is a gentleman in every sense of the word. What's more," she hesitated, "he is going to be my husband."

"My dear, I had no idea how deep your feelings were. I know of course that you and Levoir have been seeing a fair amount of each other. But truthfully, I thought it was only a matter of convenience with you. A solicitous, good-looking escort during your visit; nothing more. I hope I have not offended you, Samantha. It would be the last thing in the world I would ever want to do. You know that I held Marie, your mother, and your father in the highest regard. Their daughter is a sacred trust to me, besides being a joy and a beauty."

Thomson's face was truly contrite, although his heart was troubled, and Samantha took his hand and squeezed it warmly in hers.

"Don't look so abject, Uncle Peter," she smiled. "You know I could never be angry with you, after all those wonderful times you showed me in Paris—you the sophisticated man-about-town and me the gawky schoolgirl, although at the time I thought the Empress Josephine paled in comparison. I value your opinion and advice even more now that my father is dead. But I have changed a great deal on this trip. China—the very air here—seems to have done strange things to me. Perhaps I am only now beginning to feel the full effect of Father's death; perhaps it is other things as well, but I feel lost, almost, and Jean makes me secure again. He makes me feel like the girl I was in Paris. He reminds me of that world I loved so well, and that now seems so remote."

Samantha paused to choose her words carefully. "I know you have known Jean longer than I have, Uncle Peter, but I don't think I have misjudged him. Life with Jean in Paris could make me forget all that has happened in the last terrible months."

Soft, big tears began to course silently down her cheeks. She reached out with her tongue and caught them, licking the salt as she had when she was a little girl.

"You criticize Jean," she sobbed through her tears, "and yet you stand up for that terrible man. How could you and Father want me to meet Mallory Jones, want to put Aunt Maude and myself in the hands of that monstrous man."

"Samantha, Samantha," Thomson soothed, "don't judge so harshly. You've barely met the man, and evidently the circumstances were not the most propitious. I don't know exactly what happened in the garden tonight. Maybe when you are feeling better you will tell me. But I would imagine that it had to do with two young men finding the same young lady very beautiful and, wishing to monopolize her attentions, exchanging sharp words that may well have led to a few well-chosen insults, the results of which I arrived in time to bear witness to."

Thomson put his arm around Samantha. "When two men and one woman combine, it has been my observation that very often fireworks erupt. At my advanced age, I must admit, I have seen—even been a party to—more than one heated disagreement over a beautiful woman. So you mustn't judge Mallory Jones too harshly from this one evening. He has been away from our Western society for a long time now and his manners have perhaps grown a bit rusty from disuse.

"Let me tell you a story, Samantha, and at the end I will be surprised if you do not think a little more kindly, at least, of our Mr. Jones. It begins some forty years ago, long before you were even a glimmer in your father's eye. The year must have been 1781. Ezekiel Jones was wounded fighting us at Yorktown and your father carried him from the battlefield in his arms, risking his own life to do so, I should add.

"Ezekiel returned to Boston and, at first, seemed to recover well. He married and fathered a son, but before the boy was even walking, Ezekiel's wound began giving him trouble again. He lingered on for almost fifteen years, little more than an invalid. Your father and Ezekiel had grown up together, and Jonathan felt a certain responsibility for his friend's young wife and child. He took the boy on trapping trips, taught him to fish, gave him his first hunting knife. He

89

was almost a second father and the boy looked up to him.

"Ezekiel had always been a weak sort. Your father had protected him when they were boys and he continued to do so when they were men. The lad sensed this I think. Although he loved Ezekiel, I think he secretly dreamed that Jonathan was his father. Anyway, Ezekiel died a few years after your mother. Your father's life had changed by then. He couldn't spend as much time with the boy as he had. On the other hand, your father was not the kind of man to abandon his friend's widow and son.

"Ezekiel's brother-in-law was a fairly prosperous merchant with a small trading company in Canton. Although the two men had had a falling out some years before and had not spoken since, Jonathan prevailed on Thomas Porter to take on his young 'nephew' as a cabin boy on his next trip to China.

"Mallory was fifteen by then. He was a strong, bright lad, a far different sort from his father. On the voyage out, Porter's appendix ruptured. None of the usual sailor's remedies helped and, although he lived long enough to reach Canton, after a week in China he was dead. Young Mallory was left alone to carry on the family business. You can imagine the fear and loneliness the boy must have felt—and the courage he had. But he never returned to Boston.

"Instead, the young boy filled the position left vacant by his uncle's untimely death. He assumed complete responsibility for the future of Porter & Co.

"Ten years later, Mallory Jones was the most successful, wealthiest and most powerful Westerner in China. He was a glorious specimen of manhood—handsome, brilliant, ambitious, with an easy grace and warm humor that made him the most popular man in Canton. Of course, there were those who were envious of him; it was hard not to be. But it was even harder not to like him. His vitality and youth were contagious, and he seemed to blend the Occident and the Orient with ease. He bridged the two worlds in a way that I have never seen anyone else do in all my years in China.

"Mallory Jones was to all appearances equally at home in the salons of Macao and in the palaces of the powerful Cohong merchants. Houqua, the most powerful of them all, treated him like a son. An invitation to Houqua's palace is a special occasion among the European traders. But Jones was a regular visitor.

"I recall one dinner I was invited to. It was a fabulous feast and, as I later discovered, a fateful one. The dinner moved through thirty courses, each more perfectly prepared than the last—bird's nest soup, plovers' eggs, *beche de mer*, shark fins, roasted snails, and pastries, washed down with green pea wine. As we finished the feast and sipped fruit wine in delicate silver cups, Houqua toasted his young friend: 'May all your days be as one,' he said.

91

"But that touching sentiment came too late. On his way to the dinner, Mallory had caught a glimpse of a girl—a Chinese girl—bathing in a lily pond. I only know this, because one day, months later, I saw Jones. I had known him, of course, ever since he came to Canton as a boy and I liked him, but he had never confided in me. We were business friends and colleagues, social acquaintances certainly, but not confidants.

"You can imagine then, Samantha, how surprised I was when one evening he came to my room. He seemed very distraught. We had a brandy and I asked him if business was going badly. He said it wasn't business that brought him. It was a personal matter. I still remember his words: 'Business was never better, Peter. I am sorry to have disturbed you at this time of night. Please excuse me.' He flashed that dazzling smile of his and stood up to leave. I have seen enough of life in my time to recognize a troubled man when he knocks on my door at two o'clock in the morning. I knew Mallory was a very private young man in spite of his popular image, but I liked him and I wanted to help if I could. So I refilled his brandy snifter and asked him to tarry a while longer.

" 'Nothing you say will ever leave this room,' I assured him—and it never did until this moment."

Thomson paused and took a deep breath. He didn't know just why he felt it was so necessary for Samantha to hear Mallory Jones's story, but now that he had begun he plunged ahead.

" 'Thank you, Peter,' he said simply, but something about the way he said it moved me deeply. 'I have to talk to someone and I don't know who else to turn to. It is a very personal, very delicate matter,' he hesitated. 'You see I am in love.' "

Samantha's cheeks flushed and her heart raced at his words, but Thomson did not seem to notice and continued his story as before.

" 'Well, my boy,' I said, hoping to lighten his mood with jocularity, 'that is traditionally a cause of rejoicing, not gloom.'

"It was almost as if he had not heard me at all, because he went on in the same tone, staring out the window at the lights from the flower boats that still flickered on the river. What trades, what commerce of the flesh, I wondered idly, are taking place behind those glimmering starpoints.

" 'It happened quite by accident,' he said, 'the night of Houqua's dinner for me. You were a guest, I remember, but there is little else I recall about that meal, although by all accounts it was sumptuous.'

"I was all ears as he went on. 'You see, on my way to the palace, I strolled through the gardens because I was early and because their order and formal beauty have always filled me with a wonderful tranquility. Or they had until that evening when, much to my amazement, as I stepped across the bridge, I came upon a scene that is etched forever in my memory. An Oriental girl with long, silken black hair and fine porcelain skin was bathing unattended in the lily pond. She must not have heard me come along the path, because she went on with her washing quite undisturbed.

" 'I was hypnotized. Never had I seen such graceful movements before. It was more like a ceremonial dance than anything as mundane as a routine ablution. I stopped and stared. Everything left my mind—the impropriety of a man watching a woman at her most private moments, the scandal if anyone saw us, the shame that would befall my greatest friend and benefactor if I was discovered—all this was forgotten. I was transfixed, standing stark still, when she saw me.

" 'Our eyes met. I bowed deeply to her. She laughed—the sound was like the tinkle of a waterfall—and pushed a lily pad toward me. I walked to the edge of the pool and stooped beside it to receive the lily. I picked up the flower, held it to my nose and pressed it against my cheek, as if it were her fair face.

" 'She called me her master and stood up from the water. She was naked. Her long hair covered her breasts, but she was naked and unashamed of her nakedness. She walked to me and bowed deeply, until I touched her shoulders and raised her again. There was no boldness in her nakedness. She was submitting to me in the traditional way of Oriental women. It was as if all her life she had been preparing for this moment—except

I was a stranger to her, and worse, more shocking, I was a Westerner.

" 'But all of this I thought later. At that moment, I touched her cheek lightly. I told her she was more delicate than the lily and I took her hair and slipped it back exposing her breasts. She stood before me small but perfectly shaped, like a raindrop. I was afraid that she was a mirage, that she would disappear. I picked up the kimono that hung from a nearby cherry tree and draped it across her shoulders.

" 'I asked her if we could meet the next day. She said there was an ancient temple on the east edge of Honam, and behind it, by the bayam tree, a hidden cave. She promised to wait for me, bowed, and was gone.

" 'The rest of the evening passed like a dream. It was madness and worse. I was betraying the trust and affection of the man I cared for the most, because the girl was Houqua's youngest and favorite daughter. But I was like a man possessed. I did not sleep at all. I couldn't wait for the morning to come because it would bring the afternoon and the girl.

" 'She was there as she had promised and she gave herself to me without reserve. We have been meeting there at her secret place ever since. I don't know how she slips away. I don't want to know the practical details. It is too much like a dream and I don't want practical concerns to intrude, although they do anyway.

" 'I am happier than I have ever imagined possible. Even the back alleys of Canton glow with life and beauty. Yet, at the same time, I am tormented, more anguished than I thought a man could be and still go on living. If she were anyone else's daughter, I would proclaim our love openly and make her my wife, and the prejudices of her people and my people be damned. I would give up Porter & Co. if I had to and take her from China. We would make a new life—a perfect life—on some island where neither culture could intrude.

" 'I know this sounds hopelessly romantic, but I mean every word. I would do anything to proclaim her as my wife. I want to honor her, not force her to sneak to clandestine meetings like some cheap flower girl. But her father is Houqua. I cannot hurt him publicly, even though I am deceiving him in secret. Each day that deception seems worse. The torment, the conflict grows.

" 'I have come to you, Peter, because I don't know what to do. I can't give her up. I love her, but I love her father too. Help me, Peter, help me.'

"He sat white and still, bent over in the chair, his face buried in his hands. His shoulders shook as if he were wracked with sobs, but I heard no sound.

"Frankly, Samantha, I was at a loss what to say to him. My heart went out to him, because I knew, in part, what he was suffering. I had loved once, as he did, and lost her."

Samantha looked questioningly at Thomson. She always thought of him as somehow apart from the pangs of love and heartbreak. Although he always had attractive women around him, he seemed to like them all equally, in the same, undemanding way, almost like spring flowers on a table. But he went on without a pause, without so much as recognizing her unframed question.

"I said, 'Mallory, I think you already know what you have to do, no matter what it costs you, and I think you have made the right decision.'

"He looked at me with those blue eyes that seem to penetrate like swords. I could imagine them piercing a woman's heart easily, as they had probably pierced the girl's. He was young and I hoped he would find another woman one day. Youth has a way of healing the deepest wounds. There is a scar, of course; there is always a scar, but the throbbing grows less frequent as the years pass.

"I didn't see him again for some time. It was the height of the trading season and I was even busier than usual with five ships in Whampoa to fill. I caught bits of gossip, vague hints that he was involved in some mysterious business. But he must have been very discreet, because as far as I know, there was never any rumor of his romance with the girl.

"Then, just about a week before most of the ships were scheduled to sail home, a great fire broke out in the American factory. It spread swiftly, destroying about one third of the foreign residences in Canton. The blaze was immense. Huge flames leapt from the windows.

"There was a general meeting of the major merchants at the East India Company that night and most of us were attending. We all gathered in the street, of course, to watch the blaze. The fireboats were almost helpless to control it. Luckily for us most of our ships were already loaded, so great cargoes would not be lost.

"We were talking like this among ourselves, when suddenly I saw Mallory Jones push his way through the crowd and run toward the blazing building. It was his factory that was burning. Several men tried to hold him back, but he broke loose.

"The roof looked like it might collapse at any moment. The flames were terrifying red tongues of heat. It seemed like we waited for hours, although only minutes passed before we saw him again. He stood framed for a moment in what had once been the doorway. Then he staggered out carrying a bundle in his arms. His clothes were on fire. His face was bloody and blackened with soot. He staggered down the road, cradling his bundle gently in his arms. Someone doused him with water to kill the flames. He seemed not to notice. Several of us moved to follow him. But he turned and shouted at us to stay back. He was a frightening figure, and he was obeyed. Something in his cry demanded obedience. No one followed. And no one saw Mallory Jones for the rest of the year.

"I sailed to England soon after the fire. When I returned the story in Canton was that Houqua's daughter had died in the blaze. I don't know if it is true, or how it got started. But Houqua has worn mourning clothes ever since that night. Mallory Jones has become a hermit. And many people, myself included, believe there was something very suspicious about the blaze. Although I have no proof of who started it or why, I have my suspicions.

"In the fall when I returned to Canton, I hardly recognized Jones. He had given up Western dress entirely. On the rare occasions when he came to Canton, he wore the long robes of a mandarin. Even his features seemed changed. He'd grown to look more Oriental than American. I know this sounds ridiculous, but I swear to you it is true. Maybe it is the inscrutable mask he puts on to face the world, the curtain he seems to have drawn over his emotions. In any case, I tried to talk to the man. I wanted to help him if I could, but he was unapproachable. Without being rude at all, he made it quite clear that my concern was not welcome.

"This night was the first time since the fire two years ago that Mallory Jones has made a social appearance, and the first time I have seen him dressed in Western clothes. I must say, it pleased me immensely to see him here tonight. It was almost like witnessing a resurrection. For that brief moment when he entered the ball and greeted you and your aunt, he was again the charming young man I'd once known—the golden boy of Canton.

"You have no way of knowing, my dear, what a difficult step it must have been for Jones. He did it, I am sure, because of his affection for your father. I just hope the trouble in the garden has not driven him away again. He can't punish himself forever. Love's fatal fires burn many hearts—many innocent hearts. I hope you will be spared, dearest girl," he added.

Peter Thomson squeezed Samantha's hand lovingly, never suspecting how his words had scorched her soul. She still sat on the settee in stunned silence, but he mistook her quietness for exhaustion.

"You must forgive an old man's windy stories," he sat standing up and taking her hand. "You have had quite enough—too much, probably—for one evening. Come, my dear, I will see you home."

Samantha allowed herself to be led outside to the waiting carriage, too numb to speak or react in any way. Finally, as they rode back toward Mallory Jones's villa, she spoke slowly.

"Uncle Peter, do you think the girl died in the fire?"

"I don't know, though I imagine she did. No one could have lived through that inferno."

There was a long, pregnant pause and then Samantha spoke again. "Do you think he lit the fire?"

"Samantha, no! I am positive he did not. What a terrible question!" Thomson sputtered in surprise. "I have known Mallory Jones since he was a youngster. He is a very gentle man."

"People surprise you, Uncle, even the ones you think you know best," Samantha said softly. "Only he could have known she was there. Perhaps he even brought her there and set the fire to destroy the thing that was destroying him. When it was too late, his heart cried out and he tried to save her."

Thomson strained in the darkness to see Samantha's face, but she was leaning back in the corner of the carriage, lost in shadows. Although her voice sounded intense, he could not believe she meant her words seriously and he answered her lightly.

"I think you've been reading too many of those Fielding stories. But if you want to know my theory, I believe that, when Jones tried to end the affair, the girl came to the hong to plead with him. She must have been desperate to do that, because it is a terrible offense in China to consort with the 'foreign devils.' By a terrible coincidence, someone who wanted to destroy Jones set fire to his factory. He discovered too late that the girl was inside and has been blaming himself ever since."

They rode the rest of the way in silence. A

CHAPTER EIGHT

The Proposal

It was high noon when Samantha awoke. The sun streamed through the shutters, angling against the ceiling just as it did in her room at home. For an instant, half-awake, aware only of the light on the ceiling and of feeling young and vibrant and anxious to taste life fully, she thought she was back in Boston.

She wondered if her father was in the library. He had probably been up for hours, muttering to himself about his lazy daughter. That was just his stern Yankee exterior. She had been scared by it once, mistaking his gruffness for a lack of love, until she saw his stern façade crack for the first time.

She remembered it clearly. She was nineteen. Five years before she had left Boston an unbridled filly; now she was returning an elegant young lady. Her gown was the latest Parisian fashion. Her hair was swept high on her head. When she stepped off the gangway, her father took her in his arms and wept. For Samantha had become as arrestingly beautiful as her mother.

From that moment, Samantha and her father had begun to grow close to each other. She had never been happier before and was looking forward to the grand trip he was planning.

To travel with her father! In her wildest imaginings, she had never thought he would count the time they spent together as anything except a duty to fulfill, and now, he said himself, he wished he had not lost the pleasure of her company through all those years.

Samantha was determined to make up for all the time they had lost together, for all the sadness he had suffered, and, most of all, for taking her mother from him. She only knew her mother from the beautiful portrait in the library, which she had studied and talked to for long hours when she was a child. Maude would never tell her exactly what had happened. Still, she was keenly aware that her mother had died giving birth to her, and that her father had never been the same again.

"I will make it up to him," she promised herself with the sunny assurance of youth.

She sat up in bed and stretched vigorously, catching her reflection in the mirror over the dressing table. She stopped as if frozen, her arms still raised over her head—a wilted rose in her hair, a teakwood mirror, a lacquered chest instead of her Hepplewhite vanity—it all came back to her in an instant. She was thirteen thousand miles from Boston, her father was dead, and she had been violated, insulted, and humiliated by the man he had loved like a son.

Samantha sat on the edge of the bed, her bare feet hanging over the side, while she waited for the maid Chin-Chin to draw a hot bath. The sun that moments before had glowed so warmly now seemed to glare harshly. She had been so emotionally drained by the night before that she had fallen immediately into a deep sleep. Sinking into the hot tub in the clear light of day, she began to think over the long, troubling evening.

As she ran the soap over her breasts and stomach and along her lithe, milky legs, Samantha thought of the girl in the lily pond and of Mallory Jones's hands on her body. *Did he make her feel what I felt?* she wondered. *Did he make her hunger for him with desire?*

She was sure that the lovely statue, the alabaster bust, was of the girl. *Why else would he be so angry because I touched it?* she asked herself. *He loved her. He would have died for her. He hasn't lived since.*

Once you have loved like that, Samantha was sure, you could never love again. His cruel words came back to her. "Not here, nor anywhere again. Go back to your dancing beaus!" And she understood at last his full meaning. He still loved Houqua's daughter.

He had ravaged Samantha in a flush of animal heat. He was the slave of an uncontrollable need, which he had to release, and she had been his luckless victim. His need coarsened her, Samantha thought. He had been living like a wounded beast. He had forgotten or lost touch with the ways of the civilized world. He had used her like a beast, and reduced her to his level.

Yet Samantha was jealous. Although she tried not to admit it to herself, she was sick with jealousy over the woman whose wedding ring waited in the drawer across the room—the woman who had come before her and had taken Mallory Jones's heart with her into the grave. She was jealous and angry and ashamed.

Why did I go back to him? What madness possessed me? she asked herself. *He must think I am a disgrace to my father, no better than those girls in the boats, his for the asking to use as often as he likes during the few weeks left of my visit.*

Realizing from her Uncle Peter's story what she must seem to him, Samantha's humiliation deepened, and with it her resentment. Brokenhearted and confused, she asked herself, "Is it this man I want, or could any man make me feel that way?" But Samantha had no way of knowing the answer because no other man had ever touched her.

Sinking deeply into the tub, she wondered if all women experience the tumultuous passions Mallory Jones had awakened in her. She was lying with her eyes closed, the warm water lapping her breasts, when Chin-Chin returned bearing an elaborate scroll and the news that Jean Levoir was waiting in the parlor.

Samantha broke open the seal and unfurled the scroll. Although the words were English, the beautifully formed letters inscribed on heavy parchment paper with a black quill pen had a distinctly Oriental feeling.

"My dearest Samantha," she read. "If it were in my power to right the wrong I have done to you, please believe I would do so. I can not. Neither can I watch silently while you pursue your plans to wed Jean Levoir. I would be failing in your father's trust, if I did not warn you that such a match would be most undesirable. You will be hurting yourself as much as you will be hurting me. Please take a word of advice and return home to Boston where you belong. My warmest regards to your aunt. Your faithful servant, Mallory Jones."

Samantha flushed a deep crimson as she read his audacious words and her fiery temper boiled. Throwing the scroll across the room, she screamed aloud, "Who does he think he is? The arrogance, the conceit of the man giving me orders and flaunting his love for that woman in my face!"

Then suddenly she leaned back in the tub and laughed bitterly, remembering the fury in Mallory Jones's eyes when he saw her bend over the injured Levoir and cradle his head in her arms. The memory made Samantha feel triumphant. She would give Mallory Jones his answer today. She would go downstairs and make her feelings known to Jean, without being forward or presumptuous. They could announce their engagement the same afternoon.

In this mood Samantha prepared to meet Jean Levoir. She chose her most provocative day dress, a sunflower blue with a tight bodice, pushing up her breasts to show off their snowy contours, and did her hair up in a loose chignon with a velvet ribbon around it. Dabbing her finest scent behind each ear, she went to pledge her future.

Even with a bruised jaw, Jean Levoir was as agreeable and charming as ever. He brushed off the affair of the previous night as if nothing had happened and apologized profusely for not seeing Samantha home.

"I trust Peter Thomson saw you safely to your door. He assured me that he would," Levoir said.

"Of course, Jean, Uncle Peter is such a dear, old friend. He seems always at hand when I need him most. He has been very kind to me through the years. But let's not talk about Uncle Peter," she smiled warmly. "I had been looking forward to a wonderful evening with you, Jean, and it was spoiled terribly before you even had an opportunity to tell me the surprise you had for me."

"It is not exactly a surprise, Samantha," Jean hesitated, "and I don't really know how to tell you . . . I don't know just how to begin."

"Would it help if you started with a kiss?" Samantha asked boldly. "You know we have spent so much time together and been so close, and yet you have never kissed me, even once."

"I was waiting, *ma cherie*, waiting and hoping for the day when I would have that right."

"I was sure that was why you hesitated, Jean, but your kiss could not offend me," Samantha said, turning toward him on the sofa and offering him her full lips.

Jean cupped her chin in his hands and kissed her expectant mouth, lightly. "I hope I will never have to deny myself this pleasure again," he said gallantly.

Samantha was disappointed by his kiss. She had imagined that the touch of his lips would banish all memory of her secret passion. Nothing stirred within her at his kiss, nothing moved. But his next words swept every reservation from her mind.

"Samantha," he said, "I have known many charming women but none like you. Since I first saw you at the masked dance, I have wanted to own you. Will you do me the honor of becoming my wife?"

Samantha did not want to be owned by any man. Jean's words bothered her, but she was sure it was just an unfortunate choice of words in an unfamiliar tongue. If he had proposed to her in his own language, he would not have chosen such words, she thought as she smiled into his soft brown eyes. "Oh, Jean," she murmured, "it is I who will be honored."

She enchanted him—this independent, beautiful American, always so cool and confident as if she were born to be worshipped. He called her his goddess. She touched something in him that he thought no woman could. She was like fine porcelain. He did not hunger for her. Samantha sensed this and it troubled her sometimes. She sensed that he wanted to possess her as he possessed a fine work of art.

He took her hands in his. "We can be married in Paris, Samantha. We will have a glorious wedding. Everyone will come. There will be a huge ballroom strewn with rose petals, and you the fairest rose of all. You will be the toast of the Bourbon court and every man in France will envy me because my bride will be the most beautiful creature in all of Europe."

He pressed her fingers to his lips. "Of course, if you prefer to be wed in Boston, I will come to you there. But then we will have to wait another six months because I must go to Paris from Canton."

Samantha's eyes danced happily. "Oh no, Jean, I would like to be married in Paris. I spent my school days there and, although Boston is my home, Paris is my heart. It is my mother's city and mine. I would like to be married in my mother's city, although I never knew her. And besides," she laughed mischievously, "I don't want to wait an extra six months to become Madame Levoir."

CHAPTER NINE

Jean Levoir

In the two years since she had left Paris, Samantha had grown more beautiful to the loving eyes of Peter Thomson. She'd lost the quicksilverness of youth, but in its place he sensed a deep current of strength and a passion that was boundless. She was haughty and aloof when she chose to be —that was Jonathan in her, he suspected—and a volcano of smoldering passion, like her mother.

He was in love with her. There was no point in deceiving himself, and, if he could not have her, the least he could do for the sake of that love and for the sake of her mother and father was to warn her of the dangers that might lie ahead with Jean Levoir.

Thomson didn't know anything definite about Levoir, but he suspected a great deal, and he was old enough to trust his instincts as surely as most men trust the gospel. Levoir had made a great deal of money in a hurry—that much was indisputable. And he was smart—slippery was probably a better word. But the Chinese Cohong did not trust him. Houqua would have none of him, and for Thomson that was reason enough to be suspicious.

Levoir had built up a fleet of clipper ships, the very newest and swiftest vessels available. They were twice as fast as the old frigates and Thomson was shrewd enough to realize that they could revolutionize the China trade. With the wily Bonner for a partner, Levoir was using the fast boats to build up a booming opium business in Lintin.

More than that, Thomson always wondered about the man himself. Levoir's business dealings, however questionable they might be, were bound to make him a very rich man in no time. But apart from that, his mannerisms bothered Thomson. Although he was too much of a gentleman to admit even in his own mind what worried him, Levoir, he sensed, was always a little too solicitous, too perfectly turned out for every occasion, too certain to be found at the side of the best looking woman in the group.

When the engagement of Samantha Shaw and Jean Levoir was announced in Macao, Thomson took his fears to Jonathan's sister.

Even before she talked to Peter Thomson, Maude Shaw had not looked kindly on her niece's prospective marriage. It was not that she disliked Jean Levoir. She had to admit that he was attractive and attentive. But he was too suave for her straightforward New England temperament. His over-elaborate courtesy and flowery compliments annoyed her, and, after Jonathan's old friend confirmed her worries, she stepped in.

Rather than forbid Samantha from marrying the Frenchman and risk alienting her fiery young neice, Maude tried to steer Samantha away from Jean Levoir. At the last ball, she had been quite taken with her brother's friend, Mallory Jones, and she tried to interest Samantha in him, hoping to give her second thoughts about her marriage. But when she mentioned the man, she was taken aback by her niece's vehemence.

Maude knew that when Samantha set her mind to something, she was as stubborn as her father. But even with that, she could not understand the girl's violent antipathy toward Mallory Jones. Fearing to aggravate the situation further, she decided to keep her mouth shut. Samantha was old enough to chose her own husband and too stubborn to be changed in any event.

Maude realized that there was nothing she or Peter Thomson could do to make Samantha reconsider her decision. She had never seen her niece so steely and unyielding before. She refused even to listen to her Uncle Peter's admonitions, for the first time in memory.

There was only one person who could make Samantha change her mind—and she would not even hear the sound of his name.

Mallory Jones could offer Samantha nothing. He had given his heart once. He did not think he could ever give it again. He had destroyed a woman once. He was afraid to destroy another. And yet, his passion kept drawing him back to Samantha, wounding her, forcing her to submit to him. He could not control himself. He never thought he would feel such stirrings again. This was different. With Ming-la it had been his first, innocent love, completely trusting and giving. With Samantha it was a violent, dangerous passion. He had thrust himself on her, forcing her to succumb to his desire. He wanted to drive her wild, to break her cool demeanor. He was like a different man with her. She awakened passions he never knew he had. His whole being hungered for her. But he dared not take another woman. Not again.

Yet, he could not let Levoir have her. The sight of Samantha holding Jean in her arms in the garden had driven Mallory Jones into a white, unquenchable fury. *I should have destroyed Levoir before*, he thought dangerously. *My old friend, Jean! Of all the men in China why did Samantha have to pick him?* And what . . .what did Levoir want from the girl?

Mallory Jones and Jean Levoir had been close friends once. Jones knew the Frenchman was weak and ambitious, but he was also witty and entertaining, a good companion through the long tea season when life in Canton was so severely circumscribed. The absence of women and the lack of liberty never seemed to bother Levoir.

He thrived on the bonhomie that characterized life in the foreign factories.

But their friendship began to sour the night Jones took the young Frenchman to the flower boats for the first time. They could never again be easy and comfortable together. Although Jones did not blame Levoir for his actions, he drew away from him and avoided his company as much as he could in the limited quarters of Canton. Soon after, Levoir joined forces with Pierre Bonner.

Bonner was well known in Canton as a scoundrel and a cheat. None of the respectable Chinese merchants would deal with him, so he was forced to operate on the fringes, frequently resorting to the other side of the law. Jones warned Levoir not to get involved with the man, but Jean always countered his warnings with some offhand remark.

By then Mallory Jones had other things on his mind. He was so torn by his love affair with Houqua's daughter that he had time for almost nothing and no one else. When he did see Levoir again, it was just a week before the fire. His eyes were glazed, his speech slurred. It was obvious that Jean was not only trading opium, he had begun to use it. Jones suspected that Bonner was behind his friend's addiction.

They had heated words that day. The Emperor had just issued a new decree, making the Cohong chief responsible for any opium that was smuggled into Whampoa. The punishment was harsh. The Chinese merchant's estates would be confiscated and he would never again be permitted to trade with the Fan-kwae. But Levoir and Bonner did not care. They planned to continue bringing the poppy juice in anyway.

Jones tried to change his friend's mind, pleading with him not to jeopardize Houqua's delicate position in China. Levoir had laughed derisively. He was going on with his scheme. It would bring him a fortune that would make the wealth of Porter & Co. seem like dirt. Nothing could stop him, he asserted, and then, in a bitter, insolent tone he added, "And who, Mallory Jones, are you to preach about jeopardizing Houqua's place —from your position on top of his daughter?"

Jones had turned white. He seized the Frenchman by the lapels of his waistcoat and all but lifted him off the ground. "What are you talking about?" he demanded.

"About you and that slant-eyed whore. You thought you were so clever, that no one knew. But I am just as clever, Mallory. I knew you had found something—someone. I followed you one day. I saw you. I watched you."

Jones's grip tightened on the man's throat.

"Don't worry, I haven't told anyone—not even Bonner. It is our secret." There was a pleading note in Levoir's voice, a sad, wistful look in his eyes. "You should not have deceived me, though. You should have told me."

"What are you insinuating?" Jones demanded.

"If I do not help you smuggle in the opium, you will spread a rumor about Ming-la?"

"That would be a sensible bargain, Mallory, now that you offer." Levoir smiled a faint half-smile. "It was not in my mind, but since you suggest it, how can I refuse?"

Mallory Jones looked at the Frenchman with withering contempt.

"Because of the friendship I once bore for you, I will not kill you here and now with my bare hands. That is the only deal I will make with you, Levoir. If you so much as breathe a word, if I catch even a hint, a suggestion, about Ming-la from anyone in Canton, I will kill you. That is a solemn oath which I swear to you."

A week later the American hong went up in flames. Mallory Jones suspected arson. He was pretty sure that Levoir had set the fire to revenge himself. But he had no proof and, afterwards, he had no heart to pursue the matter.

He was sure Levoir did not know Ming-la was in the factory. He did not know himself until her servant drew him into the alley, and by then it was too late. If he thought for a moment that Levoir knew the girl was there, the Frenchman would be as good as dead. But he did not believe that.

Jones pitied Levoir more than he hated him. He had been fond of the young man who had come to Canton five years before and it made him sad to see what Jean had become.

After the fire, Levoir moved his opium business to Lintin and Jones retreated into the hills of Macao. The next time they met was in the garden with Samantha. Mallory Jones was amazed that this man was coming to claim the girl, even for a dance, and when she informed him that he was interrupting their engagement party he was first stunned and then infuriated. Perhaps he could let her go to another man, but never to Levoir.

Mallory Jones was certain that if he had not mistaken Samantha in the garden that first night, she would never be pledging herself so fatefully. There was one way he could stop her, but it would be tantamount to a proposal of marriage, and he could not pledge himself to another woman. Not now or ever. His pledge lay buried somewhere in the Celestial Empire from which he and every other foreign devil was excluded.

CHAPTER TEN

China Farewell

Samantha Shaw was leaving China a bride-to-be. Her bags were packed and loaded aboard the waiting ship. Basking in Jean Levoir's gentle affection, she had almost forgotten the anger that had prompted her to accept his proposal. Now as she made the final preparations for the voyage to Paris, she was sure she had made the right decision. In spite of Aunt Maude's disapproval and Uncle Peter's admonitions, no doubts assailed her. Jean's tender love was the perfect antidote to Mallory Jones's violent passion.

Although she sometimes wished that Jean revealed more desire for her, Samantha was confident that he was suppressing his deepest feelings until she was rightfully his. She longed for the day and threw herself happily into plans for the voyage to Paris. She was already planning the wedding. Madame Desrochere would design her dress. She wanted a bodice and long sleeves of Chantilly lace and yards and yards of train.

There would be countless fittings and discussions, and a whirl of parties for the handsome couple.

Samantha was disappointed that Jean would not be on the dock to say goodbye when she left China. In fact, she was dawdling a little in the hope that he would be back from Lintin in time to see her off.

She recalled their last meeting—she had wanted him to tell her nothing could keep him away. But instead he said apologetically that his business was urgent and he would be unable to attend her sailing.

She responded lightly to hide her disappointment, "I understand, Jean. When we are Monsieur and Madame Levoir I daresay we will see more than enough of each other."

"I hoped you would understand, Samantha," he said relieved. "I will try to be back if I can, but don't hold the ship for me."

"*Toujours Paris,*" she said in parting.

Samantha was remembering that last conversation when there was a knock on the door. Her heart jumped. The uncharacteristic daring that brought him to the door of her boudoir excited her.

"Come in, *mon cheri,*" she called.

She was standing against the dresser, her lovely face glowing with anticipation when Mallory Jones entered the room, closing the door firmly behind him.

"What do you want?" she cried, surprised and

angered by his intrusion. "How dare you come into my bedroom?"

"I believe this is still my house," he answered. His ice blue eyes bored through her, bringing a flush to her cheeks. "I just came to return this. You forgot it somewhere," he said coldly, thrusting a velvet ribbon into her hand.

Samantha blushed with the memory of how he had come by it. "Thank you, but it was unnecessary," she said.

She had almost succeeded in closing him out of her mind entirely in the happiness she had found with Jean and in the flurry of preparation for the voyage to Paris. But now that he was standing directly in front of her, his fierce eyes pinning her to the spot, she could not seem to draw away from his stare. His bold, cold gaze made her uncomfortable and stirred memories she had tried to destroy.

"Now, if there is nothing more, Mr. Jones, will you please excuse me," she said, hoping her voice sounded calm and unconcerned.

But he stepped closer. "Who were you expecting?" His words hissed out at her like a snake's tongue.

From the look on her face, Mallory Jones knew instantly that Samantha was waiting for someone—and he knew it wasn't him. He tried to control his anger. What was there about this woman that drove him to such fury? But the thought that someone else would—or maybe already had—possessed her, that Levoir of all people would have her, filled him with a raging jealousy.

"My fiancé, of course, Jean Levoir. I believe you have met," she responded cooly, but her heart was running wild. For a moment she thought he could see it thumping in her chest, it was beating so rapidly. His sudden, unexpected appearance had caught her completely offguard and his controlled, smoky anger and burning eyes awoke those passions in her that she had tried to quench, to bury forever, and with them her shame, by marrying Jean.

"You can't go through with it, Samantha, not with Levoir. I won't let you," he said fiercely.

"And what do you think you can do to stop me, Mr. Jones?" she asked, a ring of triumph evident in her voice.

"I will make you remember," he answered gruffly, "whether you want to or not." And he took her in his arms.

Samantha knew it was useless to fight him. He was too strong. So she tried to remain ice cold. She would blot out the demand of his lips with thoughts of Jean, gentle Jean.

But Mallory Jones did not try to kiss her. He just held her in his arms, fiercely, possessively, his mouth pressed against her ear, murmuring her name, his hot breath tickling and exciting her, until they were one. She forgot about the ship. She forgot time and her fiancé and lost herself in his embrace.

127

He was rough and gentle at the same time, caressing her body and crushing her against him, tracing her lips lightly with his tongue, then bruising her mouth with deep, violent kisses. His tender, urgent passion touched the deepest recess of her heart and Samantha knew at last the meaning of love. A strange, unfathomable destiny had brought them together, now nothing could part them again. Mallory Jones was the man she was born to possess and to be possessed by and she surrendered willingly to his sweet, savage desire. His caress, his touch, his kiss aroused deep, ungovernable passions within her as Samantha answered his demanding body with abandon. Aching to know again the full thrust of his desire, she pleaded, she beseeched him to take her.

"There isn't time," he whispered huskily. But she was already unfastening her bodice, and lifting her breast to his lips. "There isn't time," he murmured again as he drank hungrily from her fountain, biting her breasts, sinking his teeth into her erect nipples, then, when she cried out, soothing the pain with his cool tongue.

"Take me, my darling, make me yours again," she begged.

He raised her skirts and petticoats and lifted her up on the dresser. "There isn't time, Samantha," he whispered, but his fingers were caressing her thighs and fondling her juicy lips through her lacy undergarments.

Samantha's desire was so intense she could deny

it no longer. "I love you, Mallory," she moaned, "I want your love again."

With trembling fingers she unbuttoned his breeches and unsheated his terrible, sweet sword. When he felt her fingers on him, he lost all control. Tearing away what lay between his hand and her treasure, he drew her to him. He was standing in front of her and she could see him disappear slowly inside her.

He withdrew, then entered her again. Each thrust seemed deeper than the first, until, spreading her thighs wider, he brought her to a climax. He stayed within her, holding her against him until it had passed and then he drew her forth again, and a third time until she thought the joy could not be greater. But he waited again until she was quiet and then he began once more, driving into her. She locked her legs around his waist and answered his urgent thrusts, the one fulfilling the other, until, like a single body, they exploded together in an absolute fullness, achieving a bliss so intense they could hardly bear it.

Samantha leaned against the mirror limply, her tired thighs wet and glistening, and smiled lovingly. Her eyes glowed. Her bare breasts were rosy from desire. Mallory Jones took her hand and wrapped it around his now weak member, then he brought her fingers, wet with his seed, to her mouth.

"You will remember me," he said, then kissing her passionately, he turned away.

At the door he stopped. She was still sitting on the dresser, her dress caught up around her waist.

"I love you, Samantha," he cried, his voice hoarse and choked, and then he was gone.

Samantha walked to the boat like someone in a trance. Jean was there, after all, and Peter Thomson, but she hardly noticed. Her eyes kept searching the crowd, sweeping the docks for a glimpse of summer blue eyes. She bade her farewells as if she were sleepwalking.

"Are you expecting someone?" Jean asked.

"Of course not, only you," she answered, but she knew Mallory would come to claim her. He would not let her board the waiting ship, not after the morning. But there was no sign of him, no message for her.

The fireworks from the pilot boat drowned out Samantha's sobs as she sailed into the South China Sea, on a ship bound for Paris. Not even her Aunt Maude, in the tiny adjoining cabin, was aware of her suffering.

CHAPTER ELEVEN

Samantha Remembers

Although the voyage of the *Wind Song* was smooth and uneventful, Samantha was ill most of the time. She felt oddly weak and sensitive, and spent long hours alone in her cabin, away from her aunt or anyone else, sorting out the memories of the trip and the tumultuous passions it had aroused in her. Lying on her narrow berth, Samantha resolved that marriage to Jean Levoir was what she wanted most in the world. She dismissed her madness for Mallory Jones as shameful carnal desire—nothing more—and was more determined than ever to subdue the terrible passions that he had awakened.

Samantha hated Jones as she had never hated before. And she hated the fire that he kindled, that even the thought of him still kindled within her. She had made up her mind to forget him— no matter what it cost or how long it took. But she found out all too soon that forgetting Mallory Jones would not be an easy thing to do.

After weeks of calm water and balmy temperatures, the sea turned cruel. Storms buffeted the ship for days, transforming the blue blanket into a terrifying black menace. But Samantha barely noticed the weather. The storm inside her was infinitely worse. Like some Oriental demon, Mallory Jones had worked his will on her body. She had to remember him now every morning. Her body forced her to, for, Samantha discovered, she was carrying his seed!

Her plans were ruined. She detested Jones and she loathed the life he had put inside her. He had planted it purposely, she was sure of it. He had seduced her and forced his child upon her, so that she could not marry Jean Levoir. What man would wed a woman who was bearing another man's child? The most glorious wedding of the Paris season would be the most ignominious humiliation. Everyone would assume the baby was Levoir's. Except Jean. What would he think of her? What kind of a woman would he think he had fallen in love with?

Samantha could not imagine how she would ever be able to explain her fragile condition to Jean. Confessing to Aunt Maude would be difficult enough. She could never admit to her upright Yankee aunt that, while affianced to Jean, she was carrying another man's child. Maude would blame Samantha's Latin blood. She had never liked Marie. She was jealous, Samantha suspected, of the woman who had claimed Jonathan Shaw so completely and had left him so desolate at her death. But she loved Marie's daughter like her own.

But she did tell her aunt, for as her sickness persisted, she had to. To her amazement, Maude took the news far more gracefully than Samantha would have expected. And in the excitement of learning she was to become a great-aunt, Maude never asked who the father was. Nor did Samantha volunteer the information.

Bad weather continued to plague the voyage. After surviving a treacherous passage around the Cape of Good Hope, the *Wind Song* sailed up the coast of Africa into violent seas and hurricane gales. Captain Crawford tried to ride out the storms, hoping for a break in the weather, but the storms did not abate. The compass broke; the mast splintered. Water poured into the holds. Finally, far off course and desperate, the captain gave the order to abandon ship. Lifeboats were lowered into the angry sea. As they leaned on the oars, pulling away from the empty vessel, the hapless *Wind Song* splintered in half and sank in the sea.

By morning the ocean had calmed. The only signs of the wreck were a few planks from the *Wind Song* that bobbed on the water's surface, and a single lifeboat. Two other lifeboats and the complete cargo were lost. The survivors drifted miserably for three days before they sighted land. As they rowed eagerly toward the shore, two deep canoes came out to meet them, each carrying some twelve or fourteen men.

Their skin was the color of betel nuts and was painted a bright blue, and they were completely naked except for a small square of leather, which covered the groin and was tied by a vine rope around their waists.

Turtles as large as footstools snapped at the shoreline, adding an eerie sound as the men chattered excitedly in their strange tongue, pointing and laughing at the small band of survivors. Signaling the lifeboat to follow, they turned around and rowed to the opposite side of the island, where they beached their canoes. As the survivors disembarked, the native men crowded around Samantha and Maude, trying to touch their fair skin and look under their long, tattered skirts. Captain Crawford pushed away their curious hands and ordered his men to form a protective circle around the women. The natives pointed their long sharp spears at Captain Crawford, but he would not be intimidated.

"Don't worry," he reassured the women, "we will die before we let these barbarians lay a finger on either of you."

Weary, thirsty, and frightened, the survivors of the *Wind Song* were led at spear-point into a village of straw huts. At the largest hut they were ordered to stop while their captors crowded around a short, squarely built man who wore a necklace of shells. They talked animatedly, pointing at the white women. It was obvious that he was their chief and they were asking him

135

for the women. Looking over his captors swiftly, the chief settled the dispute to his own liking.

"That one," he seemed to be saying, pointing to Maude, "is too old. This one I gratefully accept from you, my brothers, as a gift from the sea." The chief strode over to the fire and kicked the old slave who was bent over a steaming kettle. "Speak to them," he ordered.

The old man straightened up and approached the Americans slyly. "This is Chief Wanda, you poor unlucky souls," he said in perfect English. "Would that you had perished at sea."

The survivors gazed in astonishment at the old man. He looked like an ancient betel nut, brown and wrinkled. "Don't you recognize one of your own?" he cried. "I am an Englishman— God Bless King George—for ten years the slave of these cruel islanders. I was the only survivor. Six of us made it ashore, but only I have survived the horror and torture of life on this island. I was a strapping lad ten years ago and look at me now. You'll be looking like this before long yourselves, unless we bury you first," he cackled crazily.

"As for you, my pretty lass," he turned to Samantha, an evil glint in his old eyes, "the chief has claimed you for himself. You will be his slave, his to violate at will and share with his pals."

"Do you know what you are saying, man?" Captain Crawford spoke up angrily.

"Don't worry," the old man leered, "the chief will marry the girl in his fashion. When the chief takes a new woman, the whole tribe gathers. There is feasting and dancing and great ceremony. While the men are gorging themselves with food, the older wives prepare the new bride. First they paint her body in bright colors, then they work on her maidenhead with their hands and sometimes their tongues until she is open and wet for the entrance of the chief.

"When the girl is prepared, the whole tribe forms a circle around her, and she dances naked, the bright paint glittering in the firelight, faster and faster, until the chief is excited enough. Then he rises, grunting like a pig, and mounts her in the center of the circle. Everyone closes in, urging their chief on again and again. His humping excites the others, and when he tires, his brothers take his place on the blushing bride."

An impatient grunt from the chief interrupted the old man's soliloquy. "He says to tell you all that tonight, in honor of this lovely white spirit here, there will be an enormous celebration. The whole village will be invited to share the lass, and, as a special courtesy, you white men will be bound to stakes and allowed to watch the marriage being consummated. The chief is quite proud of his private part and he doesn't mind showing off what he can do with it." He turned to Samantha.

"Now, me girl, raise your skirts and give us a peek of what you've been hiding," the old man wheezed, sidling up to Samantha. "The chief wants to see if you are the same as his brown women down there, so he'll know what preparations to make for his wedding." He laughed insanely and grabbed her skirt.

Samantha had stood ashen as the wizened old man described her fate in all its revolting detail. But when he tried to raise her skirts, she cried out in horror and swooned in a dead faint. Captain Crawford caught her in his arms as she fell and shouted to the natives to keep back. They hesitated, sensing the note of command in the white man's voice. The chief grunted again.

"He wants to know if she's dead," the old man translated.

Maude Shaw could hold her tongue no longer. She remembered all too clearly Captain Stevens's ominous warning, but she would kill Samantha herself rather than allow the girl to submit to such a fate. "You tell that filthy man to listen to me," she ordered the old man, stepping forward. "You tell him for me that my niece is in a very delicate condition and cannot be touched by anyone. She is carrying a child, and no man will lay a finger on her until they kill me first."

"Aye, aye, ma'am," the old sailor snapped smartly. Maude's bold, honest words seemed to have awakened a fleeting memory of civilization. He spoke hurriedly to the chief who seemed to be responding with disbelief. Then the chief yelled loudly and a handsome, middle-aged woman appeared at the entrance of his hut. She was naked and enormous with child; another was in her arms. The chief pointed at the woman.

138

"He says that is what a woman with child looks like," the old man translated.

"Be that as it may," Maude insisted firmly, "my niece is also carrying a child."

After more discussions and exchanges between the chief and the old man, the woman walked over and stared wondrously at the slim white goddess who sat in the grass, resting against Captain Crawford's knee.

"He wants the woman here to tell him if your niece is in that condition, ma'am," the old man said.

"Very well," Maude replied curtly. "Captain Crawford, carry Samantha into that . . . that hut over there. Then please wait outside. You too," she added to the old man, "we may need you to translate." Maude took the native woman's arm and they followed Captain Crawford, Samantha in his arms, into the chief's hut.

The others waited anxiously until the native woman appeared again at the mouth of the hut. She spoke briefly to the chief, who questioned her sharply. When they were through, the old Englishman translated.

"The woman says she is sure the child is due in six moons. At the seventh moon, the chief will take the girl in two days and two nights of feasting. The old goat is drooling just thinking about it," he cackled. "Can't say as I'd mind being in his shoes. She's a choice morsel, that one, probably the sweetest piece of meat that's ever come to Pagalu."

139

CHAPTER TWELVE

Island Enslavement

While the chief waited for the child to be born, he kept Samantha and Maude apart from the other survivors, isolated in a small straw hut, a short distance from his own. Aunt Maude was made to work in the fields from dawn to dusk. But the strain of the trip and her pregnancy had been too much for Samantha. For much of her confinement she was too weak to leave her grass mat and so remained in the hut, watched over by one of the chief's young sons.

Samantha grew fond of the boy Owino, and he was enchanted with the beautiful white goddess from the sea. Most days he would try to bring her a special present—some sweet, ripe berries one day, a beautiful bird's feather the next. Samantha began to teach the boy English to make the time pass and to give her someone to talk to. She knew Owino was falling in love with her, but she was helpless to spare him and too distraught by the prospects of her enslavement to think clearly about the boy's emotions.

Each day that passed, Samantha grew more desperate, knowing that it brought her closer to her native wedding date. One day, as she went into her seventh month, she asked Owino about the dreaded ceremony. The boy picked up a stick and drew a picture on the sand floor of the hut. He drew figures dancing and eating, and, in the center, he drew a naked woman, lying prone. On top of her he drew the chief with the necklace of shells around his neck, and then he just kept drawing figure after figure over the first one until Samantha cried aloud. The boy brushed out the drawing quickly, his dark eyes wide with alarm, and tried to calm the beautiful lady. But she would not stop crying, her cries soon turning to screams.

Owino ran to the fields and fetched his mother. By the time they reached the hut, Samantha was already in labor. The chief was ecstatic that the birth was early, and immediately issued orders to begin preparations for the wedding ceremony even as he gave instructions to throw the new-born baby into the sea. Premature babies, the villagers believed, were born too early and there-fore too weak to ever grow into strong men. With the help of Owino, the chief's number one wife delivered Samantha of a male child. Owino took the infant to the cliff as he had been ordered to do.

When Maude returned from the fields that night, the old sailor told her the child had been born dead. She grieved inwardly, even though she knew the infant was better off dead than born into enslavement on the desolate island. But her immediate concern was Samantha. She had lost consciousness during her labor and had never regained it. Now she was burning with fever.

For the next five days, Maude refused to go back to her work in the fields. She and Owino stayed at Samantha's side, guarding her through her delirium until the fever broke and her temperature began to drop. They had saved Samantha's life, but Maude wondered if they had done the right thing. What had she saved her niece for? she asked herself as she looked down at the girl lovingly.

Finally Samantha opened her eyes and smiled weakly. "Aunt Maude," she whispered.

"Yes, dear, what can I get for you?"

"May I see the baby now?"

Maude took the girl's hand and squeezed it tightly.

"You lost the child, Samantha," she said as gently as she could. "It was born dead."

Samantha lay back and closed her eyes again. She wondered if it had been a boy or a girl, but she didn't ask and she never spoke of the child again. To her it was as dead as the strange passion she had felt for its father.

As Samantha gradually regained her strength, she grew to dread more and more the forthcoming wedding celebration. Her illness had slowed down the preparations, but now that she was gaining rapidly, she could no longer postpone the inevitable. Each night when Maude returned from the fields, they would consider plans of escape from the desolate island prison. But in her heart Samantha knew their only real hope lay with Owino.

Samantha had spent more time alone with the boy than she ever had with any man, and a natural intimacy had developed between them. When she was too weak to care for herself, Owino had done it. He had fed her, he had bathed her, he had tended to her most personal needs. He had rubbed her aching limbs with palm oil and washed her matted hair. Without his gentleness and care, she probably would have died. Owino had never had a woman and, although he never said it, Samantha knew there was only one woman on the island he wanted. How much would he do to possess her? she wondered.

A year ago Samantha Shaw would have sworn on her mother's grave that she would give herself only in love, and only to the husband that she cherished. But that time seemed so distant, it was hardly more than a dream. The girl she had been was dead. The woman she had been forced to become would use all her powers, even her body if she had to—and use them well—before she would ever be violated again. She had submitted to Mallory Jones. She would never submit to any man again. If this was the only way to escape from the brutal rape this band of savages was planning, then she would do it.

The next afternoon, Samantha called Owino

into the hut and asked him to rub her back with oil. She was lying on her stomach on the grass mat, as she had done so many times before, her back bare, a cloth held across the sides of her bosom modestly. The boy rubbed her back skillfully, his strong young hands working the palm oil deep into her skin. When he had finished, she turned over on the mat, leaving the protective cloth underneath her.

"Owino," she said softly, "would you mind rubbing my breasts, too? They are sore and tender from the drying milk."

The boy's dark eyes grew wide with wonder as he stared at the pure white globes still heavy and ripe with the unused milk. They are whiter than the moon, he thought, as he shyly began to rub the oil into the valley between them. Samantha smiled at him encouragingly and moved his hand onto the dome of her breast. The oil and his young hands felt so sensual on her unsucked mother's teats that gradually she gave in to the sensation, murmuring low moans of pleasure. Then she smiled up at him.

"There is more to do, Owino," she said and, untying the grass skirt he had woven for her, she stretched naked before him. The boy caught his breath. His wildest dream was within reach.

Emboldened by Samantha's sighs, Owino rubbed the oil into her stomach, so smooth that one could never tell just a few weeks before she had given birth, and down the front of her long slim legs. He rubbed her feet, working his way

146

back along the inside of her calfs up to her thighs. When his brief loincloth could no longer disguise the fact that he was a man, Samantha drew him toward her. Like a mother bird teaching her chicks to fly, she showed him a man's pleasure.

The boy's excitement was too great to contain long enough to satisfy Samantha, but she did not care. When he was finished, she held him in her arms as she would a child and let him drink the milk from her breast. Samantha stroked his hair as he suckled.

"Owino," she murmured softly, "I am so frightened of the celebration your father is planning for me."

"There is no need to be afraid," he answered. "All the wives of my father have done it. It is a great honor for a woman to be chosen."

"In the land where I come from, the chief takes his wife in private, as you have taken me," she said, still stroking his hair fondly, "and he never shares her with his brothers. A woman gives herself to one man only, and she is his to honor and obey until death." Owino did not answer, but she knew she had given him something to think about.

The next afternoon, Owino came to her again, and after he had taken her, she held him quietly. All her passion was in her low voice. "Owino, I am going to throw myself into the sea. I wish you had let me die with the child, let me die with my shame, instead of saving me for your father, and a far worse humiliation."

"My shame," Owino repeated softly. He looked at Samantha strangely, as if he wanted to comfort her, but he said nothing more. He just stroked her cheek and sang a sad native song.

Each morning the chief came to Samantha's hut to check on her health and make sure she would be strong enough for the wedding. Each afternoon, his young son came to lay with her. Samantha often wondered what the chief would do if he found out that his son had already claimed his prize. She had grown fond of the alien boy and had begun to look forward to their afternoons together. His love-making did not excite her. Quite the opposite, it quieted her, calmed the fears that grew hourly more palpable. When they were finished, he would ask her about the way white ghost men take their wives.

"In my country," she said one day, "each man has one woman and each woman has one man. They choose each other because they love each other above all others. The man shelters the woman, the woman bears his children. They nourish each other with their affection, and they grow old together."

"The father of your child, the man you belong to, did he die in the shipwreck?" Owino asked.

Samantha hesitated, unprepared for the boy's question. To her Mallory Jones was dead, as dead as the child she had borne. The man she belonged to was Jean Levoir. But how could she explain to Owino that the man she was bound to was not the father of her baby?

"No," she said finally. "He didn't die in the wreck. I was on my way home to wait for him."

"Then you have broken the law of your people by lying with me." His voice was more curious than admonishing.

"Yes, I have."

"If you could go back to him and be with him again, if you could be free tomorrow would you go to him?"

"Yes, Owino, I would go."

Samantha was afraid she had hurt him with her words. He is just a boy, she reminded herself, a very young boy infatuated by a girl for the first time. He thought she was more than a woman—a goddess, his white goddess. "Don't you see, Owino," she said, "if I stayed here I could never remain with you. In another week your father will claim me, and then your uncles and, who knows, probably their sons—all of them taking their pleasure from my body while you watched. We would never lie here again in each other's arms and I would never again know your gentle manhood."

The boy lay quietly beside her. His eyes seemed to drink her in for a long moment before he spoke. "There is a great ship lying off the eastern shore. They came today to trade for fresh fruits. Tomorrow, I think, they will come again. Perhaps this great ship would take you back to your home . . . to your people."

Samantha's heart leapt wildly at his words. A ship! A ship at last! "Yes," she said, not daring

149

to reveal the extent of her excitement, "it might. But your father would never let me go."

"I will come for you after dark tomorrow," he said simply.

"And your father . . . " she hesitated. She didn't want to weaken his resolve, yet at the same time, she didn't want any harm to come to the boy. "What will he do if he finds out?"

"Owino will not find out," he said flatly.

Samantha clasped him tightly to her breast for the last time. He was just a simple native boy, but his tenderness had struck a sympathetic chord within her. "We will be ready."

She could hardly wait for her aunt to come back from the fields that evening. Maude Shaw was used to a staff of servants. Now she was less than the least of them herself. The hard physical labor in the fields had taken its toll. Her hair had turned snow white. Her back was stooped. After so many hours in the field she could barely straighten up at the end of the day. Her feet were swollen, her hands calloused and raw. The forthright, tart-tongued woman who had sailed out of Boston harbor was barely visible in the drawn, old woman who shuffled into the hut. Fearing any sudden shock might be more than her aunt could bear, Samantha decided to break the happy news to her gently. She made her sit down while she fixed some hot water and betel-nut juice. While Maude sipped the hot drink, Samantha told her what Owino had said.

"Can we trust him?" Maude's old curtness had not changed.

"Absolutely," Samantha answered enthusiastically.

"How can you be so sure?"

Samantha avoided her aunt's sharp eyes and began to wrap their few pathetic goods in a bundle. "He is our only hope. We have to trust him."

"Yes, of course we do," Maude said, "but have you thought of what the consequences will be if we are discovered?"

"Could they be worse than this? Or worse than what will happen next week?" Samantha shuddered involuntarily at the thought of it.

"I will find a way to talk to John Temple in the field tomorrow. He will pass the word to the others—there are only five left, you know. Poor Captain Crawford, God rest his soul, died of the fever, and two others as well." Maude sighed heavily. "I don't sound very excited, my dear, but believe me, it is the best news I have had since . . . well, since you came home from Paris. It seems like so very long ago now."

"Yes, yes, Auntie," Samantha said embracing the old woman, "but tomorrow we will be on our way back."

The next day seemed to stretch on forever. The chief made his usual morning call and, with gestures so crude she could not possibly mistake his meaning, he indicated that he thought she was more than ready to be taken by himself and his brothers. Samantha did not deign to respond in any way, but when he had gone she shook uncontrollably with repugnance.

Owino did not bring her noon meal, and by midafternoon, Samantha was watching anxiously for him. But he was nowhere in sight. As the hours passed, her nervousness increased. *Has he changed his mind?* she wondered. *Is he afraid of his father's punishment? Or is it just that he won't give me up?* Angry and disappointed, she made up her mind they would try to escape without him, if they had to. That evening Maude returned to find a fiercely determined Samantha. All her excitement of the previous day was gone, and in its place was a grim resolve to get to the unknown ship at any cost.

"Has something happened, Samantha? Has something gone wrong?" Maude asked anxiously. She was very tired, so tired she could not fully enjoy the idea that they might be sailing home in the morning. The old woman had two wishes—to see her niece away from this barbaric island, and to see Boston once more. She wanted to spend whatever days remained to her there where she had been born and lived her life, and to be buried in the North Church graveyard beside her parents and her brother Jonathan.

"The boy has disappeared," Samantha answered. "I have not seen him at all today."

"Maybe he is making preparations for our escape," Maude said, more to encourage Samantha than because she believed there was any truth in her words.

"Or maybe he has gotten scared."

"Samantha, the good Lord has brought us this far. I don't think he will abandon us now that hope is in sight." Maude was not convinced by her own words. She had been taught to believe that the ways of the Lord are strange indeed and that it doesn't behoove mere mortals to try to understand them, but she wanted desperately to give her niece hope.

"The good Lord has nothing to do with it," Samantha said bitterly. "We are at the mercy of a man—a young man to be sure—but a man nonetheless. If he doesn't come at dusk, are you willing to try the escape without him?"

"We must, dear," Maude said evenly. "John and the others will be waiting for us at the eastern point. They are counting on us."

"We might have to try to swim to the ship. It will be a long, difficult swim. Do you think you can . . ."

"Samantha, my dear," Maude interrupted, "I would rather die trying to escape than spend my few remaining years in this savage place."

"Oh, so would I, Aunt Maude." Samantha hugged the older woman. "We will wait until the last possible moment. Maybe the boy will keep his promise afterall."

Maude lay down on the grass mat to rest for the dangerous adventure ahead of them. She closed her eyes, although she did not sleep. She knew she would never survive a swim to the ship. She was exhausted, her body broken by the arduous work she had been forced to do. But her will was still strong. She was old, but Samantha was young, and she loved the girl like a daughter. Samantha had a full, rich life ahead of her and Maude was not prepared to see it end in the middle of this godforsaken island with dozens of savages ravaging her. She had not brought the girl up so lovingly to see it all end like that. All those years away in school had been lonely ones. But Samantha's happiness had always been the most important thing in Maude's life.

She lay on the grass mat with her eyes closed tightly and prayed for a safe escape, until Samantha shook her lightly.

They could wait for the boy no longer. Grasping their pathetic bundles, the two women crouched in the entrance of the hut, listening in the darkness for some human sound. They heard nothing.

"It seems unusually quiet," Maude whispered, "too quiet. Maybe they have lain a trap for us."

"We don't have to try it, Auntie, if you don't want to."

"It is our only chance, dear. I am ready for whatever comes."

Stealthily, the two women crept out into the clear night. For a brief second they were silhouetted in the light of the full moon. A high bird whistle pierced the night. Samantha stopped. The bird trilled again.

"Aunt Maude," she whispered, "it's Owino."

Maude squeezed her niece's hand in silent communion and they inched their way toward the bird sound—Owino. The boy motioned them to follow him and they crept through the sleeping village towards the rough headland. Each foot they traveled seemed like a mile. Each twig that snapped under their feet seemed to resound like thunder. Samantha feared the sounds would alert their captors. At every step she expected to see blue-painted bodies leap out from behind the next shrub and seize them.

She could smell no hint of the sea and this confirmed her worst suspicions, for she imagined that the boy was leading them in a wide circle and that they would end up in the center of the village with all the natives assembled to take their horrible revenge.

As these frightening thoughts raced through her mind, Owino turned and their eyes met for a moment. His face was set and intense. She felt a terrible guilt for distrusting him, but she had no time to brood about it because a few paces more and they emerged from the undergrowth onto a rocky cliff.

Samantha's heart skipped excitedly as she gazed out at the black sea. Straining her eyes, she could glimpse, in the moonlight, the outline of a dark object along the horizon. The ship was there just as the boy had said. What flag was she flying? Where was she headed? Would she take on unexpected passengers? None of these questions occurred to Samantha as she peered happily at what, she was sure, was their salvation.

Owino watched her intently, her joyful face imprinted indelibly in his heart. He wondered who the white man was she was returning to and whát powers he possessed to make her overflow with such happiness. Wordlessly, the boy picked up the bundles so the women's hands would be free for the difficult climb, and motioned them to follow him down the side of the cliff.

Looking down at what appeared to be a face of sheer rock, Samantha realized sadly that her aunt could not make the descent. One glance at her aunt's face and she saw immediately that Maude knew it too.

"Go ahead, my child, I will remain. I am old. No harm will come to me. My life is behind me and I have lived it well. But everything is ahead of you, Samantha. Go now while you have the chance. We have come this far—you cannot turn back."

"No," Samantha said, tears welling up in her eyes. "I can never leave you here, no matter what is done to me." Sadly, she turned to the boy, "My aunt is too old to make the climb," she said. "We must go back."

Owino hesitated. If he said nothing, the white goddess would remain and maybe one day, when his father and uncles had tired of her, she would be his again. He looked at the pools of tears in her eyes and remembered the joy on her face moments before, and he knew he would never see that happiness again, even if one day she became his.

"Try," he said, "it is not as difficult as it looks."

"You are right, young man. There is never any harm in trying," Maude said matter-of-factly.

Her old Yankee resolve came back to her and, cautiously, she followed the boy's lead, trying to step exactly where he did. Her skirt was bothersome, but after the first gingerly steps, she gained confidence. The moon lit the path, such as it was, and an occasional shrub offered some support. Turning around carefully on the narrow ledge and walking backwards, the boy took her hand and helped her over the most difficult terrain.

Samantha followed them as best she could. But without Owino's steadying hand, she lagged behind. Then she slipped and lost her footing. Her ankle twisted beneath her and she felt an agonizing wrench. But she pulled herself up and struggled on. Although the pain was severe each time she put her weight on the tender ankle, she forced herself to continue. But searching the darkness ahead for a glimpse of the boy and her aunt, Samantha did not see where the path suddenly narrowed, and she stepped out into space.

She felt herself falling, falling, to the rocky shore below. Reaching out desperately, she caught hold of a sapling that was growing out of the side of the cliff. She clung to the tree, scrambling for a foothold in the rock, but could find none. Five hundred feet below, the black sea roared and waves rushed in, crashing against the rocky shore. Samantha's grasp weakened, her hands growing raw from clinging to the bark. She knew she could not hold on much longer, and then, suddenly, she felt the tree come loose from its rocky bed. The ship in the distance might as well have been a thousand miles away, because the tenuous thread that held her life was breaking and in the next moment she would be hurled to the rocks below.

Samantha felt the tree give way and she felt herself float free and fall into space. Instead of landing on the sharp rocks, however, she felt something pliant yet firm beneath her and she was encircled in a protective embrace. *I must have died and entered the other world*, she thought dreamily as an unearthly mist enveloped her and she gave herself up to its eerie call.

When Samantha revived, she found herself in the arms of Owino, her hands still clenched tightly around the sapling. "Wake up, wake up," he was urging her, "there is little time."

With her arm around his shoulder to spare her injured ankle, Owino half-carried Samantha down the difficult path to the shore where Maude and the remaining crew of the *Wind Song* waited anxiously for her. The night would not hold much longer and there was still work to be done.

The boy led the sailors to a cave where a deep canoe was hidden. They carried the boat to the water's edge and quickly sheathed the oars in long seaweed grass to muffle the sound. Helping the women into the canoe, they pushed it into the dark sea.

Samantha sighed with relief as they began the long row to the ship. Nothing could stop them now, she thought, as the canoe skimmed noiselessly over the sea. The ship's sleepy watch never heard them approach until they drew alongside and John Temple banged his oar on the hull.

The watch walked over to investigate the strange noise. Yawning widely, he peered into the black sea and in the light of the moon saw the odd party in the canoe. He looked again, rubbing his eyes vigorously as though he thought he was dreaming. He could not believe what he saw and scurried off to find the mate.

When the second man looked down into the small boat, his mouth dropped open. Then, slapping himself on the forehead with his open palm, he gave an excited order to the watch. They lowered a rope ladder over the side and the grateful survivors started climbing to safety. John Temple went first, followed by Maude Shaw. Although the other sailors expected Samantha to go next, she insisted on being the last to leave the canoe.

When the fifth man mounted the ladder, she unclasped a gold locket from around her neck. One side was white enamel encircled with a delicate wreath of tiny forget-me-nots; the other was inscribed, "My darling girl, Samantha." Her father had given it to her when he had left her in school in Paris and, miraculously, it had survived all her subsequent travails. Samantha pressed the beloved locket into the boy's hand and kissed the fingers that closed around it. Then she turned and hurriedly began to climb the ladder.

As soon as he saw that Samantha was halfway to safety, Owino started to row back. By the time she reached the deck, he was a small figure in the moonlight. Although she knew he could not see her, she waved fondly at his distant, fading figure, and then turned to survey her new surroundings.

The ship was a beehive of activity. Every hand had crowded onto the topdeck to see the new arrivals and they all seemed to be talking at the same time in a strange foreign tongue that Samantha had never heard before. Most of the men were swarthy, with great hook noses and colorful bandanas wrapped around their jet black hair. They gazed at her with undisguised lust, laughing and gesticulating as their avid eyes measured the length and breadth of her slim figure. The boldest of them—a big, brutish-looking man with a week's stubble on his face and a gold ring in his ear—grabbed her roughly and slapped her resoundingly on the backside. Though weak with fatigue, the sailors from the *Wind Song* came to her defense gallantly and a mad melee broke out in the dark.

160

I wonder if we haven't traded one hell for another, Samantha thought as, overcome with the excruciating pain in her ankle and the excitement of the past two days, she swooned on the deck of the *Zanzibar*.

CHAPTER THIRTEEN

Pirate's Bounty

When Samantha awoke, she was lying in a cramped and stuffy berth, her swollen ankle bound tightly in a white cotton bandage. She did not know if it was day or night; if she was in the company of friends or in the grip of enemies; if they were on the high seas or still lying at anchor off Pagalu where any moment the blue-skinned natives would be approaching in their many-oared canoes to reclaim their slaves. She hoped their inauspicious reception on the *Zanzibar* was due to the surprise of men who had not expected to see a woman for months to come, and that, once they became accustomed to her presence, they would not be so loutish. If she had to, Samantha would stay in her berth until they reached a port where she and her aunt could secure a more agreeable passage. There was, in fact, no reasonable demand she would not meet to assure their safe voyage.

Struggling out of the berth, Samantha tried to

stand, but the moment she put her weight on her left foot, an excruciating pain shot through her ankle and she fell back. She was still gasping from the pain when the door flew open and a huge, ferocious-looking man filled the entrance. Pearly white teeth gleamed beneath a thick black moustache. Black eyes snapped in an olive face. A silver-handled saber glinted at his waist. He was dressed in a white, ruffled shirt with full sleeves that billowed out from tight ruffled wrists and black trousers that revealed muscular thighs. He bowed with a flourish and spoke rapidly, his mouth curled in a menacing smile. Rings of rubies and garnets sparkled on his fingers and a silver amulet swung from his neck.

Samantha could not understand a word of his guttural speech. Still, she smiled at him graciously and, enunciating each syllable carefully, she said, "American. Yankee. We are American Yankees from Boston."

"Ah, Boston," he nodded knowingly.

Pleased that he had at least heard of home, she asked, "Do you speak English?"

He stared at her blankly, the menacing smile still flickering on his lips.

"French, then, do you understand French?"

He continued to stare at her unmoving. Then, without any warning he jerked his elbow back. "Translate," he barked in perfect English.

Samantha heard a painful groan and realized for the first time that behind the dark, massive man was another so much smaller that he was barely visible until he stuck his head through the captain's arm. He was a red-haired little man of undiscernible age with a grin that stretched the width of his freckled-face.

"Welcome, fair lady, to the *Zanzibar*, the most notorious ship to sail the seven seas since Bluebeard's own," he said.

Samantha heard his sinister greeting with a sinking heart.

"This here," the man went on smoothly, "is our illustrious captain, the Honorable Abdul Laboud. Allow me to present him to you, Miss . . . Miss?"

"Miss Samantha Shaw of Boston, Massachusetts," she said warily.

"Cap'n, I have the singular honor of making your acquaintance with Miss Samantha Shaw of Boston, Massachusetts." The captain bowed again. "Miss Shaw, meet Captain Abdul."

The fast-talking, ever-smiling little man squeezed under the captain's armpit like a slippery lizard and stood in front of Samantha. "And I, fair lady, am Freddy Finckle, cabin attendant on this here shipshape bark, most lately out of the northside of London."

As the ingratiating little man raised his hand to his cap in a mock salute, Captain Abdul delivered a swift, unceremonious kick to the seat of Mr. Freddy Finckle's pants. Then he turned brusquely and stalked out, leaving the cabin boy sprawled at Samantha's feet.

Still grinning, Freddy scrambled up on his

knees, sat back on his haunches and resumed his spiel as if nothing had happened to interrupt him.

"Lady Luck has brought you to the hold of the sleekest, swiftest buccaneer vessel asail—already crammed with gold and jewels and now pleased to add one more treasure to its cargo, namely you, Miss Boston, Massachusetts." He giggled slyly. "We have a rowdy gang of shipmates, as you saw last night. That was Rudy who gave you the little lovepat that sent you swooning, though it was probably the stench of him that knocked you over."

Goaded by Samantha's obvious embarrassment, Freddy went on, "No offense, ma'am. Rudy meant no harm, to be sure. He's the sentimental sort. Why I remember a few months back when we stopped in the islands of Hawaii for a bit of excitement, Rudy found himself a willing wench. Pretty thing she was too. Rudy was so taken with her that he cut out her heart to have something to remember her by. Keeps the souvenir in a pocket at his breast to this day.

"But you have nothing to fear from Rudy, or any of the mates for that matter. Any man who lays a hand on you gets twenty lashes from the captain himself."

The news buoyed Samantha's flagging hopes. "That was very kind of Captain Abdul," she said.

"Yes ma'am, our capt'n's got the manners of a prince," Freddy said with a lecherous grin. "When he came on deck last night and found you lying there so pale and next to naked, he looked you over carefully from prow to stern, and then he gave his order. So you can deduce yourself lucky, Miss Boston, Massachusetts. You will be the captain's fine lady and all hands will have to treat you like the bloody Queen of England.

"I tell you this to spare you hurt feelings," the little man added wickedly, as he scrambled to his feet and headed for the door. "That is to say, if the mates keep their distance, you shouldn't be insulted. It's not, you can be sure, that they ain't all itching to lay their grubby paws on you. But twenty lashes from the captain can leave a man with no skin on his back from his neck to his knees."

Freddy was standing in the open door. "I'll be just outside here, awaiting your pleasure," he said gleefully. "Capt'n said not to let you out of my sight." He paused as if he had just remembered something important, "One more thing, Miss Boston, Massachusetts," he said leaning toward Samantha and whispering intimately, "your legs are a sight for these sore old salt-stung eyes."

The little man's leering face and suggestive tone made Samantha acutely aware of how seductive her brief island dress must be to these lusty sailors. Over the long months of enslavement, her ragged frock had become threadbare and Owino had made her a collar of large, flat, white shells that covered her breasts and a skirt from the long palm leaves. Beside the naked village women, her scanty dress had seemed modest.

168

But in the eyes of her new shipmates, it was an almost irresistible temptation. She had emerged from the sea like a mermaid. Her leafy skirt was soaked in sea spray and torn from her near-escape on the cliff. Her bare skin was as brown as a native girl's. Her hair was bleached by the heat of the equatorial sun.

Mortified by the sluttish appearance she had made and heartsick from the little man's lewd words, Samantha took the rough cover from the berth and wrapped it around her half-naked body. Then she limped to the door and called him back.

"Do you think you could find some other clothes for me? My own are not warm enough for a sea voyage," she said, mustering as much dignity as she could under the embarrassing circumstances. "An old shirt and breeches of yours would do well, if you could spare them."

A lewd smirk spread across Freddy's freckled face. "Excuse me for saying so, missy, but your grassy outfit was most becoming. 'Twould be a shame to cover up too much of your bounty on a pirate ship like ours."

Samantha was quickly growing to dislike the grinning little man. But she held her peace and her tongue. Like it or not she might well be stranded on the *Zanzibar* for months. "You are most flattering," she said politely, "but I do need something warmer."

Freddy laughed coarsely. "Captain Abdul's got something warm for you. You can bet on that.

But I'll do the best I can for you. Freddy Fin-ckle's always at the service of a fair lady from Boston, Massachusetts."

The little man was still laughing when, later, he pushed open Samantha's door and tossed a bundle of clothes at her. It was better than anything she had hoped for. Although both sleeves were torn off, the white ruffled shirt was fairly clean and the blue knickers had only two small patches. She slipped into them quickly. The shirt was a fair fit but her slim hips were lost in the breeches. Taking the length of vine from the waist of her leaf skirt, Samantha secured the knickers firmly. With the vine from the shell collar she tied back her long, thick hair. When she was as decently attired as she could hope to be, she limped into the narrow passage where Freddy Finckle slouched at attention.

"Old Freddy's clothes never looked so good," he said, giving Samantha his broadest grin.

"Thank you, Mr. Finckle," Samantha said formally. "Now, if you don't mind, I have another favor to ask of you. Would you be kind enough to take me to my aunt?"

"Your aunt, Miss Boston, Massachusetts, and who might that be?"

Deliberately ignoring his insolence, Samantha answered cooly, "That, Mr. Finckle would be the lady who accompanied me to this ship last evening.

"Ah, the old crone! Is that who you'll be referring to?"

"My aunt is no longer a young woman, Mr. Finckle, and she has suffered grievously in the past months. We were little more than slaves on Pagalu."

"You were slaves, were you now? From your high-toned talk I would have guessed you were the slave owner. Tell me, fine lady from Boston," he said mockingly, "are all the slaves on Pagalu as pretty in their bare skin as you?"

A year ago, Samantha would have responded to such impertinence by slapping the offender's face. But now, although her blood boiled, she struggled to control her furious temper.

"Mr. Finkle," she replied icily, "I am sure that sometime during the long voyage ahead we will have occasion to discuss my experiences on Pagalu. But right now, I would be most grateful if you would take me to my aunt."

"If you insist. But I don't know that she'll have time for you," Freddy said slyly. "Just follow close behind old Freddy and no harm will come to you."

Limping painfully, Samantha followed the little man down to a lower level where rows of open berths lined both sides of a narrow passage. The air was close and stale. "Why has my aunt been put down here?" she asked in dismay.

"She came down herself last night in the middle of all the commotion."

"What commotion? I don't remember hearing anything?"

"One of your companions took sick," Freddy

171

volunteered. "He was raving and screaming. Scared everyone out of his wits. The captain wanted to throw the man overboard before the evil inside him infected the whole crew. But the old lady would hear none of it. Stood right up to the captain braver than any man on board and told him there was nothing wrong with the boy. 'It is a perfectly understandable reaction to a very perilous escape,' she said, bold as could be.

"A spunky old dame, your aunt," he added with grudging admiration. "There she is, over there," he pointed.

Maude was bending over the last berth at the end of a long row. Samantha was struck by how thin and drawn her aunt had become.

"Aunt Maude," she called, limping slowly toward her, "are you all right?" She put her arm around the older woman and felt an unnatural heat in her body.

"I am just tired, Samantha. The boy died moments ago. I was up all night with him. He was burning with fever." Maude's voice was so faint, Samantha had to strain to pick up each word. "The Lord was good to take him before the fever could spread to the other men."

She squeezed the girl's hand with what little strength was left in her old body. "We have a long journey ahead of us, my dear, and I am very tired." Her thin voice trailed off and she slumped limply in Samantha's arms.

"Aunt Maude, Aunt Maude," Samantha cried tearfully. Her ankle throbbed from the weight

172

of her added burden but she did not care. With Freddy's help, she carried the old woman up to her cabin. While he went to find water and clean cloths, Samantha tried to make her aunt as comfortable as she could in the cramped quarters.

Samantha was stroking Maude's veined hand when Freddy returned with a bucket of murky water and a pile of soiled rags. "Here you are, my girl," he said, "just what the doctor ordered, and," he said winking broadly, "I have a surprise for you too. The captain wants you in his cabin on the double." He laughed lewdly. "He'll have you purring like a cat in an hour."

Ignoring the little man's wicked words, Samantha picked through the rags and with the cleanest fashioned a compress for Maude's fevered brow. *The captain wanted to throw the man overboard* . . . she thought as she bent over her aunt's wasted body. *If he finds out about Aunt Maude . . . he cannot. He must not.*

Realizing that her aunt's very life hung in the balance, Samantha tried to make herself attractive to meet Captain Abdul. She dipped a rag in the pail of water and wiped her face gingerly, and then she smoothed her hair with her hands as best she could.

"Here you go, Miss Boston Massachusetts, will this help make you beautiful?" Freddy said, gallantly offering her a brush of grimy, black bristles. "It's a little dirty, mind you, but a bit of water will take care of that." He dipped the brush in the bucket then shook it out briskly. "There you are, clean as a bone."

Undoing her hair, Samantha brushed it vigorously until every snarl was out and her thick locks glistened richly. Then tying it back again, she followed Freddy to the captain's cabin.

CHAPTER FOURTEEN

Alone at Sea

Captain Abdul's quarters were like a king's chamber compared with Samantha's miserable berth. The cabin was paneled in teakwood and furnished elegantly. At one end was a plush divan upholstered in rich red velvet, a deep leather armchair, and a matching ottoman. At the other was a wide, intricately carved mahogany bed made up with a cool gray satin coverlet.

Captain Abdul did not move when Samantha entered his cabin. Lounging on the divan like a pampered potentate, he acknowledged her presence only with his black eyes, which appraised her critically from head to toe.

Samantha blazed furiously under his bold gaze, but she was determined to maintain her composure—and her temper—for the sake of her aunt and their uncertain future. *If I can put up with Freddy's insolence*, she told herself, *I can withstand this man's arrogance.*

"You called for me, Captain," she said, hoping

her words would bring an end to his appraisal. But he continued his viewing as if she had not spoken. Thoroughly satisfied with what he saw, he barked out a guttural command that sent Freddy scurrying out the door.

When they were alone together, Captain Abdul rose from the divan and walked over to Samantha. "We have a long voyage ahead of us. I hope you will enjoy it," he said smoothly and lifted her fingers to his lips.

Samantha's mouth dropped open in surprise, for the captain spoke English with a crisp British accent.

"I thought . . . " she stammered.

"You thought," he interrupted her, smiling suavely, "that a pirate like me could not know the King's noble language."

"I, sir, am an American," Samantha bristled, "not a subject of any king—or any man."

"You may soon find that it is an honor, and a great pleasure, to be the subject of a king," he responded sharply. "On this ship, I am king. The *Zanzibar* is my realm and you have come to it uninvited. That in your civilized world makes you my subject, does it not?"

"Sir, I have been raised on the sea. I had my first sailing boat when I was five years old, and by the laws of the sea a captain never fails to help voyagers in distress and to treat those he rescues as guests on his vessel."

"But—Miss Shaw, is it not?"

Samantha nodded.

"You forget, Miss Shaw, that I am a pirate whose law it is to break the law of the sea." He laughed deeply. "But you have nothing to fear from me, as long as you obey me. I like a woman with fire in her." He grasped Samantha's wrist and pulled her toward him. The strain on her ankle was agonizing and she cried out in pain.

"Ah, your poor foot. I am sorry. I forgot your injury," he said soothingly. "Sit down by me on the divan and rest it."

"This will be more comfortable, I think," Samantha said, breaking away from him and limping over to the armchair.

His face clouded with anger for a second, and then cleared. "Very well, if you find it more comfortable. When your ankle is quite well again in a day or two, then perhaps you will discover that this divan is the most enjoyable spot on the ship." His lips curled in the gleaming, menacing smile and Samantha shuddered inwardly imagining the dark plans he was laying for her.

"Now," he said settling back smugly, "would you think it impertinent of me to ask how a beautiful Bostonian lady happened to be at the side of my ship in the dead of night in the dangerous waters off the Ivory Coast, half-naked and escorted only by a few weak and ignorant sailors?"

Samantha laughed lightly. "Not at all. We certainly owe you an explanation and our heartfelt gratitude as well for taking us aboard." Briefly, she described the shipwreck and their miserable life on the island, omitting any mention of the birth of her child, the chief's proscribed wedding ceremony, or Owino's role in their escape. *The fewer ideas Captain Abdul has about me*, she thought, *the better off I will be*.

"I was wondering," he said easily, "was there much fever on Pagalu?"

Samantha eyed the captain warily. "There was some," she said slowly. "Why do you ask?"

"One of your companions was ill in the night. Your aunt—a very strong-willed woman, I might say—insisted that he was simply fatigued, but I have my doubts."

"Yes, I know. My aunt was with the man through the night. I believe he died only hours ago."

"Ah, that is good to hear, because if he had not recovered by dusk, I would have been forced to throw him overboard, dead or alive. A fever aboard ship and the crew could all be dead in a week."

"I understand your position," Samantha began cautiously, "but to throw a live man overboard, surely . . ."

"When the choice is one death or many deaths, the decision is clear. The one is sacrificed. Is that not fair?"

"I see you have a difficult choice to make," she said, trying to sound judicious yet all the while thinking of Aunt Maude burning with fever. "But is there no alternative?"

"None. Absolutely none," he said firmly. Then

suddenly, he jumped up and stood over her, pointing his finger down in her face. "You," he said, "are you healthy?"

"Yes, I believe so," she replied. "I was sick with the fever several months ago. Once you have suffered with it, you can neither contract it again nor pass it on to another."

"Good," he laughed. "I will be quite safe then. And the men you brought with you, your companions, are they healthy?"

"Yes," Samantha said responding to the captain's question with complete honesty. "I believe all are in fine form, considering their cruel enslavement."

"Good. Then I will put them to work with my crew in the morning. Every man must earn his way—and every woman." Captain Abdul smiled. "You may go now. Freddy will keep me informed about the condition of your ankle."

Once outside the cabin, Samantha breathed a deep sigh of relief. Maude and she were both safe, for the moment at least.

For the next two days she spent every hour nursing her aunt. The fever was critical and Maude's worn body had little fight left in it. Medical aids of any sort were in short supply. The nearest port lay far in the distance. Helplessly, Samantha watched her aunt grow weaker. She was frightened that Maude could not withstand the heavy toll of the fever, but she had no one in whom to confide her darkest fears. At one point in the middle of the second night, Maude became delirious, raving wildly and tossing her frail body from side to side in the narrow berth.

If Freddy heard her aunt's delirious cries, he kept his own counsel, and Samantha was grateful to him for that. He seemed to be at her door at all hours of the day and night. No matter when she opened it, she found him slouched against the wall, a broad grin glued on his freckled face. Usually when he brought her meals, he would inquire after Maude, and each time Samantha would say only, "My aunt is suffering from exhaustion but she is coming around."

On the fourth night when he brought her dinner, Freddy asked jovially if her ankle was doing as well as her aunt.

"It is still quite painful and swollen," she said, although in her concern over Maude she had quite forgotten her own pain.

Grinning more broadly than ever, Freddy said, "Captain wants to see for himself—in five minutes. And he doesn't like to be kept waiting."

Samantha was afraid to leave Maude alone, but she was even more wary of angering the captain. "Very well then, let's go now and have done with it if we must," she said.

Exaggerating her limp, she trailed after Freddy to the captain's cabin. This time, the little man just stuck his head in the door. "Here she is," he said, giving her a push to encourage her to enter, and then he left her.

The captain was standing at the far end of the room, absorbed in a large globe that rested on a wooden stand at the foot of the bed. Samantha stood at the door, watching him silently. She was not sure how best to proceed with this dangerous man.

Finally, he looked up from the revolving world, his face sober and serious. "Ah, Miss Shaw," he said as if they were meeting at a garden party, "how nice to see you again. And what brings to you my cabin tonight?"

He began walking across the room toward her, smiling charmingly, his white teeth flashing in the candlelight.

"I believe you sent for me, Captain."

"And why do you believe I would send for you at this most intimate evening hour?"

"Regretfully, Captain Abdul, I have no experience as a mind reader or a clairvoyant."

"You are a sassy one," he said, stopping just inches away from her. "But you look very tired. Have any of my men been keeping you awake?" he asked, a sinister note creeping into his voice.

"Certainly not, Captain, but I am a little tired." Samantha was still wearing Freddy's old shirt and knickers. In fact she had not had them off her back once. Keeping the long, lonely vigil at Aunt Maude's bedside, she had had no time to think of clothes or sleep. Hoping her poor appearance would dampen Captain Abdul's lust and her obvious fatigue would discourage his advances, she said, "My aunt is suffering from exhaustion and I have grown quite exhausted myself caring for her."

"In that case," Captain Abdul said benevolently, "I will send Freddy to tend to your aunt."

"Oh no, no, you mustn't do that," Samantha blurted. "I mean, she is my aunt, Captain, practically a mother to me. Nursing her is a duty I could not pass on to anyone."

"As you wish," he said, "but now why not sit down on the divan and rest yourself."

"Thank you, Captain, but I am perfectly happy standing."

"Sit down," he commanded. When Samantha obeyed and perched lightly on the edge of the divan, his tone softened again. "A little brandy will make you feel much better, Miss Shaw."

"No, thank you, Captain."

He glared at her. "Very well, I'll have some myself. Just a drop, of course," he said mockingly as he went to a low cabinet beside the bed and poured himself a tumbler from a crystal decanter. "To a happy voyage," he said, raising his glass and downing half the cognac in a single gulp, "and to a healthy ankle." The captain refilled the tumbler and this time downed all the liqueur in one gulp. "Here," he said, filling the glass a third time and bringing it over to the divan, "have just a taste."

"No, thank you, Captain," Samantha said.

"I insist." He thrust the glass at her.

"Very well, just a sip. Any more, I am afraid, would make me drowsy."

183

"Just keep your pretty eyes open a little while longer and then you can sleep as long as you like between those satin sheets," the captain said, pointing to the big four-poster.

"Thank you for your kind offer, Captain, but my own berth is quite comfortable enough."

Captain Abdul threw back his head and roared with laughter. "You are a feisty wench; I like that."

Lunging forward, he pushed Samantha down on the divan and crushed her lips with his own. Samantha fought desperately beneath his massive weight, but her struggles seemed merely to entertain him. He rolled off the divan and lay outstretched on the rug. "You have a lot of fight in you for such a skinny girl," he glowed admiringly, "but save a little of it. The night is still young and you have hours of scrapping and clawing ahead of you."

Samantha sat up slowly. She was flushed and breathless. Her tawny hair had come undone and fell on her shoulders, framing and softening her haggard face. "Is there anything else, Captain Abdul, or may I go now?" she asked coldly.

"You are very beautiful, you know, with your hair down." He gazed at her admiringly. "I never want to see it pulled back again. And yes, since you ask, there is something else." He sat up on the floor. "Your ankle! It is quite healed, I see."

"Not quite. It is still swollen and will take at least another few days to mend."

"Let me examine this swollen ankle." He took

184

her foot in his huge hands and looked at it with mock seriousness. "It must be the other leg. A slimmer ankle than this and you could not walk on it." Stroking her foot gently, he looked up at Samantha through shrewd, narrowed eyes. "It seems, Miss Shaw, that you are quite ready to begin earning your transport like everyone else aboard ship. You are, I have no doubt, a woman of your word, and so you cannot have forgotten the bargain we struck."

His fingers strayed from her ankle up her bare calf, as he talked. When they reached above her knee, Samantha could contain herself no longer. With one almighty kick she struck the captain in his most tender parts and sent him sprawling across the rug, retching and clutching himself. Leaving him to his agony, Samantha fled swiftly and did not stop running until she reached her own cabin. Closing the door tightly behind her, she leaned her head against the frame to catch her breath.

"Samantha dear, where am I?" a thin voice called out. Samantha whirled around. Aunt Maude, frail and delicate as a porcelain cup, was sitting up in the berth, smiling at her as she had when Samantha was a little girl.

"Samantha, dear, you mustn't run in the hallways," she said. "Elsa just waxed the floors and they are very slippery. You could take a terrible fall."

Samantha rushed to her aunt, and knelt beside

her. Burying her face in the gnarled old hands, she sobbed like a little girl.

"There, there, dear," Aunt Maude said, patting the girl's head fondly, "dry your tears. I wasn't scolding. I was only concerned that you might take a spill."

Samantha looked up through her tears. Aunt Maude seemed lucid and clear-eyed, but her mind had wandered back many years. The old lady smiled at her niece warmly. "Everything will be all right, Samantha, you wait and see." She stroked the girl's silky hair, and then her blue-veined hand went limp and her eyes closed. Aunt Maude was dead.

Samantha knelt beside the bed, holding the old woman's cold hand and grieving bitterly. Now she was alone in the world—alone on a strange ship bound for she knew not where, at the mercy of a band of buccaneers. "Everything will be all right, Samantha, you wait and see." The irony of her aunt's last words made her death even more poignant.

Maude had died remembering only the happy years. She had forgotten the misery they had lately suffered, and the loss and hardship they had been forced to endure. That, at least, was some consolation for Samantha.

Wiping the tears from her eyes, Samantha drew the sheet over her aunt's withered face. With the piece of vine she used to tie back her hair, she fashioned a crude cross and placed it on her aunt's cold body. Then Samantha slipped out into the passage, closing the door softly behind her. For once, Freddy was nowhere in sight.

Samantha walked boldly out on the deck, aware that she was drawing the eyes of every man on duty, and looked for John Temple. When she found him and told him of Maude's passing, she waited at the rail while he fetched his companions, then she led the men silently to her cabin.

The men from the *Wind Song* carried Maude's body to the deck of the *Zanzibar*, and solemnly Samantha began to recite the words of the burial service as best she could remember them: "Earth to earth, ashes to ashes, dust to dust; in pure and certain hope of the Resurrection unto eternal life." Then, seven hundred miles from her beloved Boston, Maude Shaw was lowered into the Atlantic Ocean by four of her city's native sons.

None of the crew, watching silently, interrupted or questioned the melancholy service, until the men began lowering the body into the dark water. Then, all at once, Captain Abdul came storming onto the deck, shouting in his strange guttural tongue, and then turning angrily to Samantha.

"What is going on here?" he yelled. "What do you think you are doing?"

In a voice that could freeze the equator, Samantha replied, "We have just consigned the soul of Maude Shaw to her Maker. I hope he receives yours as happily as I am sure he has received my aunt's. Now, if you will excuse me . . . " She swept passed him, not wavering or pausing until she had returned to the comparative safety of her cabin. Then overcome with exhaustion and grief, Samantha fell into a deep sleep.

CHAPTER FIFTEEN

Captain of the Zanzibar

"Wake up, wake up. You've been sleeping since yesterday." Freddy's voice was urgent and for once there was no grin glued to his freckled face. "The men are dropping like flies. They're burning with fever. Half the crew is sick. The captain is raging."

Samantha listened through half-closed eyes to the rapid volley of words. Even in her drowsy state, she knew what she had to do. She was, in a sense, responsible for the crew's illness. She had to do everything in her power to save them.

"Freddy," she asked sharply, cutting through his alarm with her commanding tone, "have you ever had the fever?"

"Yes, ma'am, in the West Indies when I first shipped out."

"Good, then you can help me. We will need plenty of hot broth and tea, buckets of icy water, and lots of clean cloths and blankets. You make the preparations while I go and try to calm Captain Abdul."

190

Samantha dressed quickly and walked up to the topdeck where she had said goodbye to her aunt. She was calm and controlled, and terribly lonely. It was already dusk; the first stars were twinkling brightly. She stood in the stern looking back at the wake of the *Zanzibar* and offered a silent prayer for Maude. "Everything will be all right, Samantha; you wait and see." Samantha thought of her aunt's last words and wished desperately for them to come true. Though only twenty-two, she was already very much a woman. Mallory Jones had loosened deep currents of desire in her beautiful body and cruel fate had forged a steely independence in her soul. Only the man *she* chose would ever know her tempestuous passion, and Captain Abdul Laboud was most certainly not that man. She would kick him brutally again, if he forced her to, but this time she hoped to make a deal with the fiery captain that would be fair to both of them. She would earn her keep by nursing the sick men until the last of them was back on his feet. After that they could discuss what else she might do to earn her way.

The sky was dark and star-filled when Samantha knocked tentatively on the door of the captain's quarters. Loud guttural shouts greeted her knock. She waited until they had subsided, then she rapped again. Cursing even louder than before, Captain Abdul flung open the door.

"Ha! It is you, at last," he barked. "Get in here." He kicked the door shut behind her, his face red with fury. "You have brought nothing but bad luck to me and my ship," he shouted angrily. "This morning we sighted a square-rigger just seven miles off our starboard side. She was probably headed for China with chests of gold. But because of you," he poked his finger in Samantha's face menacingly, "we had to let her pass. I don't have enough men on their feet to take a skiff, let alone a frigate. They are all sick with the fever that you brought. I have a good mind to throw you all overboard—you and your friends—just to teach you a lesson."

"You have every right to be angry, Captain Abdul," Samantha said evenly. "We did not know when we escaped from Pagalu that Tom had the fever. Had we known, we would not have risked his life in such a hazardous adventure. Had we known," she added softly under her breath, "my aunt would still be alive today."

Samantha's voice choked, but she cleared her throat, took a deep breath and went on. "I have already had the fever, as have my four companions, so you have nothing more to fear from us. Quite to the contrary. I came here tonight to propose a deal to you. You always insist that everyone should earn his way. Well, I propose to do just that by caring for the sick men. I will nurse the ill men until the last of your crew is back on his feet."

Captain Abdul stared at Samantha in disbelief and then threw back his great head and roared like a bull. "*You* are going to make a deal with *me*? Didn't you forget something, you fine lady from Boston? Yes! You forget that I am the captain of this ship—I, I, I," he shouted, pounding his chest. "I give the commands. I say how each man—and each woman—will earn his way, and I have other plans for you.

"Of course, when I am finished with you, I may send you down to nurse my men, but now I have better plans for you and I have waited too long already to carry them out."

He grabbed Samantha roughly, pulled her head back viciously by her long tawny hair and punished her lips with his. She tried to scratch and claw at his face but he pinned her arms behind her back, holding them easily with one of his huge hands. With the other, he grabbed her shirt at the throat and ripped it open to her waist.

"You look too much like a boy in these ugly clothes. I want to see if there is a real woman under there," he laughed. Letting go of her arms, he grabbed each side of her torn shirt and ripped it off. Samantha gasped in horror as she stood before him in nothing but Freddy's old knickers.

Captain Abdul could not suppress his astonishment and delight as he gazed at the slim girl before him. Her high, firm breasts were surprisingly full and, unlike her arms and face and throat, they were as white as pearls. "Ah, you have been hiding these jewels from me for too long," he said, and he seized one in each hand and pulled Samantha to him by her milky white breasts, squeezing them cruelly until she cried out in pain.

She hated his eyes to look upon her, his hands to touch her. But the more she fought him, the harder he squeezed her breasts, until she could bear the agony no longer and she submitted weakly to his kisses, even allowing his tongue to part her lips and sink deeply into her mouth. He picked her up easily and carried her to the bed. It was the first real bed Samantha had lain on since leaving China. The satin sheets felt cool and inviting against her bare back, and, for an instant, she sank sensually into the downy mattress. Then, catching herself, she tried to roll off the bed, but she was no match for Captain Abdul.

"I want to drink from your white fountains, Samantha, and I will, whatever you do," he said, his voice thick with lust. Lying down beside her, he pinned her to the bed with his mouth on her breast, sucking her teat like a starving man, sinking his sharp teeth into the soft mounds, bruising the creamy white skin.

Samantha struck back with all her strength, pounding his head with both her fists and pulling his hair so hard she was left with a great black tuft in each hand. Captain Abdul sat up with a deep roar, cursing her roundly. "I won't waste any more sweet caresses on you," he growled angrily and, in a sudden motion, he tore open her trousers.

Samantha's stomach was as smooth and white as her breasts and, at its base, a thick, lustrous crown of tawny-colored curls glistened in the moonlight. "A treasure chest," the captain gasped in admiration, then suddenly he closed his eyes and put his hands to his head. His face flushed and his breath came in short heavy gasps.

Samantha watched him carefully, afraid to move. He sat down on the edge of the bed and slowly, deliberately unbuckled his boots. Then he stood up uncertainly and again slowly he began to unbutton his shirt, revealing a massive chest almost entirely covered by a mat of tight black curls. With each piece of clothing that dropped to the floor, Samantha's fear heightened. She could try to run but she knew she would never get by him and, if she did, there was no place on the ship where he could not reach her.

"Move over, wench," Captain Abdul commanded, and, lying down beside her, he ran his hands across her breasts and down along her stomach. Samantha shuddered with disgust at his touch but this seemed only to encourage him. He kissed her harshly on the mouth and rolled over burying her beneath his enormous weight.

Samantha braced herself grimly for her unavoidable fate. But nothing happened. He kissed her again, savagely this time. He milked her breasts and spread her unwilling thighs wider. Still nothing happened. Rolling away from her angrily, he cried, "You have put a curse on my ship, and now you have put a curse on me. This has never happened before. The kick! It was the kick that did it."

Captain Abdul laughed wildly, a harsh, mad laugh that frightened Samantha even more than his physical abuse. "You injured me, wench, now you must repair the damage or I'll throw you to the crew and then you will wish you were back in the captain's fine bed."

Still laughing madly, his eyes glowing eerily in the moonlight, he grabbed her by the hair and forced her mouth down on him. "Talk to it," he urged mockingly. "Talk to it like a fine lady from Boston, Massachusetts. Every gentleman listens to a fine lady from Boston." He pulled her hair hard. "Talk to it," he growled hoarsely. "Take it in your mouth and talk to it."

He pulled her hair again. Then suddenly, his grip slackened and Samantha's head fell forward against his thigh. Not daring to move for fear she would excite him again, Samantha forced herself to lie motionless her face pressed into his sweaty limb, for what seemed like an eternity. Finally she turned cautiously and peeked through her hair. The captain looked like he was sleeping.

Slowly, stealthily, Samantha inched off the bed. She crouched in the shadows, listening intently to the man's breathing until she was sure he was sleeping soundly, then she tiptoed over to his dresser and eased the top drawer open. As she reached in, searching for something to cover her nakedness, the captain let out a mighty roar. Samantha's breath caught in her throat. Her heart raced. She glanced fearfully over her shoulder and sighed with relief. Captain Abdul was still sleeping. Slipping into one of his fine shirts, she eased over to the door, rolling the long sleeves back over her arms as she went. Her hand was on the knob when she paused, ears tuned tensely to catch the slightest sound. The sleeping man was tossing restlessly and muttering darkly to himself.

Samantha realized that Captain Abdul was not sleeping—he was delirious. The fever that had killed her aunt had saved her from him. It had sapped his strength, leaving desire but no power to satisfy it. Samantha hesitated at the door, then tiptoed back to the side of the bed. The dark giant was stretched across its width, sprawled on his back, uncovered. He seemed even larger in his nakedness. His shoulders were broad enough for two men, his waist tapered, his stomach flat and hard. Muscles bulged in his arms and legs and rippled across his massive chest. The black hair that covered it was glistening with sweat. His useless member lay limply on its side.

Looking at the naked giant, Samantha felt a sudden tingle between her legs. Appalled, she covered him quickly with as many blankets as she could find and went out in the passage to look for Freddy.

"How are the men?" she asked anxiously when she finally located the little man in the galley where he was stirring a vat of steaming broth.

"Burning up, most of them, and growing weaker every moment," he answered grimly.

"And cook?"

197

"He's fallen too. That makes seven that're down."

"No, eight," Samantha said. "Captain Abdul has the fever too."

Freddy looked at the girl incredulously. She made an unearthly picture, standing in the reddish glow of the stove-fire, her slim figure lost in the folds of the captain's fine silk shirt. "I've shipped out with Capt'n Abdul Laboud for ten years, and never known him to have a sick day in his life."

"Freddy," Samantha replied sympathetically, "the fever strikes everyone, captain and cabin boy alike. Your master is a very sick man. I will do everything I can for him. But first you must find something for me to wear. I am no good to anyone dressed like this."

In the next few days, the *Zanzibar* became a floating infirmary, with Samantha the chief nurse. She instructed Freddy and her companions from the *Wind Song* on how to care for the sick men and nursed them herself both night and day. By the end of the second week, four men had died of the fever. The others were slowly regaining their strength.

Only the captain showed no signs of improvement, although Samantha did everything she could for him. She fed him the hot broth and tea, bathed his burning body with cool water and wrapped it in blankets to sweat out the fever. At night she slept on the red divan, so that she would be close by if he needed her. But his stubborn body rejected her ministrations. His charcoal eyes dropped back in his head. His enormous muscles slackened and shrank.

While the once powerful giant lay near death, Samantha studied the navigational charts and determined the course of the *Zanzibar*. Abdul had been heading back to the Barbary Coast and, although Samantha would have preferred to steer the vessel toward England or France, she felt it her duty to bring the sick man and his ship home to safe harbor. For now Samantha Shaw was captain of the pirate ship *Zanzibar*. She was occupying the captain's quarters. She was issuing the commands.

In the last difficult year, Samantha had grown and strengthened. Her iron will had been tested, her mettle proven time and again. She had been forced to seize opportunity when it came, to turn the slimmest hope into reality. Had she been meeker, less intelligent or determined, she would never have survived this far. So, when the captain's grave illness left the ship without a leader, Samantha readily took command and proved that she could match any man in strength of will, in the power to demand respect and obedience.

During the rash of fever, these bawdy buccaneers with their long history of bloody carnage became accustomed to taking orders from the girl. She was not a woman in any sense they had ever known—certainly nothing like the girls they ravaged gustily in every port of call—and they answered readily to her command. She was kind but not soft, fair but still demanding. She never whipped them or threatened to, but she maintained an iron discipline and they admired her for it. By the month's end, Captain Abdul's command had become little more than a shared memory. From their ribald jokes about his whippings and his sudden bursts of temper, it was clear they had shifted their allegiance to Samantha. But the first true test of her command was yet to come.

The sea had been unusually calm, as balmy as a lake in summer, and all hands knew the fair weather could not hold much longer. When the storm finally came, it struck with tremendous force. Mile-long streaks of lightning rent the black sky in two. Thunder boomed like cannon fire. Huge waves rolled over the deck. Samantha was standing at the helm, sure and confident as she issued her crisp commands, when suddenly she saw Freddy lose his footing and slip toward the edge of the rolling vessel.

Samantha never hesitated. Shouting to Rudy to take the wheel, she grabbed a rope and began to inch her way toward the helpless man. Sheets of rain beat down and great gusts of wind forced her back. Dropping to her hands and knees, she knotted the rope around her waist and began to crawl forward to where Freddy lay clutching frantically at the slippery deck. As she stretched out on the deck to slide the rope to the desperate man, a huge wave washed over the deck, submerging them completely. Samantha felt the rope cut into her stomach sharply and she held on for dear life against the weight pulling at her waist and the fury of the sea and the rage of the wind.

When the ship rose again, Freddy was dangling dangerously over the side of the deck, clinging tightly to the end of the line. Again on her hands and knees, Samantha began to crawl back toward the safety of the hold. But Freddy was much heavier than she and as hard as she tried she could make no progress. The most she could do was hold firm and try to keep them both from slipping backwards into the raging sea.

The rope at her waist bit painfully into her tender flesh. *How long can he hold on?* she wondered, *how long can I hold?* Remembering how she had felt as she clung to the side of the cliff in Pagalu, Samantha summoned all her strength and tried again. Inch by inch, she crawled back until she had gained enough distance for Freddy to work his way onto the deck. Together they slowly made their way back until strong hands reached out from the hold and grasped the soaked, exhausted girl, pulling the little man in with her. Samantha's white shirt was stained with blood where the rope had cut into her soft flesh, but she was too tired to feel the pain.

By morning the storm had passed, but Samantha's courageous act was not forgotten. She had earned her command. Even Rudy took her orders willingly and carried them out faithfully. Every man now accepted her as captain—every man except the sailor Simul.

Captain Abdul had kept the men in line with

frequent whippings, so brutal that often the victims could not move for several days after. Samantha had never used the whip, and never would. But one day her hand was forced.

Ever since the first night she had come aboard, Simul had looked at her in a way that made her skin crawl. She was well used to a man's admiring glance, but there was something about the way Simul eyed her and ran his thick tongue suggestively around his fleshy lips, that made Samantha's blood run cold. She tried to avoid the man as much as possible. But one night, after long hours at the captain's bedside, she was climbing up to the topdeck, when she felt a clammy hand on her ankle.

"Come on down, Captain," his familiar voice wheedled. "I have a surprise for you."

Samantha bit her lip and tried to keep the fear out of her voice. In the sharpest tone she could muster, she commanded, "Simul, let me go at once and you will not be punished. I will overlook this one incident."

"But Captain, I can't forget the surprise I have for you. It's too big," the slimy voice whined and the clammy grip tightened around her ankle.

Samantha felt herself fall backwards off the ladder and land in the hairy arms of Simul. Then, suddenly, Rudy was standing over her, pulling the disgusting man away from her, cuffing him roughly across the face, and booting his rear in disgust when he turned tail and fled.

Despite her abhorrence of whipping, Samantha

had no choice. Simul must be whipped, and whipped soundly, or every hand would think he could take the same liberty. In the morning, when Rudy and Freddy came in for the day's instructions, she gave Rudy the order: "Twenty lashes, in front of all hands."

The two men exchanged worried glances. Then Freddy cleared his throat loudly. "Begging your pardon, Miss Samantha," he began awkwardly, "but there's only one man on a ship that can give a whipping and that's the captain, ma'am."

"Yes, yes, Freddy," Samantha said, anxious to put the whole ugly matter behind her, "but as you can see Captain Abdul is in no condition to whip anyone. Now that's all for this morning."

"Yes, ma'am," he said. But neither he nor Rudy budged.

"Well, what are you waiting for?"

"You see, ma'am," Freddy blurted out, "since you are giving the orders, you have to whip Simul. Rudy here can't do it. The men would resent it coming from him. If you don't do it yourself, they'll think they can get away with whatever they want with you."

Samantha looked at the men in horror. Freddy was studying his boots. Rudy was shaking his big, dark head in solemn agreement. They were right of course. Samantha had known that all along. But could she do it? Could she snap a whip across a man's bare back? She trembled at the thought.

But she had to do it. She had to maintain command. If she didn't and the captain died, she would be at the mercy of these crude, rough men. Reluctantly she said, "Have Simul stripped to the waist and on deck in an hour."

The entire crew was assembled in silent, curious attention when Samantha strode on deck, Captain Abdul's cat-o'-nine-tails tucked under her arm. Simul stood in the middle of the line, a guard at each side. His bare chest and back were completely covered with long black hair like an ape. An evil smirk covered his ugly face.

Samantha fingered the black whip and felt the vomit rise in her throat. Forcing it back, she flicked the whip lightly in the air. Her eyes ran over the line of men and stopped at Simul's taunting face. "Bend over," she ordered brusquely.

Simul, with a deep bow, presented his bare back to Samantha. He knew, and Samantha realized he knew, that she could not hurt him. She raised the whip and swept it tentatively across his back. To her horror, Simul responded to the touch of the leather on his skin with the sickening grunt of an animal in heat. She raised the whip and stung him lightly again, and again he groaned. When he grunted the third time, she sensed a ripple of amusement pass through the men.

Simul looked back over his shoulder at her. Samantha saw the foulness in the man's smirking face and the pleasure he was taking in this exhibition. A cold white fury swept over her.

Raising the black whip for the fourth time, she brought it down across the small of his back with all her force. Simul screamed in surprise and pain. The men tightened their grip on his arms. Blood oozed across his back. But Samantha lashed out again. Five . . . six . . . seven . . . eight . . . the blows were raining on the man's bare flesh in rapid succession. By the time she reached the twentieth stroke, the skin was stripped raw from his neck to his buttocks. The fury of her lashes had cut through Simul's pants, and patches of the shredded cloth stuck to the open gashes on his cheeks. Great crimson welts stood up along his back. Blood streamed from his open wounds.

When she had brought the whip down for the last time, Samantha paused and let the leather lash dangle across his bloody back. She looked coldly down the line from man to man. "Anyone else?" she asked.

There was not a sound on the ship except the muted moans of Simul. Samantha dropped the whip on the deck, turned abruptly and walked down to the captain's cabin. She was sweating and trembling all over. A dreadful force had been loosed within her, a force she had never known she possessed. In the instant that she drew the first blood, all her pent-up fury—all the humiliation and degradation she had been forced to submit to at the hands of lustful men—rushed over her and she wrought her terrible vengeance on the man's helpless flesh.

Alone in the cabin with the unconscious giant, Samantha wondered fearfully what kind of a woman she was becoming and grieved silently for the innocent girl she had been.

CHAPTER SIXTEEN

'Mallory Jones' Divided Heart

Mallory Jones had watched the *Wind Song* drift into the China Sea until the ship was a tiny dot and then the dot itself was lost in the distance where the sky and the sea merged. He had watched with mounting anger Samantha's tearful farewell to Jean Levoir, never thinking that the tears she shed so copiously might not be for the Frenchman, and he was filled with a mighty rage that would never be satisfied until he had avenged his honor with the blood of Levoir.

Perverse luck had spared Levoir once. It would not spare him again. Only the terrible grief that made Mallory Jones shun all things and all people, that drove him to the brink of insanity and forced him to retreat from all commerce and society or go mad, had stopped him from demanding revenge from Levoir after the fatal Canton fire. Nothing—not the law of man or God, not the bonds of remembered friendship that had stayed his hand once before—could stop him now.

Mallory Jones had been in China so long that he had lost touch with the ways of the Western world. He had developed the same keen sense of honor by which Oriental men lived and died. Walking back to his empty villa that only hours before had been alive with Samantha's blazing passion, he planned his fatal revenge. But even as he was preparing to meet his old friend in a fight to the death, Levoir was sailing down the Pearl River and out of reach. He was stopping at Lintin to inspect his opium storage ships. From there, the *Grand Vent* would pick him up and take him back to Paris.

When Jones discovered that his prey had slipped through his fingers, his anger was surpassed only by his anguish. For, not only had Levoir escaped, but, Jones was sure, he was on his way to Samantha's waiting arms.

Samantha, Samantha—he could never let another man possess her. He knew it was unreasonable. He hated his own base jealousy. But he could not help himself. The memory of her face, her touch, just the sound of her name was enough to kindle his smoldering passions. Yet, even as he yearned for the vibrant, breathtaking beauty who had given herself to him, Mallory Jones still clung to the memory of the gentle, compliant Ming-la whose charred remains had to be wrenched from his unyielding arms. His was a soul divided—by love, by duty, by desire.

As the sun rose pale and ghostly over the land where he had grown to manhood, Jones retreated, as he had done so many times in the bitter year that had passed, to the woodland sanctuary where Samantha had come to him blushing but eager, burning to give herself to her mysterious lover. At his touch, she had awakened from the innocent, unsuspecting slumber of girlhood and been transformed into a ravishing woman of unquenchable passion. She had not only submitted to his desires, she had taken her fill of him. She had lusted for him—he felt it in her touch, tasted it in her sweat. His pulse quickened with the memory. He could never give her up. Yet he had. Torn between two loves, he had let her sail away into the waiting arms of the dangerous Jean Levoir.

He pictured her face as it had been when he entered her boudoir unannounced just hours before. Resolved never to betray again the love of his sweet Ming-la, Jones had sought one last glimpse of Samantha before blotting her out of his life forever. The velvet ribbon she'd left behind was only an excuse to win one final moment alone with her. Then all at once, he was in front of her, thrusting the ribbon at her, speaking coldly, threatening her harshly. For he had known with the utmost certainty that she had been waiting for another. His firmest resolves vanished when he thought of her giving herself to any other man. He remembered the flood of fury that led him impetuously, uncontrollably to seize her. He remembered her valiant though vain efforts to resist his touch, and then her passionate capitulation, as she begged him, pleaded with him, entreated him to take her.

The memory of Samantha's words rang in his ears, "Take me, my darling, make me yours again," and he was engulfed once more in the intensity of desire that drove her trembling fingers to his throbbing member. "Oh, Lord," he cried aloud in his silent room, "can I ever get enough of this woman? Can I live with her, or without her?" He picked up the alabaster head and ran his hands fondly over the perfect likeness. "So unlike the gentle affection I have for you, dear heart," he murmured. "Could you ever forgive me for this fatal passion? Would you quench it from my heart if I stayed here with your memory? I have become passion's slave . . . little more. First I betrayed your father who was closer to me than my own. Then, by allowing you to submit to my impure love, I murdered you as surely as if I had stabbed you with my own dagger. And now I have ravaged, brutally violated the daughter of my father's closest friend. One of my crimes at least, sweet girl, I must try to set right. I must do the only honorable thing. I must make Samantha my wife, beg her to accept my unworthy love. Can you forgive me Ming-la? Can you understand and forgive me?"

Gently, Mallory Jones placed the alabaster statue on the table, then he lay down and slept, peacefully at last.

His torturous decision finally made, Jones lost

no time in putting his affairs in order. He spent long hours at his factory in Canton, working diligently to leave his books in perfect order for his young cousin, Andrew, who would oversee the business until a new representative arrived from Boston. He dared not stop working except to catch a few hours sleep each night, for fear his indecision would return.

Leaving Canton would not be easy. It is difficult, after all, for a man to leave the place where he has lived and loved for more than fifteen years, a place that holds his fondest memories. Jones had only the vaguest recollections of Boston, and even those were surely outdated. Every time a fresh cargo arrived from America, he heard marvelous tales of how his city was changing and his country was growing, stretching out as far as the shores of the Pacific. Now that his mind was made up, he was eager to see America again and he chafed at the ill luck that delayed his departure.

First the arrival of young Porter and then fearsome typhoons that ripped up shrubs and lashed the row of factories week after week kept him in Canton. Six months after the *Wind Song* had disappeared in the distance, Mallory Jones was still in China. There were those who said he would never leave.

After long months at anchor in Whampoa, the *Democrat* was ready to begin the return voyage. Thirteen thousand miles. Four and one half months. Then Boston. With any luck she'd be home by August.

Chests of rich, black Hyson and green Bohea tea, cases of blue and white porcelain, cassia and camphor, bolts of nankeen and the finest silks were crowded in the hold, together with the usual assortment of Oriental odds and ends: two bundles of rattan floor mats; three lacquer-ware tea caddies and one cigar box; four Canton crepe shawls; twenty-four ivory-mounted fans; sixty tortoise shell combs; six mother-of-pearl coffee spoons; one silver service with carved dragon-head spouts; three rolls of wallpaper with a border pattern of flowers and butterflies; and four tubs of sugar candy.

The candy was for the crew. The rest were individual orders Captain Proctor had filled for the bankers and brahmins of Boston. Captain Proctor went over the cargo one last time with his mate to be sure nothing had been forgotten, then slowly folded the invoices and put them in his pocket. He was trying to carry on as usual, to act as though this were a routine voyage, but time was running out.

The *Democrat* was a standard three-master, no faster, no fuller, no sleeker than twenty others. There was nothing unusual about her, certainly nothing extraordinary enough to merit the attention she was receiving. Everyone in Canton was talking about the *Democrat*. In shops, warehouses, factories, ships, and saloons, she was the main topic of conversation. And today, everyone was watching her. All eyes were glued to that space of sea between ship and shore, watching for a sampan ferrying passengers to her side.

Aboard the *Democrat*, Proctor could sense a tenseness in the air and could see a million question marks flashing across his mate's expectant face. Now more than ever, the captain had to act routinely.

"Cargo complete," he said curtly. "Prepare all hands to ship out." Proctor spoke sharply, hoping his abrupt tone would hide his own uneasiness and discourage White's questions.

White was a fine first mate, but he could hold a rudder in a storm better than his own tongue; and now he was so curious, nothing less than death could stop the words from racing each other out of his over-worked mouth.

"Then we're not waiting for Mr. Jones, sir? He's not coming? There was talk he wouldn't, plenty of talk. Got China in his blood, they say. They was taking bets on it in Hog's Lane last night. An old mate, been on more than a dozen sailings, says Jones's been here so long only his eyes are still Yankee. Says he's become one of them. Then this other sailor steps in, one I never seen before. Had an eye that went off to the side and a voice to raise the bristles. Jones has got to leave, he says. He can't stay in Canton. The sweet smoke's turned him bitter and . . . "

"That's enough of your gossip, White," the captain snapped. "There's work to be done. Get

214

those sails hoisted. A stiff breeze is blowing up and I want to catch her before she changes course."

Proctor had heard enough talk on shore. As captain of the *Democrat*, he had become something of an overnight celebrity in Canton. Everyone presumed he knew more than he was saying. But the truth was Proctor had never set eyes on Mallory Jones. His sole communication was a note received ten days ago: "M. Jones requests passage on the *Democrat*. Will board at 11:30 A.M. on the morning of departure." Proctor had dismissed the note as a practical joke, until Houqua personally verified it: Mallory Jones was leaving China.

It was already well past noon. Any moment the Comprador's ship would draw near to conduct the departure ceremony. Should he delay the sailing or keep to the schedule? Maybe White's friend was right and Houqua was wrong. Maybe Jones would never leave China, Proctor thought as he leaned on the rail, looking toward Whampoa for some sign—of what he did not know.

There were all kinds of rumors in Canton and Whampoa about Jones—rumors that he had become addicted to opium, that he had violated an ancient law and so was forced to leave China forever, rumors that linked him to the fatal Canton fire. There were always rumors, Proctor thought. But no one really knew why Jones might be leaving the country he had adopted so completely, going back to one he no longer knew.

He had come to China a poor, fatherless boy. He would leave it with a fortune equal to any in America. But fifteen years make a difference in a place—they had fought another war with England since 1808, added new states to the Union. And they make a difference in a man. But Mallory Porter Jones was Porter & Co., and Porter & Co. owned the *Democrat*. Captain Proctor would wait.

CHAPTER SEVENTEEN

Kaou-Tsze

They stood on the dock at Whampoa and watched the mainsail of the *Democrat* unfurl. If there is a way to say goodbye to a fifteen-year friendship, they had no time left to discover it. The older man spoke first.

"Good wind and good water," he said, invoking Fung-shuy, the invisible agency that influences a man's fortune, to guide his friend home.

The younger man answered softly, his deep voice low and strained. "Elder brother, kaou-tsze," he said.

Elder brother was a term of affection and respect in China. Kaou-tsze their way of saying adieu. It meant literally, "I inform you that I am leaving." The young man had used it only once before. Neither would ever forget the occasion, nor ever speak of it again.

The two men bowed deeply. Shook hands. Then turned away, neither looking back—Houqua to be swallowed in the crowd of coolies, porters, and merchants that thronged the narrow streets of Whampoa whenever the foreign ships were in port, Mallory Jones to board the waiting sampan that would ferry him to the *Democrat*.

There is a certain prescribed ceremony for every occasion in China. And the departure of a foreign ship is no exception. According to custom, therefore, the captain and crew of the *Democrat* were lined up on the maindeck when the Compradore arrived to conduct the formalities. For Proctor, the routine of Grand Chop, cumsha—the great baskets of oranges, preserved ginger, dried lychee, and Nankin dates—and fireworks was a familiar one. No ship could leave China without going through the ceremony and this was Proctor's ninth trip. On each previous voyage he had listened impatiently while the Grand Chop was read, giving his vessel official permission to leave China unmolested. But now, for the first time he felt oddly reassured as the Compradore read from the large parchment, embossed on each side with the dragon symbol of the Celestial Empire of China:

"When Western Ocean ships have been measured, paid their duties and departed, should bad winds and water drive them to the shores of another province (not being within the escorted limits of trading), if it is found that they possess this discharge, they must be allowed to continue their voyage without delay or opposition. Which is on record.

"Now the foreign merchant ship *Democrat*,

219

having loaded with merchandise, goes to the Hwa-ke country, there to manage her business. She has been measured, and duties incurred by her have all been settled as customary. As she is now departing, this is given as a clearance into the hands of the said merchant to grasp and hold fast, so that, should he meet with any custom-house, he must not be detained. Military stations to which it may be shown must also let the said vessel pass without interruption, and not induce her to remain and trade that they may be bene-fited by any charges or duties. Should they act otherwise, it will give rise to trouble and con-fusion."

The Compradore rolled the parchment scroll and handed it to Captain Proctor. They bowed to each other in the Oriental custom and then the Compradore presented the cumsha—his parting gifts to the captain and crew.

The leave-taking ceremonies could be pro-longed no further. Proctor had to act.

"My apologies, sir," he said to the Compradore. "The departure of the *Democrat* will be delayed briefly while we await the arrival of a distin-guished passenger."

"Ah yes, Captain," the Compradore responded blandly. "You would be referring to Mr. Jones, I believe."

As if on cue, a tall figure in Oriental dress appeared suddenly at the side of the ship. Proctor had imagined a small, sallow man of hurried mo-tions. But Mallory Jones was obtrusive in his handsomeness. He had acquired the impenetrable expression and fluid, almost floating movements of the East. But his build and coloring were unmistakably Western. His eyes, Proctor noted instantly, were his most compelling feature. They seemed—like rooms that have been emptied—to remember nothing, to be stripped of memories.

"Welcome to the *Democrat*, Mr. Jones," the captain said, stepping forward to shake hands.

"Thank you, Captain."

"We will sail as soon as you are ready."

"As you wish, Captain," Jones answered, his voice toneless and remote. He glided silently past the row of astounded sailors to the prow of the vessel. For a moment no one moved or spoke. Even White was speechless. Then Proctor started bellowing orders: "Raise anchor. Hoist the sails. Man the rudder."

Firecrackers to awaken the gods to the *Democrat's* departure boomed from the Compradore's ship, filling the sky with brilliant rosettes, as the pilot boat guided the *Democrat* out of the harbor, down the Pearl River, homeward bound.

Mallory Jones stood on the topdeck and watched Whampoa fade in the distance. He was not sure whether he was going home or leaving home. He knew only that he had no choice. He touched the long, thin purple scar at his temple, almost indiscernible beneath his shaggy hair.

Macao was fading in the distance. Lintin lay just ahead. It was the last speck of Chinese land, the "Solitary Nail" in the China Sea, and Jean

Levoir's old headquarters. Jones went below. He wanted nothing to cloud his last view of China, for he knew he would never return. A new life in a distant, barely remembered New World lay ahead of him—a new life he yearned to build with Samantha at his side.

His plans were set: The *Democrat* would veer from its usual course to take him to England and from there he would proceed immediately to Paris. But his hopes were flagging.

"She must despise the very memory of me," he thought to himself. "She will never accept me. I treated her like a ravenous beast. Although I tried, I could not stay away from her, could never get enough of her. In my hunger to consume her, to extinguish the flame that scorched my soul, I forced myself upon her like an animal. How could she forgive me? How could she ever love me? I am a fool to even dream that she will marry me."

Tormented with doubts, Mallory Jones kept to himself during the long sea voyage, an aloof, mysterious figure still cloaked in the long robes of the Orient. At first, Captain Proctor tried to make his powerful passenger feel like a part of the life aboard ship. But Jones made it quite clear that he wanted to be left alone. And so he was until the *Democrat* had rounded the Cape and was sailing up the coast of Africa toward their port of call in the Cape Verde Islands.

A few knots south of the Equator, high seas and furious winds forced them back. With sails furled the *Democrat* searched for sanctuary in the small island they had sighted the day before. The ferocity of the weather kept them anchored off the island for three days before a party could be sent ashore.

CHAPTER EIGHTEEN

My Shame

Mallory Jones watched silently while the first mate of the *Democrat* bartered with the native chief for fresh supplies of food. Pleased with the brightly colored scraps of silk the white men brought, the chief invited the party to share a meal with him.

A bowl woven of grass and leaves and filled with a beverage so potent it threatened to strip a sailor's insides was passed from man to man. All drank deeply of the liquor while they waited for the meal to be prepared.

As the afternoon wore on, the combination of the tropical sun and the powerful beverage took its toll on the men. They were laughing raucously and ogling the bare-breasted women who served them when a grizzled old man limped up to the boisterous group.

"Mind if I join you?" he whined, insinuating his grimy body between Mallory Jones and the first mate.

"Well now, upon my soul, an English-speaking native! What in heaven or hell are you doing in this godforsaken place?" White shouted jovially.

"Hee, hee," the old man cackled. "You'd be surprised how many white folks come to these parts—and stay."

There was something distinctly ominous in the old man's speech that both repulsed Mallory Jones and piqued his curiosity. He had drunk sparingly of the dangerous brew and had not joined in the men's ribald jokes.

"You mean to tell us, sir, that there are other white men on this island besides yourself?" he asked politely, although it had probably been years since the man's mud-caked old carcass had been even remotely white.

"Not only men," he cackled again. "Women as well—and young ones."

"Here, now? Well, then, introduce us, man, what are you waiting for?" White said, slapping the man heartily on the back.

"I would be pleased to introduce them to handsome chaps like yourselves, but they can't be found anywhere," he confided.

"Can't be found?" Jones asked quizzically.

"As I sit here beside you, they have disappeared. One day they were here, the next day they were gone. The chief sends a party to look for them every morning, but they have never been seen again. The natives think they were spirits, but if the young green-eyed wench was

227

not the prettiest piece of woman flesh I ever set my eyes on then I ain't Anthony Trollope."

White had turned back to the bowl of firewater, leaving the old man to sidle closer to Jones.

"The chief, there, he thought so too. Waited for months to get his hands on that little lady and, just as the day approached, she vanished. Gone in thin air."

"Very strange, indeed, Mr. Trollope," Jones said, trying to rid himself of the foul-smelling old man and his tall tales. "Now, if you will excuse me, I think I will take a brief walk. Maybe I will be lucky and find your missing spirits."

Mallory Jones presented a startling figure as he strolled through the native village in his long mandarin robes. The round, husky women, their bare skin as brown as betel nuts, and the spindly legged men, their bodies painted a bright blue, slunk into the straw huts as he passed. He wandered far from the village, not thinking of his safety at all, just enjoying the feeling of land beneath his feet once more. He stood at the edge of a cliff, watching the sun set brilliantly, lighting the western sky with crimson and pink streaks, and wondered for the thousandth time what it would be like to return to Boston—to be home again.

Alone on the primitive island he lingered, staring out at the darkening sea, trying to remember the place he had left as a boy. Home. He wasn't even sure what the word meant anymore. Then he heard a strange cry. It sounded like a human voice and it was very close. He searched through the low scrub for some sign of life, but all he found was a weasel. He listened again. This time the cry sounded as if it was at his feet, although the only thing within fifteen feet was a low shrub growing out of the base of the cliff. Jones pulled the bush lightly and, to his surprise, it came up easily in his hand, revealing a small opening in the rocky wall. Crouching down on his knees, he reached into the secret nest and, to his astonishment, he found a child—an infant no more than a few weeks old, a white male child with a soft fuzz of blonde hair and eyes as blue as his own, wrapped up in what looked to be a piece of a woman's dress.

Maybe, Jones thought incredulously, *I have stumbled on the mysterious white spirits the old man was rambling about.* He listened for some other sound of life, but heard only the sound of the water breaking on the shore below.

Thinking the mother, whoever she might be, could not be far away, he cupped his mouth with his hands and called, "Come out. I won't hurt you. I come as a friend." His voice echoed and re-echoed against the cliff, but it brought no reply.

Now that he had found the child, Jones was at a loss what to do. Although it seemed to be well cared for, he could not simply put the baby back in its nest and sail away. On the other hand, he dared not carry the baby back to the village, not knowing how the chief would react to the discovery of a white infant on his desolate island.

Hoping the mother would return soon, he sat down on a rock to wait. At first he was nervous, holding the fragile infant. He could not remember ever touching one before. But as the baby cooed contentedly, he began to relax, and soon he was tickling its chin and laughing delightedly when the child gurgled and waved its tiny arms.

He held the boy up on his knees and as he did, he noticed for the first time something glimmer around its neck. On further examination, he saw that it was a small gold disk with a wreath of enamel flowers on one side and an engraving on the other.

Mallory Jones strained in the fading light to read the inscription. Then his fingers locked around the disk so tightly his knuckles turned white. Clutching the child to his chest, he leaped up like a man possessed and began shouting, "Samantha, Samantha!" He shouted over and over, calling her name, his voice breaking with emotion, the child pressed in his arms. But the only answer was the pounding surf.

All his senses were tuned acutely to catch the slightest sound, a note on the wind, a whisper in the air. But there was nothing. As he stumbled back towards the nest where he had found his son, the first light of the moon illuminated his haunted face. He was unaware of the native youth who watched him from the shadows.

Owino looked into Mallory Jones's blue eyes

and knew instantly that this ghostly figure was the father of the child, this was the powerful spirit that his white goddess had returned to.

"My shame is your son, I think," the boy said.

Startled, Mallory Jones whirled around and saw the young boy crouching in the shadows.

"I take care of him for his mother," Owino said.

Mallory stared at the boy's solemn face. "Where did you find the child?" he asked, struggling to speak slowly and calmly.

"With the mother. I helped it be born."

"And his mother, is she here?" Jones asked, scarcely breathing as he waited for the boy's reply.

"No more."

"She has gone to the village?"

"No, to the sea."

"His mother went to the sea in a great ship like mine?"

"Yes," the boy nodded his head vigorously.

"And she left her baby here with you?"

The boy continued to nod vigorously, but Jones was sure he had not understood. He tried again.

"The mother," he pointed to his eyes, "were her eyes green like the sea?"

Owino nodded again. "She was very beautiful he said, "all white." He hesitated, and then, with a touch of pride in his voice, he said, "But not here." He pointed to a spot on the left side of his belly. "Here, dark circle."

Mallory Jones studied the native boy intently. It was true. There was only one blemish on Samantha's fair body. One single dark beauty mark.

"The mother," he said gruffly, "when is she coming back? When does she return?"

"No more," Owino answered.

"She has to come back for the child," Jones said impatiently.

"No more," the boy repeated, shaking his head sadly. "Gone on the big ship to find the father."

Fearing the child was too young to survive a rigorous voyage, Samantha left him with the boy while she returned to China to get me, Jones thought, until Owino added, "To Paris across the sea."

Jones looked incredulously from the boy to the tiny bundle in his arms and back to the boy. He did not believe it. Samantha had deserted her baby in this barbaric place to flee to Jean Levoir. She left her child here in Pagalu to a fate that she could not even begin to imagine—to be raised by a native boy and probably killed if he was discovered.

This was the woman Mallory Jones had left China for, forsaken the memory of his beloved Ming-la for? This was the woman he was following halfway around the world? What kind of a woman would desert her child like that—his child. Did that mean nothing to her?

"This, this charm," he said, pointing to the gold

232

disk around the baby's neck, "where did you find it?"

"The mother," Owino answered.

"Are you sure the mother gave it to you?"

"Yes. A gift from the mother."

"And the child's name?"

"My shame," Owino answered, making the words sound like an endearment. "Very pretty name."

Mallory Jones's anger was so great as he listened to the boy that the thin, purple scar stood out on his forehead.

"Who named the child?" He spoke each word slowly to keep himself from exploding.

"The mother." Owino whispered for he saw the tempest in the white man's face.

"This is my child."

"Yes, I see in your eyes."

"I will take him with me."

The boy said nothing.

"Please," Jones pleaded, "wait for me here. You will be safe as long as the child is uninjured. I swear it," he said as he commended his son to the native boy for the last time.

Mallory Jones ran back to the village, barely seeing the path in front of him, guided by some primordial desire to save his child. The evening had set in, but the stars were so bright it still seemed almost like daylight, as Jones stumbled ahead. He could hear the sailors from the *Democrat* long before he could see them. Their loud, drunken shouts and boisterous songs rang across the island, reaching his ears well before he could distinguish the blaze from the fire.

The men had been attacking a great vat of steaming food, interrupting their feast only long enough to make lewd gestures at the women who served them and grab at their bare breasts as they bent over the kettle.

Seeing the white men's pleasure in his women, Chief Wanda singled out one young morsel and, clapping his hands, demanded the attention of his guests. He stood up and led the girl to the center of the circle. The girl grinned, baring her brown stained teeth, proud to be chosen out of all the women of the village, and, raising her arms above her head, she danced to the chief's command.

Her undulating, animal movements drew forth wild catcalls from the men. More than two months at sea and this kind of temptation could drive a man crazy. The chief basked in the approval of the visitors. Magnanimously, he ordered the food removed and spoke enthusiastically to the old white man.

"Hee, hee, mates," the wizened old crow cackled, "you're in luck tonight. The chief would be pleased to share this young sweet with all men who want to join him. It's the best dessert you've been offered in many a night, I betcha."

The sailors let out a wild whoop that pleased the chief so much, he gave the girl a fresh command. Obeying eagerly, she undid her grass skirt and danced again, this time even more lewdly than before. When her naked body was steamy with sweat, she dropped on her knees in the center of the circle and raised her broad brown moon to the chief.

White pulled rank and took his place behind the chief while the other sailors pushed and shoved to line up behind him. Urged on by the hoots of his men, White rode the girl as the chief had, mounting her from behind like an animal and clutching her breasts like the horn of a saddle. He was just wiping himself off, when Mallory Jones stumbled onto the debauched scene.

The picture that he saw fueled his already monumental fury even further. The men of his ship were acting like beasts in heat, ganging up on one helpless girl in their drunken lust.

"Ah, Mr. Jones," White called, his tongue loosened dangerously and his courage fortified by the prodigious amount of spirits he had consumed, "will you join us?"

Mallory Jones icy gaze froze the words on the first mate's tongue.

"What is the meaning of this, Mr. White?" Jones demanded in a low, carefully controlled voice. Even through their drunkenness, the men sensed that his quiet tone was infinitely more dangerous than a raised voice, and their ardor softened in their pants. The girl, still on her knees, looked around, curious to see why the men had stopped after only two.

"Mr. Jones, sir. Ah, you see, sir, we were only trying not to give offense to the chief. He asked us to join him. I mean, sir, to share the girl with him. It must be a local custom, a kind of welcome mat, if you know what I mean, sir." The mate was gradually recovering the use of speech and his slippery tongue was anxious to soften Jones's anger.

"Not wanting to give offense, sir, and thinking it might be a long time, if you understand my meaning, sir, before we had another bit o' luck like this, we thought we would accept the chief's kind hospitality."

As if to confirm White's word, the chief approached them and, gesticulating broadly, beckoned Mallory Jones to take a turn with the girl. Jones looked at the girl's grinning face and at the men now cowering behind her.

"Get me one of the sacks we brought for the supplies," he ordered White curtly.

"Yes, sir. Right here, sir," the first mate obeyed swiftly.

"Empty it."

"Aye, aye, sir." Mangos and oranges rolled crazily over the ground as White turned over the flour sack. "Here you are, sir. Anything else, sir?"

"Yes, Mr. White. I want you and the men to wait for me at the skiff. Immediately."

He noted how their faces dropped at his words, but no man dared question his command. Jones was not shocked by the spectacle he had interrupted. From his long years in China, he had come to understand and accept the fact that different worlds have different customs, different mores. What is barbaric to one is quite natural and sometimes even an honor in another.

He realized that in his anger he had forgotten this basic lesson he had learned so well in Canton. When he arrived in China young and green, he had been shocked by the pleasures the flower boat girls proffered with their feathers and fans. But in time he came to understand that their exotic services were an ancient and well-accepted part of Oriental life. In fact, it was his thorough acceptance of the Chinese ways that had led him to take Samantha. If he had not mistaken her for a flower boat girl, he would never have touched her. But knowing their compliance and their subtle secrets all too well, he had his way with her.

Houqua had directed him to the most skilled girls and they had performed fantastic tricks on his body with their ostrich plumes. He was, after all, a young man with all of the natural urges and a hungry passion not easily sated. These men were as healthy as he was, Jones thought, and this ritual of taking turns in public with one woman must be a local custom. Why should they pass up their fun when no one would be hurt by it and the girl herself seemed eager to resume the proceedings?

Jones, himself, was not above sharing a willing wench with a pal. Back in the days when he and Jean Levoir were friends, they had visited the flower boats together. He remembered all too clearly how, after bathing in a warm, scented tub with two girls to wash them, and consuming far too much rice wine, they had all rolled into one large bed together. Because their heated encounter was more than he had bargained for was no reason to deny these sailors their pleasure, he thought.

Jones addressed the first mate. "Mr. White, tell the men they have fifteen minutes. No more, no less," he said. "Any hand who is not at the skiff is left behind."

Jones turned on his heel and swiftly walked back into the woods. The sailors' lusty roar, like the cries of men who have been granted a reprieve after feeling the noose of the gallows tighten around their necks, resounded behind him.

Jones hurried through the woods, the empty sack in his hand. He had wasted too much time already, he thought. He was worried that the boy might have disappeared with the child. Since the baby had clearly been well cared for, perhaps the boy had grown to love him and would not give him up. If he decided to hide with the child, Jones would have no way of finding them. He could not ask the chief for help, that much was sure, and yet, nothing could ever make him leave Pagalu without his son.

Thinking again of Samantha's desertion, he was filled with a virulent passion that he knew would burn within him for the rest of his life. But he had no time to brood over her now. He had to think of the child—his child, his son—and the boy.

It was disgustingly clear to Mallory Jones. The boy had been intimate with Samantha. There was no other way he would have seen the beauty mark on her belly. But he was little more than a child himself. She could not have fallen in love with him. She could not have been given to him by the chief, and he was too young to win her as a warrior. Samantha must have realized that the boy was enchanted with her pale beauty and used his affection. She must have given herself to him like a whore so he would help her, and then given her child to him as a reward.

Samantha paid him off with our child, Jones thought bitterly as he approached the cliff where he had left the boy cradling the child in his arms. But now the clearing was empty. His heart sank. He did not have a chance of finding the child. There were too many hiding places on the unfamiliar island. Every crack, every crevice in the rocks would be big enough to hide an infant.

Ming-la had been carrying their child when she died in the fire. That was why she risked going to the foreign quarter of Canton. Mallory Jones had lost one child. He could not bear to lose another—especially now, after he had held the little one and stroked its soft cheek. One parent had abandoned the baby, the other could not do the same.

Jones searched the cliff-side carefully for a sign of the vanished pair. Then, in the shadow of a jutting ledge, he saw them. The boy was curled up in a ball asleep, his cheek resting lightly against the baby's head. Tears welled up in his eyes as he watched their peaceful slumber. The boy, he imagined, had loved Samantha, and through the child he still poured out that love. Now it was over.

Jones bent over the sleeping pair and touched the boy's shoulder. "We must go, son. The ship awaits us."

Owino opened his eyes and gazed up at Mallory Jones, trying to understand something of this spirit man in the long skirts who had taken away his white goddess and was now taking the child. Reluctantly, he held out the baby.

Jones slipped the sleeping child into the sack and tied the mouth loosely, allowing plenty of space for air to enter. The boy did not move. He sat hunched by the side of the cliff, staring blankly at the man.

Reaching deep into the pocket of his robe, Mallory Jones brought out a peach velvet ribbon with a white cameo pinned at the center.

"Here," he gave it to the boy, "keep this. She would want you to have it, and so would the child," and then he turned abruptly and was swallowed by the woods. Moving at a half run, the baby cradled in his arms, he skirted the village entirely and, hugging the shore line, he made his way back to the skiff.

"Well now, sir, what tasty dish did you find for yourself," White called good-naturedly when he caught sight of Jones. "One of them delectable turtles by the size of it, I'd guess."

"You'll find out in due time," Jones replied sharply, well aware of the nosiness of the man and of the gossip that the sudden appearance of the child aboard ship would be sure to cause. "No time to waste now. Get that skiff in the water."

The men, still in high spirits, were all present and waiting and the boat was loaded with the fresh supplies.

"Here, sir, let me give you a hand with that," White said, his natural expansiveness aggravated by the wine and woman. "Plenty of room to just toss it on top."

"No, thank you, Mr. White," Jones demurred, "I will hold on to this one myself."

As they rowed out to the *Democrat*, Mallory Jones sat silently in the stern with his precious cargo in his arms. He turned back for one last look at the island that almost became home to his son. There, on the cliff, standing small but straight against the sky, silhouetted in the moonlight, was a small figure. He raised his arm and waved it high over his head. Mallory Jones waved back and continued to wave until he could not see Owino any more.

CHAPTER NINETEEN

Samantha's Unforgivable Sin

Samantha's son never wanted for attention on the long voyage to Boston. Although the men were clumsy at first, they were soon performing the chores of feeding and changing as if they had been nannies all their lives. In fact, White took to the woman's work so quickly and well, his shipmates dubbed him "Ma."

Mallory Jones renamed his son Jonathan—Wee Jon to the sailors who took turns babysitting, bouncing the boy on their knee and walking with him when he was upset and fussy. Gregg, the puniest hand on board who had always been the butt of jokes because he was so slim and lightly bearded, came into his own. Every night he sang the child to sleep, his clear tenor sounding through the ship and rising on the salt air. His lullabies softened the tough men and filled them with thoughts of home and families they had been so long apart from.

For many reasons, Jonathan seemed the only

name for the boy, Jones thought. Whatever Samantha had done, she was still the child's mother, and Jonathan Shaw was a man whose name anyone would be proud to bear. More than that, he had been a faithful friend.

Having the child to care for and think about had lightened Mallory Jones's spirit. He put aside his Oriental clothes and dressed simply in breeches and an open shirt. His hair was bleached almost white by the sun and salt and his body turned bronze.

Although he was still occasionally overcome by dark memories that would keep him in his cabin for days at a time, Jones joined in the life of the ship much more freely now, and his easy charm and open manner earned the devotion of all hands. Frequently, in the evening, he would join Captain Proctor for dinner and a game of cards or take up the accordion and sit on the top-deck playing for the men.

He watched each small step in his son's development with wonder and joy. When the baby smiled or reached out his tiny arms to be taken into his father's powerful embrace, he thought he had never known such happiness.

And so the *Democrat* made the Atlantic crossing, stopping en route at the Cape Verde islands and again at the Canary Islands. At each port, Jones inquired if a ship carrying a young Yankee woman had passed, knowing that such a novelty would be the talk of the port for months. But he

245

received no word of Samantha. She had stopped at neither port looking for help to rescue her son.

With each step and each response, Mallory Jones cemented his sure knowledge of what Samantha had done and he locked every thought of her from his mind. He recharted the ship's course. The *Democrat* would not stop in London. It would follow a direct route to Boston.

Once his initial fury at finding the child abandoned in the pagan and primitive Pagalu had passed, a deeper, smoldering anger took its place. He was like a fire in which the flames had died but the embers still burned, a blue, penetrating, eternal heat which he would carry in his heart forever.

But Mallory Jones could never forget Samantha, for every time he looked into the face of his son, he saw the child's mother looking back at him. Except for Jonathan's eyes, which were his father's, the child looked remarkably like Samantha and the resemblance seemed to grow more pronounced each day.

If anyone else made the connection, it was never mentioned. In fact, none of the men ever asked where Jones had found the child or whom it belonged to. He accepted paternity; whether in fact or because it was a white child that he had discovered abandoned, no one knew surely. Everyone noted the incredible similarity of their eyes, but no one ever questioned Jones or hinted about the baby's mother. And they never saw the gold disk.

All the sailors knew the rumors about his fatal liaison with Houqua's daughter. Although little Jonathan did not seem to have any Oriental blood in him, they wondered and gossiped among themselves. But no man dared question Mallory Jones.

Even though he was more open and convivial since he'd brought the infant aboard and was well-liked by all, there still remained something guarded about him, a certain distance he maintained which prevented intimacy. He would joke with the crew. He would help them out of a jam. He would treat them equitably and honestly. But he would never be one of them. Mallory Jones was, after all, the most powerful China trader, as much a legend in America as he was in Canton.

And so, with their small but precious cargo from Pagalu and their strangely pleasant but unusual voyage behind them, the *Democrat* sailed into Boston harbor safely.

CHAPTER TWENTY

The Buccaneer's Bed

While Samantha commanded the *Zanzibar*, Captain Abdul lay racked with fever in his beautiful mahogany four-poster. The powerful man had faded to a shadow. But in the long days of nursing, Samantha had grown fond of the helpless giant. She blamed herself for bringing the fever to the ship and so felt responsible for the sick man. She spared herself neither time, nor sleep, nor energy to care for him. But the captain's condition never changed. The fever neither rose nor abated. Periods of delirium and fitful sleep alternated with periods so calm that on several occasions Samantha thought he was dead. He never regained consciousness. He never recognized anyone. But in the jumble of guttural sounds he would mutter in his delirium, Samantha always caught the same phrase, an English phrase: "Barbary Rose."

Samantha thought that if only she could understand what "Barbary Rose" meant, she would unlock the mystery that kept him a thrall, would free his spirit so that he could begin the long road to recovery. She asked Freddy once if the captain had ever mentioned "Barbary Rose" to him, but he had no idea what she was talking about. She riffled through Abduls desk and found a leather-bound notebook that looked as if it were a log or diary of some kind. But it was written in a strange alphabet which she could not begin to decipher. So she waited and wondered—waited for the captain to take a turn for better or worse and wondered about the mysterious "Barbary Rose."

A month to the day after he had taken Samantha into his bed, Captain Abdul looked at the world again. Sunlight streamed through the open porthole and he blinked and covered his eyes to protect them from the unfamiliar glare. The air smelled fresh and salty. He was lying in the familiar four-poster that he had taken from a French frigate. The globe was at his feet as usual. But he felt strangely disassociated from his surroundings. He couldn't remember going to bed that night, or the events of the day. Yet he had a vague, shadowy recollection of someone soft and sweet-smelling bending over him and of cool towels on his hot brow.

From the glare of the sun, Captain Abdul judged that the day was half-spent. Blaming an excess of brandy for his failure to remember the night before, he pulled back the covers, wondering as he did why he had so many blankets over him when even in the coldest northeastern he slept under nothing but a satin sheet. But the effort of moving the heavy blankets exhausted him and he sank back into the pillows breathing heavily.

Brandy can turn a man to jelly, he thought to himself. His eyes roamed over the familiar room for clues of the drunken orgy he must have had the night before. Usually after a bout of hard drinking, he would wake up to find glasses broken on the floor, clothes thrown all over the room, a table or chair upturned. But this morning everything was in its proper place. The room was neater than he had ever seen it, except for a bundle of blankets on the divan.

As Captain Abdul was considering this curious situation, the bundle moved and tawny-colored locks tumbled out, reviving his memory vividly. Last night he had tried to take the Yankee girl, and he had failed. His devastating humiliation came back to him. He had ripped off her clothes in a frenzy of lust, but dazzled by her pearly white breasts and tawny crown he had failed.

Why is she still here? he wondered angrily. If he had torn her clothes so badly, she could have run naked back to her cabin and let the men who saw her try their luck. They would have her today anyway, he would see to that. "She must be a witch," he muttered darkly, "appearing from nowhere out of the sea, bringing fever to my ship, robbing me of my manhood, and now

252

casting me under a spell that's making me too weak to move."

He lay motionless in the bed and watched the divan like a lion stalking its prey. The girl stirred. Through half-closed eyes he saw her get up, peel off her nightshirt and, stretching sensually, walk naked to the basin. Filling it with water from his brass pitcher, she began to wash herself. He watched her with suppressed anger. She acted like she owned the ship. This was *his* cabin and, in one night, she had taken possession of it—one night that she had treated him like a dog, tearing great handfuls of hair right out of his head! But he couldn't find his voice and he began to drift off. Though she was still slim, her body seemed rounder, more voluptuous than the night before, he thought, as her figure started to blur in the fog that was rolling over him.

When Captain Abdul came to again, he could hear a low murmuring and could feel cool hands stroking his brow. He opened his eyes, blinking again at the sunlight. Her anxious face was just inches from his own and her smile was brighter than the sunlight.

"Good morning," she said softly, "you have been sleeping for a very long time."

She wiped his face tenderly with a damp cloth as he closed his eyes again and tried to remember what had happened. Why was she behaving so kindly? Because she had humiliated him? He could hear her talking to someone but could not catch her words, and when he opened his eyes again, she was across the room pouring tea into a small mug and Freddy was standing at his bedside.

"What is she doing here, Freddy?" the captain asked. His voice sounded faraway, as if it were coming through a cave.

"She is taking care of you, Captain, and very good care, I might add."

"Get her out of here. What am I, an invalid who needs a nursemaid?"

"But Captain . . . "

"Get her out!" he shouted, but his voice came out in a low, hoarse whisper that Freddy had to strain to hear and, in his frustration, he seized the compress from his forehead and threw it at the little man.

"Freddy, I will go for some porridge. It isn't good to upset him now that he is just coming around. There will be plenty of time to explain everything later," Samantha said.

Abdul heard the door close and shut his eyes. His anger had exhausted him and he sank back into a fitful sleep, but this time there was no delirious screaming for "Barbary Rose."

The worst was over. Although it would be weeks before he regained his strength completely, he was out of danger at last.

When Samantha returned about an hour later with the warm broth and porridge, the captain woke up and went into as great a rage as his weakened state would permit. Dashing the gruel to the floor, he ordered her out of his cabin.

"Freddy, will you leave us for a moment?" Samantha asked, ignoring Abdul's outburst. "Just wait outside the door and I will call if I need you."

Freddy scurried out, glad of an excuse to escape. Captain Abdul frightened him. He looked like a corpse that has come back from the grave. His olive skin was ashen, his black eyes sunken, his drawn face quivering with anger.

When they were alone, Samantha asked gently, "Captain Abdul what do you remember last?"

"You witch," he cried hoarsely. "Your evil curse is on me and my ship."

"That is just as I thought," Samantha said smiling.

The captain sensed a new aura of assurance and command about the girl that only heightened his anger. He was not a man to forget a humiliation—a humiliation worse than any other—and this woman was obviously enjoying her triumph.

Ignoring his dark scowl, Samantha went on. "That night, which you remember as last night, was really one month ago today. You have been lying in bed for thirty days and thirty nights, wracked with fever. I did not place a curse on you. It was the fever that weakened you and deprived you . . . saved me . . . that drained your sex," she finished bluntly.

"It was the fever? I had the fever? Are you sure?"

"Quite sure. I have been sitting at your bedside every day, nursing you. All the men but four

255

recovered weeks ago. But you are a stubborn man."

"You are right. It was the fever. I will prove it to you," the captain said excitedly. He grasped her hand and tried to pull her down on him, but he was so weak he could not budge her.

Samantha laughed. "You still have a long way back before you will be strong enough to have your way with innocent girls again. But if you ever want to," she added mischievously, "you had better begin by drinking this broth."

Captain Abdul submitted meekly.

In the long weeks of his recovery he grew to enjoy her tender ministrations, and became a somewhat demanding patient. It was not that he had a great many needs, but rather that he liked to keep Samantha near him. The clothes she wore now were much more becoming than the ugly rags he had once ripped off her. Just a simple shirt and dark breeches, but they conformed closely to her graceful curves. He even liked the way his men snapped at her command.

Little by little as his strength returned, Samantha told him about the fever and the storm that swept the ship and, although it was never spoken outright, he accepted the face that she was running the *Zanzibar*. Now that he was recovering, she would bring him the charts each morning and ask him to plot their course, but he usually waved her away, enjoying the way she had risen to the challenge and confident that he was now well enough to right any errors she might make.

Samantha was still living in the captain's quarters. But now that Abdul's health was returning so rapidly, and there was no more need for her to watch over him in the night, she thought it was time she moved back to her own cabin.

"Just a few more days, Samantha," the captain would say each time she broached the subject. "Just wait until I get a little stronger. You have nothing to fear from me yet—nothing for weeks more, you said so yourself. So what are a few more nights? It will make me rest easier knowing you are here."

Samantha was touched by Abdul's words. *Ill winds sometimes bear good tidings*, she mused. The man she had once thought was so sinister and had actually feared would throw her and Aunt Maude overboard had shown her a tender side. If there had been no fever epidemic, she would never have discovered the gentle man within the menacing giant.

But Samantha had another, more pragmatic reason, to stay in the captain's cabin. Once she moved back to her old cramped quarters, she feared there would be a subtle shift in power. She would lose the edge of command she had striven so hard to gain. Once the men saw her back in her old berth, they would gradually cease to think of her as captain. It was not that they were fickle or thankless. It was simply that their orders had always come from the captain's quarters. That very cabin with its elegant furnishings symbolized power to them and instilled fear as surely as the tea in Boston Harbor had spelled power to the Yankee rebels.

Although weeks of sleeping on the divan began to tell on her back and she longed for a good night's sleep in a real bed, Samantha remained in Captain Abdul's cabin. One night, as she was turning restlessly trying to find a comfortable position, she heard him call to her in the darkness. It was very late and the night was very black. She thought he had been asleep for hours, but instead, he had been lying awake listening to her tossing.

"Samantha, Samantha." Her name sung out softly in the quiet room.

"Abdul, you should be sleeping."

"I cannot rest, Samantha, while you are sleepless. Come over here. My bed is big enough for two."

"No, Abdul, don't ask me that."

"Then help me up. I will rest on the divan tonight and you can have my bed to yourself."

"No, Abdul, you will not get strong again, if you do not rest well."

Samantha lay so still she could hear the captain breathing. The even rhythm was so different from the erratic sound she had listened to anxiously through many a long and worried night. She thought he had finally fallen asleep, but then she heard him call to her again.

"Samantha, Samantha, Samantha." He whispered her name until it seemed to be echoing around the room. "Don't be afraid, Samantha,

I can't hurt you. I am too weak. We will lie like brother and sister, and I will never touch you."

His voice was low and hypnotic, and her back was so sore. Her tired body yearned for the comfort of the wide bed, and the feel of the satin sheets against her bare back once more. But something held her back.

Was it the rules she had learned so long ago and, though forced by circumstances to abandon, had never completely relinquished—the rules that taught her it was wrong to lie in the bed of a man you were not wed to, even though you never touched. Was this what held her back? Or was it fear—fear that this man who had tried to ravage her twice before would take his pleasure from her body as soon as she fell asleep? She had sworn that she would never be taken again by any man against her will, and nothing had happened to make her change that vow. Yet, Samantha knew very well that it would be many more nights before Abdul would have the strength to violate her.

What fear was it, then, that held her back? Was it fear of the tempestuous passions that Mallory Jones had awakened so brutally, so completely, so fatally?

The girl, Samantha, had known innocent flirtations, but in her young dreams she had imagined a gentle kiss that would send her heart racing, a dance that would make her breasts heave in the remembering, a quick press of the fingers through

259

lace gloves that would seal a sacred bond. But once the torrential, unsuspected fires that smoldered within her lovely breast were aroused, the flames could never be quenched. The woman, Samantha, possessed the deepest hungers, the most searing desires. Many months had passed since she had tasted the joys of the flesh, and then it had been only the affectionate coupling with the overeager boy. Her maternal emotions were stirred, but her womanly needs were left unanswered.

Her body ached with desire. At night she had begun to dream, not of Jean Levoir whom she loved, but of the hated Mallory Jones and of the passionate, burning, abandoned way he had taken her on that last day in Macao. She would dream of his consuming lust and of his ravenous hunger, and wake up perspiring and flushed, her thighs encrusted with her dry passion.

Was Samantha afraid to lie beside the man? Afraid to trust her hungry body? Afraid she could not restrain her burning needs?

Ashamed of her secret desire, determined to conquer her fatal passions, she tiptoed across the room and slipped between the satin sheets. She could not feel their sensual sheen through the thick nightshirt she wore, and it was just as well, she thought, as she sank back into the deep bed with a sigh of pure pleasure.

"Samantha," Abdul whispered in surprise and took her hand gently, raised it to his lips, then pressed it against his chest. They fell asleep like that, the two captains of the *Zanzibar*, hand in hand like children.

From that night on, without being asked, Samantha slipped into bed beside the captain, protected by his weakness and her thick nightshirt, and every morning she would dress modestly behind a curtain that Freddy had erected at the far corner of the room. Captain Abdul never told her that he had watched her that first morning— had watched her graceful naked body as she performed her morning ablutions—but he would remember the picture each day when she stepped behind the curtain and he heard the sound of splashing water.

Gradually, as the captain grew stronger, he would sit on the divan for a few hours in the afternoon and one day even took a short turn around the deck. The men cheered gustily when they saw him, but he dared not stay too long because he did not want them to know how weak he still was. After twenty years at sea, he knew all too well how precarious a captain's command was and he didn't want to give his crew any dangerous ideas. For this reason—apart from the fact that he enjoyed her gentle feminine company —he was glad that Samantha had taken command. But much about her still puzzled him.

Although she lay beside him each night, he never touched her, except to occasionally rest his head on her bosom and sleep like a baby on his mother's chest. She would hold his head lightly, then, and they would fall asleep to-

261

gether, two innocents tossed at sea. Abdul was waiting, hoping that when he had the strength to perform like a man, she would accept him. It was clear that she had grown fond of him. She had nursed him for weeks and lived with him for weeks more. And he desired her fiercely.

Yet, now that they had become friends—mates—he did not want to force himself on her. He wanted more than that. He wanted her to yearn for him as he yearned for her. And so he waited, with surprising patience for such an impatient man, until, one night, he was awakened by her violent tossings and turnings.

Samantha had kicked off the sheet and her long nightshirt was entangled around her waist. Her tawny crown shone in the moonlight, moisture glistening on her creamy thighs, her legs spread wide. He stared in awe. *What exquisite dream is she having?* he wondered as he reached over, carefully so as not to wake her, and stroked her round, smooth stomach. His touch seemed to relax her and she moaned slightly, as his fingers explored the length of her stomach, caressing the inside of her moist thighs lightly, then daringly sinking into her tawny hairs. Samantha moaned again, arching her back like a cat. But Abdul dared go no further for fear of waking her. He held his breath, his motionless fingers still tangled in her hair, but she arched her back higher and opened her legs wider, inviting him to continue his explorations. He worked his fingers slowly down through her luxurious forest until he found

262

her opening. It was wide and briny like the sea, as if she were waiting for him to discover it. He plunged his finger in, still careful not to wake her, and she received him hungrily, pumping her thighs up to meet his fingers, moaning deeply; then, with a high delirious cry, she filled his hand with her precious juices. Still, she did not wake up.

Captain Abdul pulled the sheet over her bare legs and lay back, amazed at what they had just done. He held his hand against his nose and drank in the sweet, salty fragrance of her desire. As he drifted off to sleep, he wondered if Samantha would remember anything in the morning. He was more anxious than ever now to arouse the passions in her lovely slender body and light the fires she banked beneath her cool Yankee demeanor.

CHAPTER TWENTY-ONE

Who Is Barbary Rose?

Samantha woke up from that strange night refreshed and full of high spirits.

"I've never had such a wonderful sleep," she greeted the captain in the morning, and her euphoric mood lasted for several days.

They were nearing the end of their voyage, and for most of the crew it would be none too soon. Under Samantha's command, the *Zanzibar* had not attacked a single vessel. Supplies were low and, without bounty to divide, the men were growing restless and bored. Although Captain Abdul had sensed the discontent in his crew, he had opposed any action, because he was afraid Samantha could be hurt and because he was still not strong enough to lead an attack.

It had been a long, slow recovery and only the presence of Samantha at his side had made it bearable. He'd had hundreds of women in ports around the world and many a good and lusty time. But this slender girl, whom he had only tasted surreptitiously under the cover of sleep, had gotten under his skin. When he wasn't watching her, he was thinking about her. He admired her courage, her command over his men, her calm assurance in a storm, as he would admire these qualities in a man, and he looked at her in many ways as a comrade, as trusted and true as a brother. Yet, at the same time, he longed for her. If she accidentally brushed against him in passing, if she leaned over his shoulder to study a chart and he felt her fine breath on his neck, if in their separate sleep they happened to touch, he was filled with a powerful desire to take her in his arms. He was strong enough now to have her, yet he held back. He was waiting for some sign, some signal that he meant more to her than a passage to safe port.

Since discovering to his surprise and disappointment that Samantha was not a virgin, Captain Abdul had begun to brood. Who was the man she had known, or had there been more than one—two, three, a dozen? What wild desire had driven her to them? What secret fear kept her from him? His torment drove him into bouts of melancholy, and Samantha, concerned by his sudden black moods, wondered if he was yearning for "Barbary Rose."

They were lying side by side in the darkness, each with his own jealous doubts. The only light was from the moonbeam that shone through the transom port.

"Abdul, may I ask you something?" Samantha

said, linking her arms behind her head and staring up at the ceiling.

"Anything."

"I probably shouldn't ask," she hesitated.

"Ask me, Samantha," he urged, hoping wildly that this was the moment he had been waiting for, "or we will never know and will be forced to wonder forever."

She turned on her elbow to face him. "Abdul," she said, stroking his cheek shyly. "When you had the fever, you kept crying out in your sleep. I couldn't understand most of what you said, but then all of a sudden you would say a few words in English."

"Mmm," he said, hoping she would keep on stroking his cheek, "Is that so unusual? Remember, I was speaking English with you when the fever struck me down." He smiled at the little joke he had made. If she kept touching him, he would not be able to control himself much longer.

"No, I suppose not," she said, moving closer and resting her hand on his bare chest, "but . . ."

"Samantha, let's not talk anymore," he said, leaning forward to reach the lips he could not resist for another moment. But she drew back.

"I was afraid you would not want to tell me. That's why I haven't asked you until now. I guess it is still none of my affair."

"No, no," he murmured, "I didn't mean it that way. Of course it is your affair. Everything is your affair. Please tell me, Samantha," he said, drawing her to him again, "tell me what it is you want to know," he said in the low hoarse whisper that always seemed to echo through the cabin. She was searching his face with her wide, questioning eyes and his last words were lost in her lips. His mouth drifted down to hers as if he were sailing into a harbor. He felt her lips stiffen and her mouth close against his, but he did not press her. He urged her gently with his tongue, and, when she responded, it was with such force that he never wanted their lips to part again. She drew his tongue into her mouth, deeper and deeper, sucking it with her lips, sinking her sharp teeth into it, then covering it with her own tongue. Throwing off the sheets, he searched for the tender flesh beneath her thick nightshirt. He was larger than he had ever been, harder and hungrier. This was the moment he had waited so long for. Nothing could stop him now.

"Abdul, "Abdul," she murmured against his lips, "what does 'Barbary Rose' mean?

"Later, later we will talk," he answered, barely hearing her words.

She gazed into the glowing eyes above her and impetuously locked her arms around his neck. "Tell me, Abdul, who is 'Barbary Rose?' " she insisted, even as she drew his famished body to her and opened her legs to receive him.

In the darkness of the cabin, the captain's olive face turned ashen. His passion vanished and a fury just as great replaced it. He grasped Samantha by the shoulders in a grip of iron. "Who told

269

you about that, that no-good son of a dog Rudy? What did he tell you?"

"Abdul, let me go, you are hurting me," Samantha cried. "No one told me and I don't know anything about it. It is what you kept repeating in your fever."

The captain got up and, tearing a sheet from the bed, wrapped it around himself. Muttering angrily in his deep guttural tongue, he paced the length of the cabin like a penned lion, then suddenly turned on Samantha. "Who told you? I want to know who told you."

Samantha was frightened and hurt but she tried to remain calm. A moment before she had been ready to give herself to this tempest of a man. Looking at him now, she wondered how she could have even considered such a thing.

"You told me," she said coldly, "in your delirium."

In the light of the moon he studied her face to see if she was telling the truth, then he began to pace again, back and forth, back and forth. "Did anyone else hear me?" he asked, his voice quieter now.

"No one. Freddy helped me to clean and feed you but I was alone with you during all your fevered ravings."

"If I ever find out that anyone else knows these words then, it will mean that you have told them." He sat down on the edge of the bed wearily as if he was suddenly very tired. "Then I will have to kill you. It may be the most difficult thing I will ever have to do, but I will have no choice." He squeezed her shoulder for a moment in his terrible passion, then he said gruffly, "You talk too much; did anyone ever tell you?" He squeezed her shoulder again, then he dressed quickly and went out.

Samantha lay awake until dawn, wondering what dark chord in Abdul's past she had struck, what horrible secret he was concealing. There are some things men will die for and she had, unwittingly, found the one thing—the one woman, for she was sure it had to be a woman— in Abdul's life. She was jealous of his passion for the mysterious "Barbary Rose" and frightened by the depths of his anger. And she wondered, as the sun rose slowly in the east, would he still be able to kill her, if they had consummated their union?

In the next days and nights, Samantha saw little of the captain. He kept to the deck for the most part, having resumed the responsibility of his office, driving the men hard and bursting into frequent fits of anger and impatience. He took to drinking brandy by the tumbler again and began to lapse back into other old habits. Samantha kept out of his way as much as she could and left the *Zanzibar* to his erratic command. The more she thought about it, the surer she became that his was not an idle threat.

Captain Abdul was drunk often now. Sometimes his drinking would begin with breakfast and go on long after Samantha had retired. She

271

missed the easy, amiable times they used to have together and worried that so much alcohol in his fragile condition would be dangerous. But she dared not interfere. They never slept together in the big four-poster anymore. Sometimes, when Samantha would wake in the middle of the night, she would see him lying on the divan in all his clothes, but he would always be gone when she woke up again, even if it was just dawn. Often she would be awakened by his anguished cries in his sleep or by his drunken brawling as he crashed into tables and chairs before sinking in a stupor on the divan. But one night she woke up to find him staring down at her, a deep sadness etched on his suffering face.

It pained Samantha to see the anguish she had caused the captain but she dared not try to comfort him, and she began to long for the end of their troubled journey. She had studied the globe and charted the course a hundred times—from Africa to Italy, Italy to France. Would Jean still be waiting for her? Surely he had taken her for dead by now, maybe he had even married. But Samantha tried not to think of these gloomy things and concentrated instead on his promise—the biggest, most gala wedding of the season, and she the toast of Paris.

Samantha had no idea how she, a single woman with no funds, could travel safely. Although she had never mentioned it to him, she had been hoping that Captain Abdul would help her, but now there was no possibility of that. She had to count on Freddy to help her find a way. He, she could be sure, would not desert her.

When the *Zanzibar* finally sailed through the Strait of Gibraltar and entered the Mediterranean Sea, Samantha could barely contain her excitement. Only Captain Abdul's dour presence kept her from racing to the topdeck and shouting with joy. The dream she had cherished through so many difficult months was in reach at last.

That night Samantha slept fitfully, dreaming of her school days in Paris, and of a dark, handsome man's tender caresses. He was bending over her, stroking her hair and murmuring again and again, "I love you, Samantha, I love you." Gently, he picked her up and held her tightly against his chest, kissing her mouth, pressing his lips fiercely against hers as if something within him would break if he ever let go. Then he put her down tenderly on the bed and stumbled toward the door.

"Abdul, Abdul," she called, her eyes brimming with tears, "don't leave me like this." But it was too late. The door slammed shut and he was gone.

CHAPTER TWENTY-TWO

Abdul's Secret

By dawn the *Zanzibar* was a flurry of activity. Men who had not been on land in months were whooping gleefully in anticipation of what lay in store for them in Algiers.

Samantha dressed quickly and tied her few meager possessions in a neat bundle.

"Let's go, Miss Samantha," Freddy called. "Rudy is saving room for you on the first skiff."

Samantha's heart was in her throat as she rushed to the deck. All hands were assembled to wish her well—everyone but Captain Abdul. She looked around anxiously for him. She could not shut him out of her life without a word. She remembered the long vigil she had kept at his bedside and the nights she had lain at his side. And she remembered his passionate kiss and his words of love in the night. She had to see him again, if only to say goodbye, to see his smoldering charcoal eyes brighten and his pearly teeth gleam beneath his black moustache.

"Hurry, Miss, the men are waiting," Freddy called.

"But where is Captain Abdul, Freddy? I can't leave without a word of farewell."

"If it's the captain you're looking for, you won't find him. Simul rowed him ashore before dawn. But he left this for you," Freddy said, producing a leather purse. "To give you a start on your journey, he said, and he gave me leave to go with you for as long as you need protection. Me and John, we'll stay by you, Miss Samantha."

Samantha was touched by the little speech. "Thank you, Freddy, I was hoping you would accompany me, since this land is so foreign to me and it is difficult for a young woman to travel alone."

"Don't worry, Miss, no harm will come to you with Freddy Finckle and John Temple at your side."

"There are no better hands I know of," Samantha said warmly. "But Freddy, I do want to say goodbye to the captain. Perhaps you know where I can find him in Algiers."

"Oh, I wouldn't be sure of that," Freddy said, embarrassment emblazoned on his freckled face. "The captain, you know, he's a wild one. Come now, ma'am, the mates won't wait forever, not even for their favorite captain."

As the skiff moved toward Algiers, Samantha looked back at the *Zanzibar*. In her last moments Maude Shaw had thought it was Boston. Samantha offered a silent prayer for her aunt and for the gentle boy who had brought them safely to the ship's side. She realized then, as surely as she knew her name, that a chapter in her life was ending. It was a chapter that had changed and molded her. It had forced her to become a woman—too soon, perhaps. It had awakened in her passions whose bounds she still feared to test. She had survived great losses—the loss of her father, her maidenhood, her aunt, her child. She had suffered shipwreck, enslavement, fever, and rape. She had met challenges that most women would never imagine and most men would never be called on to face. She had commanded a pirate ship. And she had discovered both the violence and the tenderness of men, and the power they could exert over her if she ever abandoned herself to her deepest desires.

Looking ahead to she knew not what, Samantha remembered her aunt's last words, "Don't worry your pretty little head, Samantha. Everything is going to be all right." Maybe, just maybe, Aunt Maude was right.

"Freddy," Samantha said, eager now to be on her way to Paris and, she hoped, the still waiting arms of Jean Levoir, "do you think we will be able to find a boat leaving for Italy in the morning?"

"I will check all the ships in the harbor," the little man answered, "as soon as we get ashore. John here can take you to the Ikavo and find rooms for us for the night. The captain said you would be safe lodging there."

"What else did Captain Abdul tell you, Freddy?" Samantha asked curiously.

"Oh, nothing else, really, Miss Samantha," he said, blushing to the roots of his red hair, "except the captain did say that you should wear my cap. Pile your hair up inside it, he said, and try to pass for a boy. That way no harm should come to you. Here you go, ma'am," Freddy said, taking off his cap and handing it to Samantha, "do as the captain says. This is a rough town for a young lady like yourself, even with me and John watching over you."

"Very well, Freddy, if you think I should," Samantha said, "but first tell me one other thing. Where did Captain Abdul say he was staying?"

"Did I say I knew where the captain was staying, ma'am? Not Freddy Finckle; never said I knew any such a thing. Why there's six or eight different places he might have gone, and none of them fit for a lady."

Freddy's scarlet face revealed more truth than his words, but Samantha knew she wouldn't get anymore out of him, and she was only distressing him by asking. *Abdul must have sworn the little man to secrecy*, she decided, *and I won't force him to break his word. The captain knows where we will be lodging tonight, if he wants to say farewell.* With her mind thus resolved, Samantha left Freddy at the dock, bade Rudy a fond adieu, and set off with John Temple to find the Ikavo.

The steep, dusty streets of Algiers were crowded with hawkers whose wares were spread in the narrow alleys. A high, monotonous music like an endless wail drifted through the jostling throngs. The air was heavy with the redolence of spices and vibrant with the cries of the street peddlers. Everything was for sale in the casbah, including women. Samantha's eyes were wide with wonder at the teeming, haggling crowds, at the men who sat cross-legged in the alleyways puffing on long brass waterpipes and the women who displayed their endowments so shamelessly. Samantha was glad she had taken the captain's advice and tried to look as much like a young sailor as she could, for she was the only woman in the streets who was not selling her wares.

Clinging closely, she and John made their way through the winding streets, following the directions Freddy had given them.

"Hello there, sailor boy, want to put your ship in my port?" a woman called to Samantha. She was old and wrinkled with a silk turban wrapped around her garish red hair. "Won't cost much for a handsome lad like yourself," she called after them. "Come on, pretty boy, no man can refuse Barbary Rose."

Samantha stopped dead. "John," she said urgently, "did that woman say 'Barbary Rose?' "

"Yes, it must be the old harlot's name. A Limey from the sound of her voice. There must be one of everything in this . . . "

"John, wait here. I have to talk to that woman," Samantha interrupted.

"Talk to Barbary Rose? You must be . . . "

But before John could finish, Samantha had broken away and was running back to the old whore.

"So you couldn't rush by Barbary Rose after all, could you sonny? None of the young ones can," the woman said with a smile that bared her gold teeth. "Just follow me, sailor boy, and old Rose will make a man of you." She laughed throatily as she led Samantha through a dimly-lit cafe into a room beyond, bare except for a dirty matress on a narrow bed and a single chair.

"You are a handsome one, all right," the old woman said, touching Samantha's cheek, "and not a trace of fuzz on your face yet. What will your pleasure be?"

Samantha lowered her voice as deeply as she could. "Begging your pardon, ma'am," she began apologetically, "but I just want to talk. I will pay you for your time, of course."

"Don't be afraid to say; old Rose has heard it all. There is nothing more that can surprise me," she said as she undid her black dress, exposing large, pendulant breasts. "My you are a shy one. What are you waiting for boy? Do you think Barbary Rose has never seen a man without his breeches before?" she laughed throatily. "Come on, sailor, I haven't got all day for you," she said, and grabbed Samantha's cap.

"A girl," the old woman shrieked, as Samantha's thick locks tumbled to her shoulders. "A girl! What are you doing here? Why do you want to humiliate me? Get out, get out!"

"Please," Samantha said, trying to calm the woman, "I only wanted to talk to you for a moment."

"You surprised me. I hate surprises; I'm afraid of them. The one was too much, too much for a lifetime." Barbary Rose sat down heavily on the dirty matress and pulled her dress around her wrinkled breasts.

"I am very sorry if I have upset you," Samantha said softly. "I was looking for a friend and I thought you might be able to help me find him. Please forgive me." She started to step backwards, working her way awkwardly toward the door, when the old woman looked up.

"Who is this friend?" she demanded.

"He is a ship's captain, a pirate captain. He mentioned you often," Samantha added, hoping to make up to the old woman for upsetting her.

"And this pirate captain's name?" Barbary Rose's sharp eyes appraised Samantha shrewdly.

The girl hesitated remembering the captain's deadly threat. "Abdul," she said in a whisper, "Captain Abdul Laboud." Barbary Rose stared silently at Samantha. "I only want to say goodbye to him," the girl explained. But Barbary Rose continued to stare with angry, accusing eyes.

"Abdul never says goodbye," she muttered finally. She seemed to have forgotten Samantha's presence and to have floated back many years. "I gave the boy to the missionary priests the day he was born and came back to the casbah. I never thought . . . " Her voice drifted off. Her body slumped in despair.

Finally she said, "He was so young, so handsome, but what a man he was already." She laughed sensually. "A wild man. He'd keep me going all night long and still want more, until at last I would have to chase him out so that the other customers would not complain. But he would always sneak back and steal more time.

" 'What would your mother think if she could see how greedy you are?' I teased one night. 'My mother's dead,' he said. 'She died when I was born. She was English like you, but a fine English lady, not a hot-blooded hussy.' He was laughing and pulling me under him when I said, 'And what was the fine English lady's name?' 'Rosemary Evers,' he answered proudly. 'Why that was my name!' I blurted out 'I was Rosemary Evers of Dover, England, way before I was Barbary Rose.' I didn't realize what I had said until I saw his eyes. He was staring down at my naked body, my legs still wet with his seed. 'You are not my mother, you dirty whore,' he cried out, slapping me across the face over and over. He was sobbing and gagging when he ran to the door, buttoning his breeches as he went."

The old lady rocked back and forth on the bed, repeating the words over and over, "You are not my mother, you dirty whore. You are not my mother, you dirty whore." She did not seem to notice when Samantha picked up her cap and tiptoed to the door.

Rudy and John were waiting outside. In the dim light of the cafe they couldn't see how pale and ghostly Samantha looked.

"What are you doing here, Rudy?" she whispered huskily.

"Why I came for Barbary Rose, of course," he answered with a low chuckle, "for old times sake."

"Rudy says he can remember when she was the most beautiful woman on the Barbary Coast," John told Samantha.

"It's true. Men would kill for Barbary Rose twenty years ago, though it is hard to believe, looking at her now."

"Would Captain Abdul kill for her?" Samantha whispered.

"Ha," he laughed, "it's likely the captain would have. He was wild for her back then, crazy with love. But they had some falling out and he never saw her again, though he still sends her a bag of gold every time we come to port."

Rudy chuckled lewdly. "It must have been some surprise when old Rose discovered you was a girl. She always liked the young ones, she did, and none was younger than Capt'n Abdul when he rode her so high and handsome."

CHAPTER TWENTY-THREE

Beautiful Byron

Samantha did not rest easily until she was aboard ship again, on a small fishing boat bound for the Bay of Naples. She wished she had never uncovered Captain Abdul's awful secret. But once she had, she was anxious to put the turquoise Mediterranean between them.

There was nothing Samantha could do or say to relieve such a torment. Captain Abdul had made love to his own mother and no woman could ever redeem him from his terrible guilt. Her heart yearned to comfort him in his anguish, but her head warned her not to put his threat of vengeance to the test.

He would find out all too soon that she had been with Barbary Rose and then . . . his wrath was too dreadful to contemplate. She had to escape before it was too late and put the hot, dusty city with its narrow, teeming alleyways and dark mysteries behind her.

Algiers frightened Samantha. Naples warmed

her heart. The bay sparkled like a jewel in the blue-green Mediterranean and the city arced above it, sun-baked and inviting. The temptation to linger was strong. For the first time since leaving China almost a year before, she had nothing to fear, and everything to hope for. She felt safe with Freddy and John at her side and protected in Naples, where Joseph Napoleon ruled as king. Just the sounds of a familiar tongue in the streets was reassuring. Yet, at the same time, it reminded her of Paris and Jean. She would not keep him waiting any longer.

With one of Captain Abdul's gold pieces, John bought three swift mounts and they rode out of Naples after only two days, north through the Campania. To avoid the worst of the scorching summer sun, they rode from dawn to late morning, pausing for food and a siesta at noon, then resuming their ride through the afternoon and evening until it was dark.

After her visit to Barbary Rose, Samantha had cut her hair short so that she could pass more easily for a boy. When they met fellow travelers, she would pretend to be very shy and the others would explain that they were three simple youths traveling north in search of adventure. At night, if they could not find lodgings, they slept in the lush fields, and in the morning they stole great bunches of sweet, juicy purple grapes for their breakfast.

The Italian countryside was green and ripe.

The vineyards were heavy with fruit, the fields a blaze of brilliant orange poppies. Cypress trees, like tall green parasols, marked their road from Naples through Tuscany. It was the most beautiful country Samantha had ever seen.

They followed the coast line from Naples to Genoa, pausing when the sun grew too strong to swim in the refreshing, blue-green sea that stretched to their left. The water was as clear as the cloudless skies and as serene as a sleeping child.

After their long, easy ride, Samantha found it difficult to accustom herself to the bustling port of Genoa. Fishing boats and vessels of every nation thronged the harbor. Sailors, peddlers, and beggars crowded the stone streets. But lying in the hills that rose behind the harbor town was another Genoa of luxurious marble *palazzi*, airy stucco villas, and gardens of brilliantly colored azaleas.

As a nameless vagabond boy with just a few gold coins in his pocket, Samantha had no entry into this other Genoa. She had to content herself with lodgings in the noisy harbor quarter for the five days they planned to rest in the town before beginning the difficult ride across the Alps.

Samantha was a superb horsewoman. She had learned to ride before she had learned to walk and loved nothing more than to give a good horse its head and feel the sudden surge of power beneath her as it began to gallop like the wind.

But Freddy and John were sailors, much more comfortable with the roll of a ship than the gait of a horse, and she was worried that the mountain crossing would be too perilous for inexperienced riders such as they.

Their only alternative was to sell the horses in Genoa and find a boat that would take them to the south of France. Once there, they could buy new mounts and ride north to Paris, bypassing the mountains completely. Freddy and John greeted the new plan with undisguised relief, and the three of them went down to the docks immediately to look for a ship.

While the men haggled with the fishermen about passage, Samantha drifted toward a sleek white schooner. As she drew closer, she saw painted in square black letters on its stern the name *Samantha Marie*. *What a happy omen for the next leg of our journey!* Samantha thought as she admired the clean, simple lines of the craft.

Just then, a slight breeze rose and she caught on the wind a few words of English.

*Maybe th*e Samantha Marie *would take us to France*, she thought daringly. *It can do no harm if I ask.* Stepping forward boldly, she called out in as deep a voice as she could, "Hello, there, *Samantha Marie*." A round, red-faced sailor stuck his head out of the hold.

"Aye, matey, what can we do for you?" he asked cheerfully.

"Would you take me and my two friends as

far as France? We're willing to pay well for the crossing."

"Sorry, lad. This 'ere is a private schooner. She don't take passengers."

"But you could make an exception this one time?" she urged, surprised at her own audacity. "We are on urgent business, you see."

"Urgent business, is it," he laughed heartily. "Get off with you, boy. You'll find plenty of ships that are willing to take you in this harbor."

As Samantha turned away, she heard a man call out clearly, "What does the boy want, Black?" That voice—she would know it anywhere! Whirling around, her heart beating wildly, she ran to the *Samantha Marie*, crying joyfully, "Uncle Peter, Uncle Peter!"

Peter Thomson's familiar gray head pushed up from the hold. "What's all this commotion?" he demanded, looking with annoyance from Black to the slim, brown-faced youth. Then suddenly, his mouth fell open. "Is it? . . . It can't be . . . " he stammered with confusion and shock.

"It is, Uncle Peter; it's Samantha!" she cried.

Before the words were out of her mouth, he was clambering up the ladder and she was running into his open arms. Crying with joy, they clung to each other.

"Samantha, my dearest Samantha," he gasped, "we had given you up for dead months ago. Let me look at you, my darling girl. What a joy you are to these tired old eyes."

Her cap had fallen off and her short, closely cropped hair accentuated the line of her high cheekbones, the fullness of her mouth and the size of her wide green eyes, luminous now with her happy tears. He held her face in his hands and wept again.

"You must excuse an old man's weakness," he said huskily, wiping his face with a broad linen hankerchief and blowing his nose vigorously. "Before I begin bawling again, you must tell me, Samantha, where your aunt Maude is and how she is and why you are dressed like a sailor."

"Aunt Maude died at sea almost three months ago and I have been forced to disguise myself as a boy so that I could travel safely." Samantha's eyes welled up with tears again as she spoke.

"Oh, my dearest child, you must have had a terrible journey. Don't try to talk about it yet, if it upsets you too much. There will be plenty of time to tell me everything that has happened to you, after you have rested yourself and put the worst behind you. For now you must come and stay at my villa in Abaro. We can stop at your lodging and pick up your things on the way." Thomson spoke briskly to keep himself from breaking down again, so overjoyed was he to have found Samantha again.

"I don't have anything to pick up, Uncle Peter," Samantha said with a blush. "Everything Aunt Maude and I possessed was lost at sea."

Thomson looked down at the girl sadly. The

gold flecks in her wide eyes glimmered with the afternoon sun. *She is still as beautiful as she ever was*, he thought, *more beautiful. But what horrors she must have suffered.* He put his arm around her shoulders tenderly. "Don't worry anymore, Samantha. From now on you will have everything you ever need or want. I promise you that. The past is behind you. No more harm will come to you."

"As soon as I saw the name, *Samantha Marie*, I knew it was a happy omen," Samantha laughed, giddy with the joy of finding her old friend and the knowledge that her dangerous journey was at last over. Then suddenly she remembered John and Freddy. "Oh, Uncle Peter," she cried, "I almost forgot in the excitement of seeing you, I must find my companions. They will be frantic with worry about me."

As they searched the docks, Samantha told Thomson about John and Freddy and when they finally found the pair, he thanked the men graciously for taking such fine care of his favorite niece, and invited them to stay at his villa as well. Then they all climbed into his waiting carriage and drove up the winding hillside rode to the other Genoa Samantha had gazed at so longingly.

Peter Thomson's villa in Abaro was a cool white palazzo with long windows on all sides, a lush garden in full flower, and a panoramic view of the Mediterranean. In such a fairytale setting it was almost impossible to hold on to bitter memories. Gradually, between the gracious surroundings and Thomson's warm affection, Samantha began to return to the laughing, lovely young woman she had once been. It was not that the steely, fiercely independent side of her character weakened at all. It merely subsided, allowing her tenderness and feminine grace to shine forth brightly.

She was more strikingly beautiful than she had ever been before in her unconventional short hair and the handsome wardrobe that Thomson ordered custom-made by the finest dressmaker in Genoa. Everyone who visited the villa was entranced, but Samantha still had her heart pinned on Jean Levoir. Sitting in the garden in the quiet evenings, she told Thomson the full story of her long journey from China to the *Samantha Marie*. She kept only Owino's gentle love and Captain Abdul's dark secret inviolate. She failed to confess only her own shameful pregnancy.

Thomson listened to every word, his heart heavy with grief at the terrors this beloved girl had suffered. Although he never questioned her, not wanting to say anything that might add to her torment, he wondered if Samantha had been violated by the brutes with whom she dealt. Had anyone stolen her innocence? One of the blue-skinned islanders? The dashing pirate captain? This young Yankee sailor whose eyes followed after her in silent adoration? Thomson was a

293

man of the world, sophisticated enough to know that even an ugly woman could not have survived such a long, peril-ridden journey untouched.

The thought of the horror she had been forced to endure made Thomson treat Samantha with the tenderest concern and so, although he had never like or trusted Jean Levoir, he answered her questions about the Frenchman as gently as he could.

The truth was that he had met Levoir in Paris the month before and had been shocked by his appearance. Once so dapper and finely dressed, he now walked through Paris in dirty linen and seedy old clothes. He had become very thin and pale, and was sharing a modest though respectable flat with Pierre Bonner.

Not wanting to add in any way to Samantha's disappointments, Thomson told her only that Levoir was well, unmarried, and still living in Paris. But, at the same time, he contrived to introduce her to other young men who, he hoped, might distract her from the memory of the Frenchman. Among those who accepted his warm hospitality was George Gordon, Lord Byron, the handsome young British poet who was living in the next villa.

At their first meeting, Samantha greeted the young lord politely, and then moved on to talk with the other guests, never suspecting that her cool dismissal was a challenge Byron could not refuse. The handsome, romantic poet with his dark ringlets, dreamy velvet eyes, and cleft chin was accustomed to having his way with the most beautiful women in England and the continent, and he would brook no exception.

In the morning he appeared in the garden in nankeen trousers and a plaid jacket, his arms laden with brilliant pink and purple azaleas.

"These," he said offering her the darker blossoms, "are the color of my desire for you. And these," he said giving her the pink flowers, "are the shade of the pretty blush now coloring your smooth cheeks."

He was so audacious, yet so charming that Samantha laughed with delight at his presentation. "Thank you, my lord, most kindly," she said gaily, "but what have I done to deserve such a rich bouquet?"

"Ah," it was Byron's turn to laugh, "that is my secret. Is it not enough that you are the most beautiful woman in Genoa?"

"Are a poet's words to be taken in truth or as evidence of his rare gifts?" she answered in kind.

"You are as bright as you are beautiful. How can I hope to resist your charms?"

Abandoning his lover, the beautiful young Countess Guiccioli, Byron pressed his suit with ardor, visiting Samantha each morning, galloping across the hills or swimming in the clear Mediterranean in the afternoons, and lying at her feet in the evenings, often reading his poetry to her.

One moment he would be full of gaiety, the next he would be filled with despair. "You appeared suddenly out of nowhere. Will you disappear the same way?" he would ask her sadly.

"How can I ever disappear when you are at my heels night and day," she would respond lightly, hoping to lift his gloom.

"I will close my eyes one moment, dazzled by the brilliance of your beauty, and when I open them you will be gone. Close your eyes and I will show you," he said dreamily.

Samantha shut her eyes and his extraordinarily handsome face filled her mind. *He is accustomed to being lionized. He is turbulent and dissolute, and he likes nothing better than to let beautiful, aristocratic ladies make fools of themselves on his account*, she thought to herself. And as she did, she felt his soft, sensitive lips press her own. But she did not resist. With her eyes still closed, she allowed him to draw her into his arms and answered his kiss with her own desire.

Peter Thomson's fondest wish had come true. Samantha had forgotten Jean Levoir. She had forgotten everything in her sudden infatuation with the moody, romantic poet. "My beautiful Byron," she murmured as she kissed his lips again and again. He urged her further, but she held back. He yearned to possess her but she hesitated.

It was not Byron's reputation that stopped Samantha, although she did not want to be another one of the women he seduced and then discarded like a soiled shirt. It was not the Countess Guiccioli whose villa he still visited, or so the local gossip had it. It was not his lameness, although she had never seen his club foot uncovered. He wore shoes when he swam and even, she had heard, when he made love. It was something inside herself, something she did not understand herself, that made her reject her beautiful Byron each day.

But each rejection only increased his ardor. The one woman who would not have him was the one he wanted most, and he was used to having his way.

"We will escape to Venice," he told her one afternoon, suddenly changing from melancholy to euphoria. "Venice, the greenest island of my imagination! You cannot resist me there," he cried. "The streets are canals, the houses are palaces, the churches are sublime. What a glorious city to consummate our love."

Caught up in his enthusiasm, Samantha agreed to follow in three days. They would meet again in the shadows of the Cathedral of San Marco. But on the trip from Genoa, her enthusiasm was suddenly forgotten as she listened to Peter Thomson's alarming words. Thomson, who had tried to make Samantha forget Jean Levoir, now felt responsible for her involvement with the wicked, irresponsible young lord.

"Samantha, my dear," he began cautiously as the carriage rolled through the farmlands of

Romagna, "since it was I who introduced you to Lord Byron, I feel it is my solemn duty to tell you how he came to be in Italy, and I pray that you will take my words in the spirit with which I give them. Shall I go on?"

"Please, Uncle Peter," she said, "although I have already heard all the gossip about Byron's numerous paramours, and it does not concern me in the slightest."

Thomson noted the edge of defiance in Samantha's voice but he went on anyway. "This is not a pretty story, but I will do my best." He cleared his throat. "When the first cantos of *Childe Harold's Pilgrimage* were published in England, Lord Byron became famous, virtually overnight. He was young, handsome, titled and talented. The country adored him, and although he was frequently drunk and often in trouble with some of England's noblest women, his transgressions were always forgiven. When he eventually married a very proper and respectable young lady, it was assumed that the dashing lord would settle down. But the very opposite happened. His licentiousness grew worse and now," Thomson paused and took a deep breath before he went on, "it apparently includes even the abhorrent crime of incest with his only sister, Augusta."

Every ounce of color drained from Samantha's face but she did not say a word and Thomson continued. "His wife left him; society, whose idol he had been, ostracized him, and he was forced into exile. I do not know if these charges are true. I know only that Lord Byron has lived abroad in Switzerland and Italy ever since."

When Thomson finished speaking, the silence in the carriage was immense, almost unbearable. Finally, Samantha spoke, her voice soft and strained. "I do not believe it, Uncle Peter. I cannot believe it. It is too . . . too heinous to imagine. So much malicious gossip about one man—it's almost too much to bear. Poor Byron, how he must suffer."

"As you wish, Samantha," the older man said soothingly, taking her slender hand in his, as they rode together silently into the fabled city of Venice, into Byron's greenest island.

In spite of Samantha's loyal words, she was deeply troubled by the accusations she had just heard, particularly since they had come from the man she lovingly called Uncle Peter. For she knew that he would never have repeated them to her unless he believed there was some truth in the reports. It was with a heavy heart, therefore, that Samantha kept her romantic rendezvous in the shadows of San Marco. But when she saw her beautiful Byron waiting there for her, a single, pure white lily in his hand to offer her as a symbol of the chaste love she would give to him that night, she dismissed all the ugly stories from her mind, and sealed their pact with a loving kiss.

Venice was more wonderful than her imaginings and she gave herself up willingly to the enchantments of the city and to the endearments of her passionate poet. As the afternoon began to fade, he led her to the elegant apartment he had taken overlooking the Grand Canal and left her with a lingering kiss that promised the joy yet to come, to prepare for the long-awaited joining of their bodies.

In a haze of romance, Samantha walked languidly through the wide rooms, undoing each button on her handsome silk gown slowly, relishing each step that brought her closer to her lord's bed. She opened the long glass doors and stepped out onto the balcony to view the city that had conquered her heart, and, as she did, her eyes lighted on the letter that was lying on the iron table, half-covered by a blotter.

"My dearest Augusta," she read. With a sinking heart, she moved the blotter aside and scanned the rest of the page. Sick with revulsion, for there was no mistaking the meaning of his words, Samantha fled through the night to the understanding arms of her Uncle Peter.

Fare thee well! and if for ever,
Still for ever fare thee well:
Even though unforgiving, never
'Gainst thee shall my heart rebel.

With these lines of his running over and over through her mind, Samantha disappeared from

Byron's life as suddenly as she had appeared. As for the dissolute lord, he returned briefly to Genoa and the Countess's warm embrace, before sailing to Greece and death at Missolonghi.

CHAPTER TWENTY-FOUR

Escape to Paris

Just as she had turned to Jean Levoir when Mallory Jones rejected her, now Samantha turned to him again when she discovered Lord Byron's incestuous love. Nothing Peter Thomson could say or do would dissuade her from making the long overland journey to Paris.

More than anything else, he wanted to ask Samantha to become his wife. He loved the girl as he had loved her mother, but he thought he was too old to ask for her hand, and so he had to watch her, as he had watched Marie, run to the arms of another man.

Although his heart was heavy, Thomson made every arrangement to ensure Samantha a safe, easy trip to Paris, and a secure, comfortable life until her marriage. The *Samantha Marie* would take her to the south of France, where the best carriage in the country and two trusted guards would meet her and drive her through Burgundy to Paris. There, she would be a guest at his apartment until she was settled. Then, if she preferred, she could move to her cousin's residence outside the city, or, he hated to even consider the possibility, she could marry Jean Levoir. He even provided her with a letter of introduction to Talleyrand himself. "If anyone could keep an eye on the girl," Thomson thought, "it's that sly old fox."

It was a tearful morning when Samantha and Thomson, Freddy and John all went their separate ways. Freddy was sailing back to Algiers to pick up the *Zanzibar* again. John was going home to Boston at last. Only Thomson was remaining in Italy. He wished he could accompany Samantha to Paris and, if it was what she truly wanted, deliver her safely to Levoir, but urgent business forced him to remain in Genoa for at least a fortnight.

Sadly, he took Samantha in his arms and begged her to be careful. "Dearest girl, I could not bear to lose you twice. For the sake of my old gray head, please do not do anything hasty or rash," he said kissing her on the forehead.

"So long, Miss Boston, Massachusetts, Captain . . . " was all poor little Freddy could stammer before his voice broke and he turned his freckled face away to hide the tears that streamed down his cheeks.

"I'll still be waiting, when you come home," John said, his voice husky with emotion, his eyes glued to his boots, blinking furiously to hold back his tears.

Samantha hugged each man tightly, than ran aboard the waiting *Samantha Marie*. She was too overcome by their emotion to trust herself to say a word. And so she left her faithful friends to return to Jean Levoir.

During the long drive to Paris, Samantha looked back on all she had been through and looked ahead to the new life she hoped to begin. No one, not even the beautiful Byron, had ever touched her heart the way Mallory Jones had. Although he was the only man who had ever kindled her hate, she still dreamed of him in the long, lonely nights, dreamed of the touch that scorched her flesh and made her passion's slave.

True, she had desired Captain Abdul. But, although she had grown to care for and respect him, her yearning had been just the needs of a woman too long unanswered. Even in her infatuation with Byron, she had held back until the last. His kiss, his caress had not driven her wild with abandon. Nor had Jean's. *He never wanted to,* Samantha thought to herself, remembering his chaste kisses. *He was waiting until he had the right to claim me as his own.* Of them all, only Jean had never demanded, never threatened. Thinking again of his quiet affection, his unfailing attentiveness, her pulse quickened. Would he still want her? In just a few more days, she would have the answer she had waited so long to hear.

Samantha's arrival in Paris was very different from her arrival in Genoa only four months before. Thanks to Peter Thomson, the vagabond boy was once again a ravishing young woman, with trunks of elegant frocks and evening gowns, two dozen pairs of lacy undergarments, fine jewels, and a substantial dowry.

"Don't worry," he had assured her. "When you return to Boston and settle your estate, you can repay me if you must. Until then I cannot see any reason for Jonathan Shaw's daughter to travel like a pauper."

Now Samantha was glad she had accepted his generosity, because she could present herself to Jean Levoir as he would remember her from Macao—a stunningly beautiful, aristocratic young woman. Little did she suspect what had become of the handsome, self-assured fiancé she had left in China.

Paris was much as Samantha remembered it. The Bourbon king still occupied the throne and wily old Charles Maurice de Talleyrand-Perigord, Prince de Benevent, still wielded the power behind the throne, pulling the strings of government like a masterful puppeteer.

Once comfortably established in Peter Thomson's spacious *pied à terre*, Samantha lost no time in getting to know the city again—and getting to know her fiancé again. Jean seemed thinner, paler, more preoccupied than he had been in China, she thought, but she soon forgot her initial concern in the whirl of parties and sumptuous soirées.

The letter from Uncle Peter to his witty and

307

cynical old friend, the Comte de Talleyrand, gained Samantha entry into the most elite salons in Paris. The beautiful and charming Madame Recamier welcomed Samantha at her glittering gatherings. Although innumerable men fell in love with her, among them some of the most brilliant writers and politicians in France, Juliette Recamier was so gentle, so unpassionate, that they were for the most part platonic relationships.

Her current *amant* was Francois Rene, Vicomte de Chateaubriand. Once the illustrious romantic author discovered there was a Yankee in their midst, he entertained Samantha with stories of his trip to America to search for the Northwest Passage. Although many of the literary gossips intimated that Chateaubriand had never gotten beyond Niagara Falls, this little fact in no way detracted from his tales.

Madame Recamier's salon soon became one of Samantha's favorite haunts in Paris. There, and wherever else she went, she was escorted by Jean Levoir.

CHAPTER TWENTY-FIVE

Jean Levoir

Samantha had never been happier. Jean's initial
aloofness soon was gone and he was pressing his
suit eagerly. Imagining that his early coolness
was nothing more than the surprise of seeing her
again so unexpectedly, she basked in his new attentiveness.

Each day brought a bouquet of fresh-cut
flowers, an affectionate note, or a small keepsake,
and each evening when he escorted her home,
he would leave her with a light kiss and a further
intimation of marriage. Sometimes he seemed remote from her, as if he were wrapped in his own
private world and she could not enter. But this
was just a slight annoyance, certainly not enough
to mar Samantha's happiness or cause her to wonder about her fiancé's intentions.

When he asked her if they could set a date for
their wedding, her happiness seemed complete.

"Oh, Jean," Samantha cried ecstatically, "are
you sure you still want to marry me? I would

never bind you by the vow you made in China, if you have the slightest doubt."

Levoir looked at her, a strange, enigmatic smile playing at the corners of his mouth. "Why do you think I would have any doubt?" he asked. "Are you afraid I would not make you a good husband?"

"Oh, no, no, Jean. I just wanted to hear you say that nothing could keep us apart again."

"Well," he hesitated, "there is one thing."

Samantha's heart sank. "What is it, Jean?" she asked.

"One of my ships is over a month late returning from China, and as a result my finances are severely strained." He hesitated again, "If you could loan me two thousand francs, Samantha, we could be married right away. I would, of course, repay you as soon as the ship comes in," he added sincerely.

"Of course, Jean," Samantha answered without a second thought. She was too caught up in the excitement of his proposal to consider the strangeness of his request. "When do you need it?"

"As soon as possible," Levoir answered, but Samantha did not notice the urgent note in his voice.

Two weeks had slipped by when he again asked for a small loan. Although their wedding date had still not been firmly set, Samantha gave him another thousand francs. Half her dowry was gone now, and she began to wonder about the propriety of her gifts. But it was too late. Jean had come to depend on her loans.

When a week later, she denied his third request, he left her angrily. The flowers and notes stopped. Was his honor offended by her refusal or had her usefulness to him ended? Samantha wished Uncle Peter would come. She needed his sound, practical advice, because her own mind was too confused to allow her to think clearly.

On the one hand, she knew Jean Levoir was not a gigolo. On the other, she had not seen or heard from him since she denied his last request, and he had never referred to their wedding again after that first time. Samantha had been tormenting herself with doubts for four days when Pierre Bonner came to her door.

Although she had met Bonner only once in Macao, she had noticed him many times. He seemed always to be standing in the shadows watching whenever she was with Jean, and if her eyes met his pale, liquid ones, he would always stare boldly until she looked away. She didn't like the man. There was something brutal about him that frightened her.

Bonner was a short, square man, with a rugged face and heavy Gallic features. The only exception was his mouth, which was thin and weak and usually curled in an ironic smile. She never understood why Jean liked the man. But they were best of friends and she was afraid to confess her distrust to him.

Now, as Bonner was shown into her drawing

room, Samantha thought she saw the same ironic glint on his face that she remembered from Macao, but it disappeared instantly and he assumed a worried, distracted expression.

"Mademoiselle Shaw," he said, "Jean has sent me to you, because he is unable to come himself."

"Why," Samantha asked apprehensively, "is anything wrong with Jean? Is he ill or injured?"

"Jean is very ill, Mademoiselle, gravely ill," Bonner said. His voice was a low, insinuating purr.

"What does his physician say? Will he get well?"

"Alas, he has no physician."

"A doctor has not looked at him?"

"We cannot get one until Jean's ship comes in from China. Our finances are too low to pay a doctor."

"The ship may be caught in a storm or wrecked on a shoal hundreds of miles away. It could be weeks before it returns." Samantha met Bonner's pale eyes squarely.

"Jean is calling for you," he purred.

She had never trusted the man. She still did not trust him. But Jean needed her now. She could not refuse him again. "I will get a shawl," she said briskly. Slipping into the master bedroom and closing the door behind her, Samantha took out the remainder of her dowry and put it in her purse. Then she put on her bonnet and shawl and returned to the waiting man.

313

As the door of Peter Thomson's elegant residence closed behind them, Samantha thought she saw Bonner's ironic smirk dance across his face. But it was gone in an instant and soon forgotten in her worried thoughts about Levoir.

Sick with guilt, she followed Bonner through the streets of Paris to the Left Bank, down a narrow alley where undergarments and sheets hung drying, into a dilapidated stucco house. *Could Jean live here in such humble circumstances?* she wondered. She had never been in such a place before. *Could his circumstances be so reduced?* she thought as Bonner began to climb a narrow circular stairway. The iron steps were steep and thick with dirt, but Samantha could not turn back now and leave Jean in such a place, sick and without a doctor.

Reluctantly, she followed, never noticing the sharp-eyed old woman who watched them through a crack in her door below. At the top of the stairs, Bonner pushed open a door and they entered a dimly lit room, enveloped in a cloud of bluish smoke. A strong, sharp odor hung in the airless room. In the smaller, even smokier room beyond Samantha found Jean Levoir.

She stared in amazement. He was not lying ill and helpless, as she had expected. He was stretched out on the chaise lounge in his dressing gown and slippers, smoking a long ivory pipe. Billows of blue smoke rose around him.

"Jean, what is the meaning of this?" she demanded. "Bonner said you were very ill."

"Ah, and so I am," he replied languidly, "and the money?"

"I have it with me," Samantha said softly so that Bonner would not hear in the next room. But it was too late. He had slipped up behind her and now his strong hand was closing around her brocade purse. He seized it roughly, and pushing Samantha out of his way, sat down on the foot of the chaise lounge beside Jean, spilling the coins in his lap.

"Three thousand francs," he whistled. "That should keep us in good supply for a spell. Here," he laughed, grabbing the ivory pipe from Jean, "let me have a puff of that." Bonner inhaled deeply. "We'll have better than this tomorrow," he laughed, "the best opium in Paris for you, Jean. Nothing less."

Levoir smiled, "And the girl, Pierre, what shall we do with her now?"

"We must keep her," he said, "or she will accuse us of stealing her money."

"No!" Samantha cried. "You can have the money. I won't say a word, if you just let me go."

"Do you think I would trust you, Mademoiselle, to keep your mouth shut?" Bonner laughed sharply.

"Jean," Samantha pleaded, "I only came here to help you. Now won't you please help me!"

Levoir stared at her with dazed eyes. "Here, Samantha," he said, holding out the pipe to her, "this will help you. Breathe in deeply. You will

315

have magical dreams and soon you will never want to leave."

"No, Jean, no!" Samantha cried, and ran out to the door. But it was locked and heavily bolted. She could hear Bonner's sarcastic laugh.

"Your fiancée does not seem to like our company, Jean. What do you think we should do about that?" He laughed again, wickedly, sadistically.

"Give her some opium, Pierre," Jean droned dreamily, "nothing you do will seem as bad then."

Samantha's blood ran cold as she listened. She was their captive. Levoir would not—or could not—help her. The only door was locked and bolted and Bonner had the key. There was no escape through the window. They were six stories up and a cobblestone street lay below. All she could do was wait. They would have to go out sometime, and then she would make her move.

No, yeah no, Samantha cried, and ran one to
the door. But it was locked and heavily bolted.
She could hear Bonner's sarcastic laugh.

CHAPTER TWENTY-SIX

Mallory Jones in Paris

Mallory Jones made the trip to Europe reluctantly. It meant leaving his new home in Cambridge before he had even settled in, and leaving his son Jonathan just as the boy was beginning to walk and talk. But he had no choice. Only one man at Porter & Co. understood all the intricate details of the shared cargo agreement with the British East India Company. And that man was Jones himself.

With his old friend Peter Thomson representing the British interests, Jones was confident that they could conduct the final negotiations and have a signed accord concluded within three weeks. He trusted Thomson as a man of integrity, reliability, and fairness, and looked forward to a speedy return to Boston.

But to Jones's surprise and dismay, Thomson was not even in London when he arrived. He had left a note pleading sudden, urgent business in Paris, and asking Jones to meet him there as soon as possible.

Jones hesitated for several days, hoping Thomson would return. He had no desire to go to Paris. The very name invoked bitter memories. Although there was little chance that he would see them on such a short trip, Mallory Jones knew that there was no city in the world big enough to hold Jean Levoir, Samantha Shaw, and himself.

But finally, after receiving a second frantic message from Thomson to come at once, he could delay no longer. Mallory Jones made his first and, he prayed, his last trip to Paris. Crossing the Channel to Calais, he hired a coach and drove directly to Thomson's *pied à terre*.

Instead of the courtly, sophisticated man he had known in China, Jones found a distraught old man. For an instant, he did not even recognize his friend, he had aged so severely. Thomson had lost a great deal of weight. His hair had turned snow-white and his face was as furrowed as a newly plowed field.

"Mallory, my boy, thank God you are finally here," Thomson said, shaking the younger man's hand warmly. "I think if I were alone another day I would go quite mad with worry."

"If only I had known you were so disturbed, Peter, I would have left London immediately," Jones said, putting his arm around his friend. "Tell me what has happened to you and I will do everything I can to be of assistance."

Thomson cleared his throat gruffly. "I knew I could count on you, dear boy," he said, deeply

319

moved by the younger man's sympathy and affection. "But it is not myself I am concerned for. It is the girl, the girl, Mallory. I am worried to death about Samantha."

"Samantha?" Jones echoed hollowly.

"Jonathan Shaw's daughter, Samantha. She and her aunt lived in your villa during your last season in Macao," Thomson said, thinking he had to refresh Jones's memory.

"I remember Samantha," Jones said. His voice was husky. His throat felt parched. "Is she here, Peter, in this house?"

"She was; that is what worries me so. I saw her off safely from Genoa, with the understanding that I would follow her to Paris in a fortnight. But business detained me much longer than I had anticipated. I arrived last week to find the house empty. All her fine things were in the closets, but the girl and the gold I had given her for a dowry were gone. The butler said she rushed out suddenly one evening in the company of a strange man, and she has not been seen or heard from since. I am so sick with worry, I can't think where to look for her or how to find her."

Thomson's voice broke and his body shook with sobs. But Mallory Jones's voice was calm and emotionless as he questioned his friend closely.

"Try to remember everything you can. Why did the girl come to Paris? Did she give you any reason at all?"

320

"She wanted to renew her acquaintance with Jean Levoir. They had been planning to marry when she left China," Thomson spoke dejectedly.

"That explains her dowry, then."

"Yes. It is my fault. I should never have left her alone with so much gold."

"It is too late now to think of that. What else do you recall Peter, anything that might give us a clue?"

"Nothing, nothing at all. I went to Levoir's flat the moment I got back, but he had moved out shortly after Samantha came to Paris. No one knew where he had gone, and, according to the servants, he had not visited Samantha for at least a week before she vanished."

"What did the man she left with look like Peter? Was the butler able to describe him?"

"Yes. He was short, square, dark, heavy features."

Mallory Jones's razor-keen brain was working rapidly, piecing the clues of Samantha's disappearance together. Listening to Thomson's story, he had drawn the Oriental curtain across his mind, suppressing his deepest feelings. Nothing mattered now except Samantha's safety, and he could allow no emotion—bitter or sweet—to get in its way. He needed to think quickly, dispassionately, or she would be lost forever.

"Peter, do you know if Levoir ever saw Pierre Bonner here in Paris?" he asked suddenly.

"He did most certainly. They shared the flat—"

Jones interrupted sharply. "Would you say Bonner was short and square with dark, heavy features."

"You don't mean to suggest—"

"I mean exactly this, Peter. Levoir and Bonner are opium addicts and worse. Pierre Bonner is a very dangerous man. If Samantha is in his hands, we have no time to lose."

"But certainly, Levoir would never allow his fiancée to be held captive, Mallory."

"Levoir is weak and spineless, unless he is scorned. Then he is ruthless. I know, I have tasted his revenge. You have friends in high places," Jones urged, "call on them now to help us find these men—before it is too late."

"I cannot accept your charges, although you have made a sound case," Thomson said slowly, shaking his head. "I cannot believe Levoir would kidnap Samantha. And yet, if we could locate him, he might be able to shed some new light on her disappearance."

"At the very least," Jones interjected.

Brightening now at the first glimmer of hope, Thomson announced, "There is one man in Paris who can uncover every secret in France, Comte Talleyrand. I will call on him at once."

CHAPTER TWENTY-SEVEN

Samantha Succumbs

"Please, Pierre, please, just one pipe," Samantha pleaded.

"No." He kicked her aside roughly with his boot. "No more for you today. We are running low and all the money is gone."

"One puff," she begged.

"I said no." He kicked her again. "Besides you would not want to deprive your dear fiancé of what little powder is left, would you?" he said, his face contorted with malevolence.

Bonner and Levoir had forced Samantha to smoke the bitter brown drug to make her more compliant. She was too fierce and fiery to handle unless she was doped with opium, and now she had become addicted to the poppy juice. Without it, she could not have borne the degrading duties Bonner forced her to perform. He had hooked her on opium and made her his slave, just as he had done to Jean Levoir.

Even through the fog of smoke that seemed

324

always to envelope her Samantha saw that Jean was a weak, self-indulgent man, completely in thrall to Bonner. She had been so blind. Now all the telltale signs she had ignored or dismissed came back to haunt her—even his gentle, undemanding kisses. What a mockery of marriage their life together would have been, especially for a woman as deeply passionate and desirous as Samantha.

On the first night that she was their captive, Samantha discovered the bitter truth. Bonner had bound her to a chair and forced her to smoke a full pipe of opium. But that was not enough. He had even more sadistic plans in mind for her.

"Now, Mademoiselle," he said, his voice lashed with cruel triumph, "you will see your fiancé consummate his marriage." Dragging her, still bound into the bedroom, he threw back the sheets and exposed Jean Levoir's body to his fiancée for the first time.

Levoir lay like a dead man. His eyes were closed. His naked, narrow body was pitifully thin and scarred. His ribs were bruised a deep purple, his crotch was swollen and inflamed.

Someone had beaten him and beaten him badly, Samantha thought, as she sat rigid and glassy-eyed, too frightened to even imagine what Bonner had in store for her. Then, to her horror, he began to undress himself until he stood in front of her totally nude, his bare body compact and muscular, the belt from his breeches in one hand.

"Jean, darling," he whispered lewdly, "your bride is waiting."

"No, Pierre, I can't do it," Levoir screamed sharply, regaining his manhood for one precious moment.

"Come on, Jean, it is waiting for you," Bonner whispered again grabbing Levoir's leg and pulling him out of bed.

Once again Jean was in thrall. He knelt in front of Bonner, clasping his bare legs and begging, "Please, Pierre, don't make me do it."

But Bonner pushed the other man's face down between his legs. "You love it, Jean. You can never refuse it," he said as he forced himself against Levoir's mouth, and brought his belt down across Levoir's bare back.

Sick with revulsion, Samantha shut her eyes against the repugnant scene. But Bonner cried out angrily, "Look at him, look at him or I will whip you too." He lashed her legs sharply with his belt, then struck Levoir's back again.

Samantha heard Jean moan excitedly, *"Plus dure, mon cheri."* His words stabbed her heart. All at once she realized that Bonner was not making him perform unnatural acts. He *wanted* to be hurt. He *wanted* to be brutalized. Her tender, considerate Jean was receiving just what he desired.

Grateful now for the opium that had dulled her senses, Samantha watched, at the same time repelled and riveted, as Levoir forgot her presence entirely and abandoned himself to his un-

326

wholesome desire. Bonner's revenge was complete. Ever since Macao when he had watched Samantha steal his lover, he had been hungry for vengeance. Now he had his triumph.

Each night Bonner forced Samantha to sleep on the bedroom floor and listen to the sounds of Jean's strange passion. Each day, he stood guard. He and Levoir never went out at the same time for fear she might try to escape.

With each day that passed, Samantha's hopes of sneaking out lessened and her dependence on the ivory pipe increased, until she was as thoroughly addicted as Levoir. Bonner beat her regularly now. The slightest excuse was enough to make him reach for his belt. If she did not obey him instantly, if she smiled at Jean, she would feel the whip on her back. But she hardly noticed the pain, she was so heavily drugged most of the time.

Once when Bonner went out after beating her severely, Jean cleaned her wounds. He seemed once again like the gentle young man she had promised to marry.

"I am truly sorry, Samantha, that I have brought you to this. I did not understand clearly what Pierre was proposing or I would never have allowed him to involve you, or even see you. But the opium dulls the brain," he added weakly.

Samantha knew that Jean was too spineless to refuse Bonner anything and yet she was grateful for his words of regret. "I don't blame you, Jean," she said, "I know you could not help yourself."

327

He smiled at her warmly. "You are still beautiful, Samantha," he said. "Even now. You were always beautiful, that is why I fell in love with you in Macao. I could never resist anything truly perfect. If I saw a perfect porcelain vase, I wanted to own it. If I found an exquisite painting or tapestry, I could not rest happy until I bought it. That was the way I felt when I first saw you at the masked ball. I wanted to possess your perfect beauty. And I almost did," he said wistfully.

"Did you wait for me at all Jean?" Samantha asked. Her quiet, unreproaching voice touched him and he opened his heart to her.

"I think even when we first met, it was already too late," he confessed. "I was young and still innocent when I arrived in China, and like most other men of twenty I never doubted that I would be thrilled by the silky touch of a woman. But in the exclusively male world of Canton I had little or no chance to test myself, and yet I was not concerned.

"I was never happier before. I liked the easy male camaraderie, and I became friends with a young American who, though not much older than myself, had already been in Canton for some years. He was handsome, intelligent, graceful, strong—everthing a man should be—and my best friend. When he discovered that I was still chaste, he took it upon himself to remedy the situation.

"We went together to the most luxurious flower boat in Canton harbor and he chose the two most beautiful girls there to service us. I did not know it then, but it was a fatal, unforgettable day in my life.

"We drank cup after cup of rice wine to relax my nervousness as we bathed in a deep pool of warm scented water. Drunk on wine and excited from our bath, we both agreed readily when the girls suggested we all go to bed together. 'Why not?' he laughed, 'What are friends for?'

"My heart rushed at his joking words, although I did not know why until it was too late. It was his body that I thrilled to, not the girls. I kept trying to touch him and, at the same time, make it seem as if I had just brushed him in passing. But he was not fooled. At first he thought I was joking, but then he sensed my desire and as quickly as he could, he brought our festivities to a close.

"But it was too late. I was already in love with Mallory Jones."

Samantha caught her breath sharply, awakened suddenly from her opium stupor by Jean's startling confession. But he did not seem to notice.

"I went wherever he went and did whatever he did, just to be near him. Although I never declared myself, he knew my secret. Ever since the night of the flower boats, his friendship had cooled. Now with each day, he tried to put a greater distance between us, and then suddenly he began disappearing entirely. He withdrew completely from the social life of Canton. I thought at the time that he was trying to avoid me, but later I found out that he had fallen in love with a Chinese girl, Houqua's daughter. In China, his crime was at least as heinous as my own.

"With Jones gone, I began spending time with Pierre. He was new in Canton and, I discovered soon enough, had two qualities which I found particularly to my liking. He preferred to take his pleasure with men and he had a scheme to become rich within a year by cutting into the British traffic in opium. We became lovers and partners. But gradually the other merchants in Canton began to grow suspicious of me. We were making too much money too fast and spending too much time together, I suppose.

"I resented their coolness and longed for the easy camaraderie I had known as Jones's friend and, at Pierre's urgings, I started to bury my unhappiness with opium. I began gradually, but, by the time I met you in Macao I was already smoking heavily, and my dependence frightened me.

"You appeared like an angel of salvation. Although I had never been attracted to a woman before, I was struck instantly by your beauty, and enchanted by your wit and grace. Pierre objected vehemently to the attentions I gave you, but you were my only hope. If I could win you, I would be able to give up my sordid ways and start anew. Or so I hoped.

"When you accepted my proposal so warmly,

I was a new man. I gave up opium entirely and left Pierre, although we remained business partners. We were both wealthy men, by then, thanks to our illicit trade. But I was anxious to move into a less dangerous business that would not keep me away so many months of the year. Pierre and I sold out our storage ships in Whampoa and sailed back to France on the same ship, immediately after you left.

"I lapsed back into my old habits on the long sea voyage, comforting myself with the sure knowledge that as soon as we reached Paris I would reform again."

Jean breathed heavily and reached out for Samantha's hand. Pressing it in his, he said, "If your ship had not been lost, if you had been waiting here for me, if we had married as we'd planned, I think I would have changed. You were my greatest hope, my fondest dream.

"But, without those hundred ifs, you see what I have become," he said, as he reached for the ivory pipe. "I am an addict who steals from a woman to pursue his addiction."

CHAPTER TWENTY-EIGHT

Samantha For Sale

Pierre Bonner returned to the dingy Left Bank
apartment thoroughly pleased with his afternoon's work. He had spent the last of Samantha's
dowry on a supply of opium and had devised a
new scheme that would keep them in gold and
silver indefinitely: he would sell Samantha's services.

With fiendish glee, Bonner described the details of how he would procure the men and
bring them to the apartment himself where Samantha would pleasure them in whatever way
they chose.

"Your first customer will be here tonight,"
he told her, "and don't you dare make any trouble.

"He is the kind of man you would like," he
added, unable to restrain his cruel nature, "fleshy
and red-faced. That's why I chose him for you
to begin with."

Bonner laughed wickedly. "Go and make your

self beautiful now for your new beau. I told him you were a real beauty—and made him pay for it too."

Although she had smoked a prodigious amount of the bitter, brown drug after Jean's confessions, Samantha's senses could never be dulled enough to make her submit to another violation. Through the billows of smoke that filled her brain, she heard her own voice and was surprised at its sharpness.

"I will not do it. You will have to kill me first."

Bonner slapped her hard across the face. "You will do as I say and you will like it."

"No!" she screamed. "This is one thing you can not make me do. Jean, help me, help me," she threw herself, sobbing at Levoir's feet clutching his legs.

"Help me, Jean, help me," Bonner mimicked mockingly, then he screamed, "Don't you understand yet? Jean doesn't want to help you."

Levoir, dull and heavy-lidded, roused himself from his lethargy. "Does she have to do this, Pierre?" he asked.

"If she doesn't, then you will," Bonner shouted angrily.

"Smoke a pipe, Samantha," Levoir said dreamily. "You won't remember anything."

Samantha looked from one man to the other desperately. She couldn't think clearly. Her mind was so foggy with opium she thought this must be a nightmare. But Bonner's bullying voice forced her to wake up to the frightening reality.

"Get up," he kicked her. "Your customer will be here within the hour and you look disgusting. Fix yourself up." He kicked her again but Samantha refused to budge.

"I won't do it. I won't do it," she screamed over and over. "Kill me and get it over with. I would rather be dead."

"You are no good to us dead," Bonner hissed, as he dragged the bed into the front room. "But you can be a gold mine alive." His voice softened. "Think of all the fine opium you will have, Mademoiselle. Before and after, all the sweet smoke you want," he wheedled.

But Samantha would not give in, and Bonner's anger returned.

"You are going to be taken tonight—and every other night—by force, since that is how you seem to prefer it," he said coldly. He turned to Levoir and snapped, "Jean, take her arm." The two men half-carried, half-dragged the screaming girl to the bed. Bonner held her down while Levoir undressed her with trembling fingers, thankful for the opium that deadened the pain in his heart.

Samantha fought them fiercely, but they stripped her naked and threw her on the bed. Bonner looked at her critically, as if he were buying a side of beef. "You'll do quite nicely, Mademoiselle, even bound and gagged."

Laughing sadistically, he flipped her over on her stomach, and with Jean restraining her, he tied Samantha to the four posts of the bed with leather straps, and stuffed a cloth in her mouth.

Jean ran his hand across the sweet, tender flesh he would never know. "The next time won't be as bad," he murmured sadly. But Levoir's caress did not escape the jealous Bonner. Throwing a sheet over the naked girl, he jeered, "You can take your turn after the customer, if you still want her then."

But before Levoir could answer, there was a heavy knock on the door. The man was just as Bonner described him, and out of breath from the stairs.

"Where is the girl, Pierre?" he huffed, one hand on his pounding heart. His voice was high and nasal. His bald head shone with sweat.

"Don't be nervous, Monsieur, the girl is right here," Bonner purred. "I took the liberty of preparing her for you myself. As you can see, she is ready and waiting for you."

Samantha's body tensed, as Bonner stripped away the sheet. In the warm glow of the candlelight, her smooth white back and long slender legs gleamed seductively.

"*Très bien,*" the fat man leered, licking his fleshy lips and digging into his pocket for a gold coin to give Bonner.

"I thought you'd like her trussed, Monsieur," Bonner said, an evil grin on his square face, as he and Jean retired to the next room.

Alone with the girl, the fat man rubbed his sweaty palms together eagerly and drew closer to the bed to feast his bloodshot eyes on this oasis of pure white flesh. "Bonner delivers on his word," he cackled appreciatively, pinching the pale moon that rose round and full on the bed. In his wildest fantasies he never dreamed that Bonner would deliver a pale beauty so well primed that she could not fail to submit to whatever his sordid mind devised. Feasting his eyes lasciviously on Samantha's bare buttocks, the eager fat man stripped off his jacket and waistcoat and, rolling his sleeves up, he unbuckled his broad leather belt. Then as he felt an uncontrollable swelling in his trousers, he bent over Samantha and whispered vilely in her ear, "I am going to make your white cheeks blush for me."

He was so close his foul spittle sprayed her face. But she did not move, and she did not flinch when he brought his wide belt down across her buttocks, for Samantha had surrendered herself to the potent poppy and had drifted back to Macao.

Old memories stirred by Jean's confessions, she dreamed they were escaping in each other's arms, each fleeing a love that seared the heart. She was an eager young girl in a white muslin dress, and he was a dashing young man, and they were running toward each other across a wide rice paddy. But the closer they grew to each other, the faster they ran and they swept by each other, unable to stop. Only their arms grazed in passing.

CHAPTER TWENTY-NINE

The Rescue

Drooling lasciviously, the fat man finally mounted Samantha. He had beaten her smooth buttocks with his belt until they were a bright crimson. Now, as she lay defenseless beneath him, bound naked and spread-eagled, he prepared to sodomize her. With his fleshy fingers he spread her blushing cheeks.

Just at that second, Mallory Jones burst in on the sordid scene, sending the entire door frame flying in front of him. Seizing the fat man who perched, frozen with fear, on Samantha's haunches, he pulled him off the bed and shook him mercilessly, until every roll of flesh on his corpulent body was in violent motion. Then Jones flung the fat man across the room. "If you ever touch this woman again, if you ever look on this woman again, if you ever think of this woman again, you are dead," he warned fiercely.

Bending tenderly over Samantha, he drew the sheet over her nakedness and took the gag from her mouth. "Samantha," he murmured, gently stroking her face, "you are safe now." But she stared at him with vacant eyes; the clear green wells he could never forget were now glassy and opaque.

White with fury, Jones stormed through the second room, shouting for Bonner. The brutal sadist relished beating his helpless victims, but he had no stomach for a fair fight, and was cowering in the corner.

Jones pulled him up violently. "When I finish with you, Bonner," he promised in a voice so cold with anger it made the blood curdle, "you will have paid twice over for every hand you ever laid on that girl, for every abuse, every humiliation, every degradation you made her suffer."

When he had beaten Bonner to within an inch of his life, Mallory Jones faced Jean Levoir. The Frenchman was lying back on the chaise longue. He had smoked all afternoon to erase the memories of China he had awakened, and smoked all evening to blot out Samantha's agony. Oblivious to the melee around him, he lay in a drug-induced stupor, his unseeing eyes locked in space, his face an unearthly pallor.

"Get up, Levoir," Jones commanded. Something in the voice, and in the memories that had been stirred that day, broke through the opium fog and Levoir looked up at the American. Smiling happily, he reached out his hand. "Mallory, you have come to me, at last," he said.

Minutes later a breathless Peter Thomson reached the top of the stairs with two of Talleyrand's agents at his heels—just in time to hear Jones's furious cry: "I should have killed you the first time I had you by the throat."

Rushing in, they found Jones squeezing Levoir in a murderous stranglehold. "Stop it, Mallory," Thomson shouted, "let him go! Can't you see that he is killing himself in his own way. He doesn't need any help from you."

Slowly, Jones opened his fingers and Levoir crumpled to the floor.

"As for these other two," Thomson said briskly, "what remains of them we will leave in the hands of Talleyrand's men. I've no doubt their minds are as fertile as ours when it comes to inventing punishments."

The depths of fury that had been unleashed in this usually gentle man shocked Thomson and he hoped by the brusqueness of his tone to stay the murder in Jones' heart.

"Now," he said, barely able to control his revulsion at what his sweet Samantha had been reduced to, "let's get the girl as far away from this foul place as we can."

Kneeling at the bedside, he said lovingly, "Samantha, it is your Uncle Peter. I am taking you home now." But the girl did not respond.

"Samantha, Samantha," he called to her urgently this time. But her glazed eyes never even blinked.

"It is the opium, Peter," Jones said bitterly.

"It was not enough for them to smoke it. They made her an addict as well."

Sadly Thomson cut the leather straps that bound Samantha, and Jones wrapped her bare, frail frame in the sheet and carried her down to the waiting carriage. As he cradled her in his arms, pressing her close to his heart to keep her warm, he could no longer deny the truth. This was the woman he loved, the woman he would always love.

But this was also the woman who had left his child for dead and returned to marry Levoir.

Jones and Thomson waited together for three days while the best physicians in Paris hovered over Samantha trying to save her, and as they waited, Thomson related her long, difficult story —or as much of it as he knew.

But Samantha had never told him about the child or the island boy, and these glaring omissions struck Jones deeply. He waited until the doctors had assured them she was out of danger and then he returned to Boston without ever looking at her again.

Mallory Jones knew that if he saw Samantha again he would not leave. Yet, remembering little Jonathan, he could not stay.

Only the faithful Thomson remained at Samantha's bedside. He stayed in Paris and nursed her back to health again. No wish was ever refused her. No whim was too small, no demand too great for him to meet. Under his patient care,

Samantha recovered her health fully. The evil power of the poppy juice was broken and the bruises from Bonner's beatings healed without a scar.

During her long convalescence, she told him what she could remember of her life in the dingy Left Bank apartment, and he related the story of her rescue.

Rescued by Mallory Jones from the deadening grasp of Jean Levoir! Had it ever really happened? Samantha had no recollections to conjure up. She remembered only Levoir's confession of love. Unknown to each other, she and Jean had both been in love with the same man, and had sought refuge in each other's arms from the searing passion that he would not answer. Then, in her hour of darkest need, he had appeared suddenly to rescue her.

Mallory Jones had searched for her, saved her, and vanished without a word. His strange rescue only heightened the dreamlike quality of the entire experience. The opium-shrouded days and nights as Bonner's captive held no reality for her.

Samantha felt as if she was waking up from a long nightmare, with her devoted Uncle Peter at her side to guide her through the new day. Wrapped in the security of his care and affection, she allowed the past with all its cruelties and conundrums to fade away like sleep.

Thomson, for his part, was content to attend and cherish Samantha for however many years remained to him. He was unwilling to ever let her out of his sight again. He had lost her twice before and each time she had fallen victim to a fate the full dimensions of which he did not know and could not bear to imagine. Now, more than anything, he wanted to make sure it could never happen again; he wanted to make her future secure; he wanted to make Samantha his wife.

Thomson regretted his reticence in Genoa. If he had pressed her then to accept him, she would have been spared the terrible suffering she endured at the hands of Bonner and Levoir. Now, he resolved that as soon as she was strong again he would beg her to accept his love. He wanted nothing more than her happiness. He would make no demands on her as a husband. If she were unwilling to be a complete wife to him, he would not insist.

To Thomson's delight, Samantha accepted his proposal happily. Although he was as old as her late father, there was no one in the world to whom she felt closer. Her gratitude to and her fondness for him were too deep to measure. After her torturous travails, she was content to rest quietly in his secure embrace.

And so in a small civil ceremony, Samantha Shaw became Mrs. Peter Thomson. It was far different from the big, gala wedding that she had dreamed of when she sailed from Macao for Paris. But she was at peace with herself at last and Peter was radiant. *Samantha has never looked more beautiful*, he thought. The light green gown she chose to be married in was the color of the first new leaf of spring. *Did she choose it because it was such a perfect symbol for the life they were beginning together*, he wondered, *or because it contrasted so alluringly with the darker green of her eyes*? Kissing his smiling bride for the first time, he was struck again by her extraordinary beauty. Her sufferings had not diminished her loveliness in the slightest. They seemed to have deepened it, ripened it, and each day now she grew to look more like his beloved Marie.

Immediately after the short wedding service, the Thomsons sailed for Boston. Samantha had been longing to see her home again, and Thomson was eager to grant her every wish. They sailed from Le Havre on their honeymoon trip. But no sooner had they left France behind them than Thomson began to feel weak and light-headed.

The strain of the last weeks and the excitement of their marriage had caught up with him, and he spent his wedding night cradled gently in his bride's loving arms. Happiness had come too late for Peter Thomson. His over-taxed heart was not young enough or strong enough to bear the surge of emotions that engulfed him when he took Samantha as his wife. Midway across the Atlantic Ocean, he died, his marriage unconsummated, and was buried at sea.

CHAPTER THIRTY

The Beautiful Widow Thomson

Three years after she and Maude had sailed out of Boston Harbor on the Canton-bound *Carol Anne*, Samantha Shaw Thomson returned home a wealthy, beautiful, young widow.

With no close family left to turn to in her bereavement, she sought the good offices of Joseph Potter. Like Peter Thomson, he was an old friend of her father, a man she could rely on and lean on while she recovered from her sudden loss.

Joseph Potter had started out working on his father's farm in Essex County. As a young man he traded the agricultural life for seafaring adventures and became a privateer, a ship's captain, and, finally, one of the leading East India Traders in Massachusetts.

Now, a scion of Boston, he welcomed Samantha home as if she were his own daughter. He remembered vividly the fresh, vibrant girl who had set off to fulfill her father's dream, bearing her grief bravely. But the girl who had finally returned was much altered.

A veil of sadness as fine as the mist that cloaks Cape Cod on a summer evening seemed to envelop Samantha now. The shock of her husband's death so soon after their wedding, and the loss of her dear Aunt Maude, whom he had courted too many years ago to mention, were cause enough for her sadness. Yet Potter sensed there was something more.

Although he did not question her closely, not wanting to pry into what must have been difficult years for the girl, he saw that she had suffered grievously and his heart went out to her. He invited Samantha to stay in his large brick mansion in Salem for as long as she liked, assuring her that she was not to think at all about the future until she was thoroughly rested and recovered from the shock of her husband's sudden death.

As the days and weeks passed, Samantha settled comfortably into the easy, gracious routine of the Potter household. Encouraged by the Potters' sympathetic ways and warm hospitality, she began gradually to tell them about her years away from Boston.

She described her excitement at arriving in China, her romance with the dashing Jean Levoir, and their plan to meet and marry in Paris, which sank with the ill-fated *Wind Song*. And she told them about her rescue by the pirate ship *Zanzibar* and her unexpected, blessed reunion with Peter Thomson.

But Samantha never told them the worst of her tale—never told them about Mallory Jones or his child, about Jean Levoir's treacherous heart or Pierre Bonner's sadistic cruelty. She could not. How could they ever understand— kind and supportive though they were—as they sat comfortably in their upstairs sitting room, white-haired and serene, a warm fire glowing in the grate? How could they ever look at her with the same affectionate eyes if they knew what she had done—what she had been forced to do! And so Samantha kept the worst of her secrets locked in her breast.

As he listened to her perilous adventures, Joseph Potter marveled at the strength of the girl and at her beauty which, if anything, had increased with the years. He remembered her as an open, eager-faced youngster. The face that he looked on now was stronger, thinner, finer, with a suggestion of smoldering passion around the sensual lips and a glimmer of mystery in the cavernous green eyes. Instead of weakening her, he saw that her suffering had given her a sharper edge, had steeled her, and he wondered sometimes now if there was anything that this young woman could not endure.

Samantha assured the Potters that she was anxious to start a new life in Boston. There was little of her old one left to pick up. Because she had spent so many years in school abroad, she had few friends in Boston, and what close family she had was gone now.

Although she spoke often of a new beginning, she did little about it. After her nightmare with Levoir and Bonner, Peter Thomson was Samantha's only tenuous thread to reality, and when that thread broke with his death, she withdrew into herself.

Samantha would lock herself up in the Potters' library and read for hours or sit alone in the garden staring into nothingness. Her reclusiveness worried Mrs. Potter. If no one interrupted Samantha, she would sit all day and all night, alone and silent. Yet whenever Mrs. Potter joined her, she was always gracious. She never seemed annoyed at the disturbance.

"Joseph, I am worried about Samantha," Mrs. Potter would say to her husband every night before they fell asleep. "It is just not healthy for a young girl like that never to go out or see anyone."

But he would wisely answer, "Leave the girl alone, Martha. She will come around when she's ready to."

In spite of her husband's words, Mrs. Potter made sure that Samantha was included in the numerous invitations to dinner parties and dances they received. But Samantha always declined politely. On several occasions, she made a special point of inviting young women Samantha's own age to tea. And, although Samantha was a charming hostess, she always declined their return invitations.

While Mrs. Potter fretted, Samantha sank

deeper into her cocoon. Safely home at long last, she felt like a man who had stood up staunchly under a terrible blow and when the danger passed and all was safe, felt his knees buckle under him. The Potters had given her a safe, secure haven and she was loathe to stray from it.

Although she knew she could not stay on forever, Samantha could not bring herself to think beyond the next day. She seemed unable to formulate any plans for her future, or make any but the smallest decisions. Under the thrall of Levoir and Bonner, she had surrendered to the balm of opium and allowed her mind to drift far away. Then, secure in Peter's devotion, she had willingly placed herself in his hands, allowing him to do the thinking and planning for both of them, for the present at least.

Now, Samantha was still not ready to face the world again, in spite of Mrs. Potter's discreet urgings. The formalities of social discourse she would have to go through to make new friends seemed fruitless. What would she have in common with the young matrons who had never been as far as New York or even Providence? What did she want with the young men who would inevitably come calling? She had not the slightest desire to ever be touched by a man again. The very thought of it had become so odious to her that it made her stomach turn and sent cold shivers up her spine.

Concerned over Samantha's continued withdrawal, Mrs. Potter asked Dr. Swift to drop by for tea and have a look at the girl. He was a jovial, easy-going man who had been the Potters' family doctor for years and shared Joseph's sensible belief that nature should be allowed to take its course. One look at the girl and his diagnosis was made: "She looks beautiful to me, Martha." But to ease his old friend's worry he prescribed a tablespoon of tonic before each meal.

No amounts of Dr. Swift's medicine, however, could do as much to restore Samantha to her old self as the unexpected arrival of Joseph Potter's young nephew George.

George Potter, Sr., had moved to London years before and established an international banking firm there. Now he was grooming his son to take over the business, and had dispatched young George to America to master the Boston branch of the firm. He would live with his uncle and aunt so that Joseph could keep the irrepressible lad out of mischief—or so his father hoped.

George Potter, Jr., was a tall, strapping young man, about five years Samantha's junior, with an enthusiasm and *joie de vivre* that was as contagious as the measles. His boyish charm brought new life to the old Potter house and new life to Samantha.

One look at the beautiful Mrs. Thomson in her black widow's weeds that contrasted so dramatically with her tawny hair and fair skin, and young George lost his heart. But he was wise enough to conceal his love. Instead, George concentrated all his energies on entertaining Samantha. Slowly, with his winning ways and boyish high spirits, he drew her out of her shell, and often now Samantha would catch herself laughing gaily at his antics or smiling spontaneously when he entered the room.

George was the younger brother she had always wanted and she responded to his attentions playfully. He, in turn, seemed content just to make her laugh and drop her mask of sorrow. Afraid of upsetting the fragile relationship he had built with the beautiful, withdrawn widow, he kept his true feelings to himself, and watched hopefully, patiently, as Samantha gradually began to come alive again.

The Potters were delighted with the change their nephew had brought about in Samantha and, with the holiday season fast approaching, they decided to celebrate their happiness with a fabulous Christmas party. The old house would ring again with Christmas cheer, just as it had when George was a boy.

"Samantha dear," Mrs. Potter said one evening as they sat at the dinner table talking enthusiastically about their party plans, "you will have to get a new dress made for the occasion. You've been in mourning quite long enough and I am sure dear Peter would, if he were still with us, be the first to tell you that himself."

"But . . . " Samantha began to protest.

"No buts," Mrs. Potter went on blithely, "I will make an appointment with Madame Margot for you tomorrow. Just leave everything to me."

"I am more grateful than I can ever express for all the kindness you have shown me," Samantha said hesitatingly, "but if you would grant me one more favor . . . please. I—I will just stay in my room during the party and read, and I will never even be missed."

"You will be missed by me," George retorted. "How could you imagine that we could have a party in this house, knowing that you were upstairs locked in your room like a mouse? I, for one, would not have any fun at all."

"George is right," Mrs. Potter said, a note of disappointment obvious in her gentle, old voice. "We could not possibly give a party if we did not all attend. If you feel strongly that you must continue to mourn for your husband, Samantha, we simply won't have the party at all. We will have a quiet little Christmas, just the four of us."

She rang for the maid, and an awkward silence settled over the table while the dishes were cleared and the dessert served. Samantha had not meant to spoil the party. She had only hoped to be excused from the festivities. For, although she had opened, like a beautiful flower, in George's irrepressible company, she was still wary of reentering the world, where she had found it so difficult to distinguish friend from foe.

George toyed with his water tumbler. "I can still remember," he said wistfully, "an enormous pine standing in the stairwell in the front hall, reaching up two stories high. I must have been eight or nine then, and I thought it was the biggest tree in the entire world. Underneath were heaps of presents of every shape and size, wrapped in bright shining paper and gingham bows, and on top a beautiful clear crystal angel hung suspended, as if it had flown down from heaven and perched on the tree to rest for a moment."

"Do you know, George, I still have that angel. Joseph gave it to me the first Christmas we were married. We haven't had a tree big enough to put it on in years. But I take it out each Christmas season just to look at it for a moment, and then I put it away again carefully to save—for what, I don't really know," Mrs. Potter said, her voice drifting off sadly.

"You two seem to be doing your level best to make this lovely girl feel guilty," Joseph Potter said, a hint of quiet admonition in his tone. "She has every right—"

"No, no, Uncle Joseph," Samantha interrupted, ashamed at her selfishness. "I am sorry, truly sorry. You must all think that I am the most ungrateful woman in the state of Massachusetts. Let's have a merry Christmas this year, all of us together." Her voice choked and her eyes filled with tears. "It has been so long since I had a Christmas, a true . . . "

Before she could say another word, George was scooping her up in his arms and twirling her around the dining room, whooping and laughing like a little boy, until Samantha had forgotten her tears and was caught up in his exuberant holiday spirit.

The Potters' Christmas party was going to be the biggest and gayest the old mansion had ever seen. For weeks before, Mrs. Potter and George pored over the guest list and menu, checking every detail to be sure no one had been overlooked, no traditional dish forgotten. Samantha left them to their checks and balances and concentrated her attention on the decorations, while Mr. Potter made it his personal business to locate the tallest spruce in Massachusetts.

As Christmas Day drew closer, Samantha lost herself in the decorations—stringing garlands of laurel leaves and twining them through the bannisters of the front stairway; making wreaths of pine cones and red velvet ribbons; hanging mistletoe on the crystal chandelier in the main entrance hall; and generally letting herself be caught up in the flurry of preparations and in George's contagious enthusiasm.

"Samantha," he said as they finished arranging the last sprigs of holly in the centerpiece for the long buffet table, "I wish it could be Christmas Eve every day to have you like this." He looked at her lovingly and ran his hand through her hair, pushing back the loose strands from her face and tucking them behind her ears. His face was serious. The laughing boy was gone.

"Well, it wouldn't do us much good," she answered lightly, "if, as soon as I get silly, you get serious. Come on, one more garland to twine and

357

then I think I will retire early so I'll be bright and gay for the party."

Samantha knew what was in George's heart, but she did not want him to tell her. She did not want him to say anything that would change their special relationship.

CHAPTER THIRTY-ONE

The Potters' Christmas Party

The Potters' great hall was a blaze of candlelight when the guests began arriving in their carriages and fur wraps. Everyone remarked in amazement at the tree, for Joseph Potter was a man as good as his word. He had found the biggest Christmas tree anyone could remember, a full, fragrant blue spruce, and, just as George described, a clear, crystal angel was suspended from the topmost branch, looking as if it had dropped down from heaven to attend the party.

From her room Samantha could hear the first guests arriving and the sounds of merrymaking begin. She was all dressed in her new gown, designed with a closely fitting lace bodice, long tight lace sleeves, and a high neck, the ecru shade contrasting subtly with her fair skin. Since she was still in mourning, she had not wanted anything too colorful and yet she did not want her appearance to dampen the holiday mood. This seemed to be a perfect choice. Life at the Potters' had brought back the lush contours of Samantha's breasts and hips, while her face, waist and legs remained as slim as ever, and her figure' was shown to its best advantage in her new gown.

Samantha had piled her hair up in a soft pompadour. She had studied herself from every angle in the mirror a dozen times, and was now seated on the bed. All the apprehensions she had pushed aside in the excitement of preparing the party now rushed back.

Samantha had not been to a proper party since Jean Levoir had been her escort in Paris. The ghastly nightmare that followed those brief days of happiness still made her apprehensive. Memories that she had blotted out of her mind returned to torment her and she trembled on the bed, unable to force herself to join the gaiety below.

Just as past terrors threatened to engulf her, a loud knock brought her back to the present. Over the din of the merrymaking, she heard George's excited voice. "Samantha, are you decent?" He poked his head in the door.

Seeing the old veil of sadness drawn across her face, he guessed what had happened and determined not to let her slip back.

"Come on, slow poke," he called gaily, "my arm is getting tired waiting out here to escort you to the party."

He took her by the hand and pulled her up, pressing a soft kiss on her forehead. "Merry Christmas, Samantha," George smiled, and before she knew what was happening, she was descending the broad staircase on his arm and he was patting her hand reassuringly and pointing out who was who with an amusing remark about each guest.

George was so charming and witty that, by the time they reached the hall, Samantha's fears had all but vanished and she was easily swept into the merry Christmas spirit.

All the guests were curious to meet the beautiful, young widow who had returned to Boston so mysteriously, long after she had been presumed dead in a shipwreck, and Samantha never looked more exquisite. Her new dress was alluring in its very modesty and simplicity, and she did not want for attention. In fact, she had scarcely a moment to be sad or fretful. If, even for a second, she hesitated and thought of fleeing to the safety of her room, George seemed always to materialize at her elbow with a cup of eggnog or a sweet cake or a funny word whispered in her ear.

Samantha was finally beginning to relax completely and enjoy herself almost as she had in Macao, when Joseph Potter took her arm.

"My dear, I have a very special guest and admired colleague whom I have wanted to introduce you to for a long time," he said, leading her into the great hall. "My friend spent many years in China, leaving, if my memory serves me, just before your arrival. I am sure you will have many memories to compare. I have told him so much about the devastating Widow Thomson that he is anxious to meet you," he went on as he steered her toward a tall, blond man who stood admiring the tree with one of the young women guests.

"Miss Martin, if you will pardon my interrupting," Joseph said, graciously. The couple turned. "Allow me to introduce the Widow Thomson whom I have told you so much about, my friend. Samantha," he smiled warmly, "may I present Miss Jane Martin—I think you ladies have met before—and Mr. Mallory Jones."

"Mrs. Thomson," Mallory Jones said, bowing stiffly. There was not a trace, not a glint of recognition in the ice blue eyes that bored into hers.

Joseph Potter did not notice that Samantha turned a ghostly white when she found herself facing Mallory Jones. "Come, Miss Martin," he said easily, "let us leave Mrs. Thomson and Mr. Jones to their memories of Canton. If you can put up with an old man's whimsy, I would be enchanted to take a turn on the dance floor with you."

The reaction that passed unnoticed by the older man did not escape Jane Martin. She saw Samantha's sudden pallor and felt Jones stiffen at her side. But she could not very well refuse her host, and so, wondering where and how the Widow Thomson had met Mallory Jones, she left them to their memories.

Jane Martin was plain, but she was not stupid, and she was very much in love with Mallory

Jones. She knew he did not return her deep affection, but he was fond of her and it meant a great deal to him that she loved young Jonathan as well.

The little boy had been too long without a mother's warmth and gentle discipline. Jane would be a good mother to him. It did not matter to Mallory that he felt none of the passion for her that he had for Samantha, and none of the pure devotion he had felt for Ming-la. What mattered was Jonathan, and the boy needed a mother.

"The Widow Thomson, is it," Jones said coldly when they were alone. He had received news of Peter Thomson's death but no word of his marriage and he never imagined that his old friend had wed Samantha. "Your husband took the only means possible to escape your tenter-hooks. Others of us have not been as fortunate as he."

Samantha did not even know Mallory Jones was in Boston. She thought he would never leave Canton. Now the shock of seeing him again so unexpectedly and the harshness of his words were too overwhelming and she felt herself float slowly away. In the distance she heard his low, urgent voice, "Samantha, you can't faint, not here."

Grasping her firmly under the elbow, Mallory Jones led Samantha to the library. He caught her as she fell on the threshold and kicked the door shut behind them. For an instant, before putting her down in a deep leather chair, he looked into

364

her exquisite face, the same lovely face that had once driven him mad with desire. It was subtly changed and strengthened. The softness of youth was gone. The ripe, sensual woman was now more than a suggestion; it was a promise that beckoned irresistibly. Lost in her loveliness, he was aware of nothing except the woman in his arms, and his lips reached out to hers as to a magnet. But he caught himself just in time.

As if to punish Samantha for his temptation, Mallory Jones slapped her cheeks with the flat of his hand. His quick, sharp blows brought her around and she cried out when she felt their sting.

"I am not striking you solely for the pleasure it may give me," he said coldly. "It seems, Mrs. Thomson, that you fainted either from too much grog or too much shame. I think you would be the best judge of which. Now, if you will excuse me."

Without another word, Mallory Jones turned abruptly and left.

Samantha was still weak and dazed when George burst in a few minutes later. "I have been hunting for you everywhere. All the best-looking men are asking where you are hiding," he said merrily, none the worse for the eggnog he had consumed.

But seeing her pale face sobered George quickly. "Are you sure you are well, Samantha?"

"I felt a little dizzy, George. I came in here to rest for a moment. It is nothing," she said.

"Can I get you anything?" he said. His voice was tender and concerned.

"No, no, George, I feel much better now," Samantha replied, steeling herself to return to the party. If Mallory Jones could greet her like a stranger and insult her contemptuously, she could—and she would—show him that he had meant even less to her.

Forcing herself to speak brightly, she said, "There is one thing you can do for me, George. You may escort me to the party—for the second time tonight—and we will dance until morning."

"That's my girl," George said too heartily. He sensed her studied gaiety and wondered anxiously what had happened to upset her so much. But his worries were soon forgotten as he held the most beautiful girl at the party in his arms and twirled her around the ballroom.

For the rest of the evening, Samantha seemed even more enchanting than he had ever seen her and, if he had fallen in love with her before, now he was thoroughly infatuated. But she was much too sought after for George to monopolize her attentions all evening. As Mrs. Potter beamed approvingly from the doorway, Samantha danced and danced with partners old and new.

Samantha did not see Mallory Jones again that night. She did not know whether he had stalked from the library and out of Joseph Potter's house, or if he had returned to the side of Miss Jane Martin and eventually left with her. Her very uncertainty forced her to keep on dancing and smiling, pretending that she was enjoying herself.

Completely deceived by her false gaiety, George was more taken with her than ever. In a moment of merriment, he grabbed her by the wrist and pulled her laughing behind him into the great hall.

"There's something I have wanted to do all evening," he said only half joking, "and now's my chance. You can't get out of it now, Samantha no matter how much you squirm."

"Oh, yes, I can, George," she laughed, when she realized where he was taking her. "No one is getting me under the mistletoe, young man." As she twisted away, the eggnog got the better of George and he lost his grip. Samantha flew backwards.

"Ah, the Widow Thomson; we meet again," a cool, low, familiar voice said and Samantha landed once again in the arms of Mallory Jones, who stood chatting with Joseph Potter and Jane Martin.

"What a choice spot to meet my beautiful young ward, Jones," Mr. Potter chuckled. "I must say I wouldn't mind being in your shoes right now myself. Well, sir, what are you waiting for? Don't just stand there, do what any man in his right mind would do. Miss Martin will not take offense, now will you?" he said patting the girl's hand paternally.

What stupid foolishness prompted me to hang it here? Samantha thought, as Mallory Jones looked up and saw the mistletoe dangling from the chandelier. Through clenched teeth he whispered, "Be assured, madam, this is no more to my liking than it is to yours, so let us do it and be done."

"Come now, Samantha, don't be shy," Joseph Potter urged encouragement from the sidelines.

"Hurry up, Jones," George called, "Make it short and sweet because I cannot bear to wait for my turn much longer."

The voices and laughter reached Samantha in a jumble and worked to seal her in the arms of Mallory Jones. She raised her face to his and, for a moment, there were just the two of them. No one else existed. The universe was empty except for them.

She could feel the strength of his hands at her waist as he drew her to him and pressed his mouth to hers, not lightly as she had expected, but firmly, fully. At the touch of his lips, all the tempestuous passion she had guarded against, the searing desire she thought had been burned out of her body, flamed again. Her breasts heaved inside the confines of her tight bodice and the rough wool of his coat scratched her throat.

At his touch every sense, every pore in her body came alive, like the first buds of spring after a warm rainfall. He was the only man who knew the unquenchable fire, the consuming hunger, that smoldered beneath her aristocratic demeanor, the only man who could awaken her sensuous desire.

Samantha answered his lips with hers, tasting his special taste that she could never forget—or resist. Her arms tightened around his neck. Her fingers entwined in his blond curls, and she surrendered to his kiss.

"Woman, have you no shame?" the lips that she kissed so passionately hissed. "Stop it, Samantha. Let me go." She felt his breath against her mouth and his strong hands pulling her arms from his neck.

Flushed with passion and mortification, she shrank back. But no one seemed to have realized that their kiss was more than perfunctory.

"It's my turn now," George laughed, grabbing her by the hand, and holding her under the mistletoe again. "You can't get away that easily."

Over his shoulder, Samantha caught a glimpse of Mallory Jones's back at the front door. But, by the time she broke away from George, the door had closed behind him.

The remainder of the evening passed in a blur. Samantha was only dimly aware of what she was doing and saying, or what was going on around her, until, finally, pleading exhaustion, she kissed Mrs. Potter goodnight and, thanking her for the Christmas party, fled with relief to the blessed solitude of her room.

Flinging herself across the bed heedless of her beautiful new gown, Samantha buried her face in the pillows. *Why did I do it?* she chastised herself. *How could I ever allow myself to be shamed by Mallory Jones again? After all I have suffered am I still nothing more than passion's abject slave? Why did he come?* she wondered. *Why did he have to burst into my life again, unannounced and unwanted?*

In the long night hours, Samantha confronted herself and what she had become. She would not succumb. If they ever had the misfortune to meet again, she would not allow even a spark of desire to escape, but she would not be driven away again just because Mallory Jones was here.

Boston would have to be big enough for both of them, because Samantha decided to reclaim her father's house.

CHAPTER THIRTY-TWO

A First Lady's Wise Words

Samantha had little time to dwell on her unexpected and disturbing encounter with Mallory Jones. No sooner was the bustle of the Christmas and New Year holidays over, her first such festivities since her father's death, than she was caught up in the Potters' plans to attend the inauguration of the new President, John Quincy Adams, in Washington City.

The trip would take twelve days with an extra day's stopover in Philadelphia to visit Mrs. Potter's sister, and Samantha was looking forward to seeing something of her own country. George would be going along as well, which filled Samantha with a sense of contentment.

Each day she grew more dependent on the amiable, adoring young man, who could always raise her spirits and dispel her deepest gloom. Since that Christmas Eve when they were finishing the party decorations, George never again pressed his suit or indicated that his attentions were anything more than those of a dear friend.

Intuitively, though, Samantha knew that he was just biding his time, hoping she would give him some indication that he meant more to her than a brother. But she also knew that, for all his high-spirits and boyish hijinks, George was a gentleman through and through. He would never force his attentions on her.

Assuring herself that she was not encouraging his false hopes or leading him on intentionally, Samantha, nonetheless, took advantage of his good nature. Now, more than ever, she welcomed his friendship. He was a blessed distraction from memories of Mallory Jones, and she was looking forward to having his company on the exciting trip ahead.

If the elder Potters had any knowledge of their nephew's intentions, they never mentioned them to Samantha. They seemed to accept the young couple as devoted companions, and gave them complete freedom to come to their own decisions, watching fondly but never interfering in their young lives.

They would have had to be blind not to see that their nephew was head over heels in love with the enigmatic young widow who had taken refuge under their roof. In the months that she had lived with them, the Potters had grown very fond and protective of Samantha. Although the exact nature and extent of her misfortunes were still a mystery to them, they knew she had suffered severely and they would do nothing to burden her further. For these reasons, the Potters did not press Samantha to accept their nephew, nor did they indicate to George that they recognized his deep feelings.

They watched silently, wishing all the while that George would win the girl, but deciding that the best thing they could do was to leave the young couple alone and let their hearts decide. George was so young and simple compared with Samantha, Mrs. Potter thought, that she sensed the boy could never be more than a friend or brother. While she would be overjoyed if his suit was successful, she was not optimistic about his chances, and she prayed that Samantha would be gentle with darling George and let him down softly.

These were the Potters' thoughts as they started off on their journey to Washington City to see one of Massachusetts's native sons sworn in as the sixth President of the Republic. A light snow was falling when they left Boston, but, bundled in thick fur rugs and secure in their spacious carriage drawn by a brace of dapple-grays, they were protected against the cold.

Samantha was glowing with excitement. She had never really seen any of her own country except Boston and the stark beauty of the wintry countryside excited her. Joseph Potter was like a youngster again himself, explaining to her and to his English-bred nephew for the one-hundredth time the route they were taking down the Post Road.

Much of Washington City had been destroyed, of course, when the British troops came down the Potomac fourteen years before and set a torch to the town. But the damage had been repaired after the war, and the city, by all reports, had become quite cosmopolitan.

By standards of Boston, Paris, or even Macao, Washington City was still almost a frontier town, or the closest thing to it that Samantha had ever seen. She was fascinated by the earnestness and bustle of the young town and by the colorful assortment of Congressmen they met as guests of Daniel Webster, the fiery senator from New Hampshire. Talk at the Websters' table turned inevitably to politics and, quite naturally, to the coming inauguration of one of their former colleagues.

John Quincy Adams was a complex man, they all agreed, difficult to know and even more difficult to pigeonhole. Some thought he was cold and aloof, much more so than his father, but everyone seemed to concur on one thing. The new President-elect was a highly intelligent man, and Samantha was curious to meet him.

The week before the inauguration was filled with teas and dinners and, as guests of Daniel Webster, the Potters were invited to the most interesting and elegant parties. On their second night in Washington City they attended a dinner at the F Street home of Congressman Cutts in honor of his aunt, Mrs. Dolly Madison, and her husband, former President James Madison.

Mr. Madison was small and quite fragile looking, Samantha thought, much more reserved than his ebullient wife who immediately charmed the girl. A circle of adoring admirers surrounded the older woman and Samantha could not help but notice that even in her sixties Dolly Madison was an astonishing beauty. Her head was wrapped in one of her famous satin turbans of violet. Her fashionable gown of dusty rose and violet subtly enhanced her still enviable complexion. Even her delicately slippered feet were graceful and pretty.

But Samantha exchanged only a few words of greeting with her. The elderly Mrs. Madison was encircled by a coterie of devotees and the young Widow Thomson was cornered by a big, angular frontiersman.

"Andrew Jackson, ma'am," he introduced himself, and Samantha took an instant liking to Old Hickory. General Jackson's valor at the Battle of New Orleans was renowned throughout the Republic, but it was his simple, country ways that appealed to Samantha. She found his rustic manners and backwoods humor oddly refreshing after the steady flow of senators and ambassadors.

While many of them were pompous and affected, Daniel Webster was the exception that proved the rule. With his galvanizing personality and sparkling intellect, he made a most gracious host, and the week passed all too quickly.

Inaugural morning dawned crisp and clear.

Lively military bands entertained the large crowds that gathered early on Pennsylvania Avenue and the Capitol laws. Samantha and the Potters watched Mr. Adams take the oath of office from the gallery of the House of Representatives, where Daniel Webster had reserved them front row seats. Senators and Congressmen filled the main floor of the hall, as the sixth president of the United States was sworn in.

At the Inaugural Ball that evening, Samantha wore the same ecru lace gown that had been made for the Potters' Christmas party. With its high neck and slim, fluid lines, she made a striking contrast to the other women, who for the most part were adorned in provocatively low-cut dresses that stood out stiffly from their bodies with layers and layers of crinolines. Even the inestimable Mrs. Madison, a fashion setter in her own day, made a point of complimenting Samantha on her gown.

"You look exquisite, my dear," the handsome old First Lady said, taking Samantha's hand in hers and tucking it protectively through her arm. "I recognize you from the reception at my nephew's where Old Hickory bent your ear the entire evening. But I cannot guess why I have not met you before. It is probably because the President and I lead such a quiet life now that we have retired to Virginia. You must visit us there, Mrs. Thomson, at our home in Monticello. I love young people and am delighted to see such

377

a pretty one adorning our capital again. You must tell me all about yourself."

"There is really very little to tell, Mrs. Madison," Samantha answered modestly. "This is my first visit to Washington City and I am fortunate to have Senator Webster for a host."

"I must confess, Mrs. Thomson, your beauty is so striking that I took the liberty of asking the Senator about you," Mrs. Madison went on. "You remind me a little of myself at your age, although it sounds as if you have already had more adventure than an old woman like myself finds in a lifetime."

Samantha looked warily at Mrs. Madison, trying to discern how much of her disgraceful story Daniel Webster knew and what he had told this delicate First Lady. Seeing the girl's discomfiture, the older woman patted her hand reassuringly.

"You need not have any fear, my dear, Daniel told me only that you have lived in Europe and the Orient and only recently returned to Boston where, since your family is sadly deceased, you have been staying with your old friends, the Potters."

She looked at Samantha squarely. "You must never be afraid that people will come to know you. If they don't, if you do not allow them to, you can never be happy. We all have our little secrets, moments we are ashamed of. But if you have done the only possible thing you could to survive, your friends will understand this and not judge you too harshly. As for the others, you would not want their friendship. It would mean nothing. Now, my dear," she smiled warmly, "if I monopolize you any longer, all the young men at the ball will think that I am a most selfish old woman. But do remember that you cannot hide forever. What you have done is in the past— all part of what you are now. It is better to have lived with passion than never to know the depths of your heart."

On the trip back to Boston, with everyone pleasantly exhausted from the gala week, Samantha had ample time to think over Dolly Madison's wise words. Of all the wonderful memories of the Inauguration, the one she treasured most was that candid moment with the beautiful old lady.

"Come to visit us in Virginia, Mrs. Thomson," she had repeated. "You will always be welcome in Monticello. James and I are kept vigorous by the exuberance of our young friends."

Samantha marveled at the older woman's insight. She had used the sanctuary of the Potters' warm home to hide—to hide from herself and from the world for fear that her dangerous heart would reveal her for what she was: a woman of torrential passions. She was afraid of the fatal fires that burned in her heart and afraid that others would discover her secret desires and disdain her for them.

More than that, Samantha was grateful for Mrs. Madison's wisdom. "Better to have lived with passion than never to know the depths of your heart." There were still depths in her heart that she had yet to explore, but now Samantha would have the courage to discover them.

"Aunt Martha and Uncle Joseph," she said as the carriage trotted along the Post Road just outside Providence. They were on the last lap of the journey home and Samantha had decided to make a stand on her own again at last. By telling the Potters her plans, she hoped to strengthen her own resolve. "I think when we get back to Boston, I will open up father's house on Beacon Hill. I have taken advantage of your gracious hospitality far too long already. It is time I started to live responsibly again."

"Dear girl," Joseph Potter said, "our home is your home. I hope you do not feel that you have outstayed your welcome."

"Oh, no, Uncle. When I thought I was alone in the world, you gave me a new family. For this I can never thank you or dear Aunt Martha or darling George enough. But I cannot live with you forever, hiding away in your home, shirking my responsibilities. I have been very selfish, thinking that no one has had as difficult a life as I. Now I see how indulgent and stupid I've been. I have been living too long in the past. What is done is done, and, no matter how much I brood over it, I will never be able to change it. It has taken me a long time to accept that, but now I think I have learned the lesson."

Joseph and Martha Potter were smiling broadly by the time Samantha finished speaking.

"Nothing could make us happier than these words of yours, Samantha," Mrs. Potter said. "You are so young and have so much life to look forward to. So many good things can be yours again, if you will truly let the past—whatever it may be—bury itself."

The distance from Providence to Boston flew by in a flurry of discussion about opening the handsome Georgian home Jonathan Shaw built on Beacon Hill. Mrs. Potter decided that Nora should go with Samantha, since she was an excellent maid, experienced enough to manage a household and, no less important, she had become devoted to the Widow Thomson. And Mr. Potter insisted that she take Snowstar, the frisky colt she had trained, as a remembrance of all the happy times they had spent together.

Samantha was so overwhelmed by their kindness that her eyes filled with tears and she hugged them both lovingly. "How can I ever repay you for all you have done for me?" she said.

"I can think of a marvelous payment—that is, if I am allowed to collect on behalf of the family," George joked, and soon they were all laughing and chatting again, and planning for Samantha's new life in Boston.

CHAPTER THIRTY-THREE

Samantha Slips Again

By late spring Samantha had moved into the Shaw mansion on Beacon Hill. The inheritance that Joseph Potter had invested wisely for her after her father's death was enough to make her one of the most affluent and independent women in Boston. Her beauty made her one of the most desirable.

"A fine catch," all the gossips noted as Samantha Shaw took her place at long last in Boston society.

She was as slim as she had ever been. Her tawny hair was still long and lustrous, and most of the time she let it fall loosely around her shoulders. Her face was more sharply chiseled now that the roundness of youth was gone.

But Samantha did not plunge immediately into the social life of the town. She lived quietly, serenely, shopping with the faithful Nora at her side or riding across the bridge to Cambridge where she could give Snowstar his head and let him gallop freely through the open fields.

Except for Nora, George Potter was her most frequent companion, still devoted, still in love, still waiting for her wounds to heal. With each day her fondness for him grew and she wondered if she could do without him. When he returned to London in a few months, she would feel his absence sorely. Each day she grew more convinced that this kind of affection might be what she was best suited for, that, rather than the passionate tempest that Mallory Jones had once aroused in her bosom, this warm caring might be the basis for a happy, long-lasting marriage, two people growing old comfortably together. The tranquil life—so refreshing after the years of turmoil she had suffered—was attractive to her and, suppressing the wild, passionate side of her nature, she began to believe that she wanted this serenity, and nothing more.

Most of all Samantha liked to either browse through her father's ample library, reading at random from his leather-bound volumes, curled up on the window seat until the afternoon light grew dim and Nora would come in and light the candles, or to fly through the fields of Cambridge on Snowstar's back, the two of them moving as one. George often warned her of the danger of riding alone with such abandon but she laughed off his worry.

"Snowstar and I understand each other," she'd

tease. "We're both free spirits and try as you may you will never be able to harness either of us."

If the truth were known though, Samantha was beginning to seriously consider a life as Mrs. George Potter and she did most of her best thinking while she was out riding. She gave Snowstar his head one afternoon, when her thoughts were filled with George and her heart was as untrammeled as the horse's hoofs. It was a glorious, breezy spring day. But the wind whipped her face and stung her eyes so that she did not see a low hanging maple branch. A second too late, Samantha realized she would have to flatten herself against the horse's neck to clear it. The branch caught her squarely in the forehead, knocking her unconscious.

Samantha dreamed she was bathing in a pond of cool, fresh water. She was floating as easily and gently as a lily pad and a stranger on the shore was gazing at her, murmuring that she was the loveliest flower he had ever seen. Gradually, as she regained consciousness, she still felt the cool water on her face and neck.

"Don't try to move yet," a low voice soothed. "Lie still, my love," and she floated away again on those whispered words.

When she regained consciousness, strong, cool fingers were caressing her cheek, and when she opened her eyes, unforgettable blue, troubled eyes were gazing into hers. Samantha thought she must still be dreaming, but his eyes smiled gently.

"You took a terrible fall," the familiar voice said, "but you should be all right in a little while more." Samantha struggled to sit up.

"Lie still, you are still in shock," his caressing voice commanded. She sank back and, for the first time, realized that her riding jacket was folded to pillow her head.

Tenderly, soothingly, he wiped her forehead with a damp cloth, pushing her hair off her face. "You will have an ugly bump here for a few days." She winced as he touched the bruise. "But not enough to mar your beautiful face," he said. He bent and kissed her forehead where the tree branch had struck.

"Where is Snowstar?" Samantha asked weakly.

"He is grazing right down there at the river bank," he said pointing toward the easy flowing Charles where she had learned to sail as a child.

Samantha lay quietly and closed her eyes. She half believed she was dreaming. Mallory Jones was nursing her in an open field. Harsh, brutal, hated Mallory Jones. His evident concern, his worried eyes, his solicitous manner confused her. She could never think clearly when his hands were touching her.

Mallory was wiping her neck and shoulders with the wet cloth. The water was calming and refreshing and she gave herself up to her senses. Samantha felt the cool water trickle down her breasts. She felt his warm breath on her bosom and realized for the first time that her breasts were bare. He must have opened her blouse while she was unconscious.

What else had he done? she wondered, but in the very next instant she didn't care. She didn't care what he had ever done before. She cared only for the feel of the cool water trickling over her breasts and his warm breath on her bosom. Wherever his breath lingered seemed to burn.

He put aside the cloth and kissed her bruised forehead again. "You will have a mean bump the size of a silver dollar." He kissed her closed eyes. "But now you must wake up, Samantha. I will ride with you as far as the bridge."

She opened her eyes and lost herself in his. "I owe you a kiss," he murmured, his lips only inches from her own, "May I give it to you now?

Her lips, white and drained from the shock of the fall, reached up to his and they lingered and blended together in a moment suspended from all time and place, a moment that surely, Samantha thought, must be as close to eternity as she would ever come in her lifetime.

"Mallory," she whispered.

"Don't try to talk, Samantha," he said. But his words were drowned by his lips, hungrier this time.

His hands reached under her blouse and pressed into the tender flesh of her back as he clasped her tightly to him. Wherever his fingers or mouth touched, her skin seemed scorched.

Snowstar whinnied in the distance. The afternoon sun dropped behind the hills. The lovers noticed neither one. They, and only they existed, suspended in time and place. What had gone before, what would come after, was forgotten.

Their lips locked in an endless kiss, their hands explored each other's body, yearning, searching for the bare flesh beneath their riding clothes. Only one thing could satisfy them now.

Mallory Jones's hungry mouth covered her face and hair with kisses. Her beautiful breasts heaved beneath his touch. She forgot the bruise on her forehead. In his expert hands her whole body tingled and came alive with a passion that she had buried deep within her. Now, she knew only the desire that had become uncontrollable, a desire to possess him again, to feel the thrill of his body on hers, the agonizing bliss of receiving him.

When his mouth fell on her breasts, the nipples were already standing as erect as daggers. His tongue explored her milky mounds and his hand sought the treasure between her legs. He felt the wetness of her passion and still he held back. He reached behind her, his forearm pressing against her, and stroked her buttocks. His body was shrouded by the dusk as he knelt over her. She could only see his face, just inches from her own. His eyes glowed with their own fire, revealing his hunger to have her again. Why then was he holding back, driving her wild with desire?

"What do you want, Samantha?" His voice was deep and urgent. "Tell me what you want." His hands were on her breasts again. His mouth was covering her neck with kisses.

"I want you," she whispered, "only you."

"Then take me, Samantha," he said softly, "Take me, my darling."

He took her fingers and drew them to him. She felt his enormous desire throbbing in her hand. Fueled by his firm, looming, undeniable need, she closed her fingers around him and, locking her ankles around his waist, she guided him to her door.

He entered her slowly at first, but in the instant that she received him fully, both were lost, abandoned to the love they had denied themselves for so long. All the passion they had suppressed was loosed again in that field in Cambridge as Snowstar waited patiently and the sun sank lower in the evening sky, until they reached a point of such ecstasy that their love burnished the heavens and made the stars come out to shine.

Mallory Jones lay quietly with Samantha cradled in his arms, staring up at the star-studded skies. Lying there in his strong arms, the taste of his sweat sweet on her lips, Samantha knew at last that she could never belong to any other man. She finally admitted to herself what she had known in Canton so many heartaches and tribulations ago. Her great fear was that he had never felt the same way about her and she shuddered thinking that perhaps she had just been used again by this passionate, turbulent man.

"Are you cold?" he asked, drawing her closer and rubbing her back with his open palm to warm her. "I should be getting you home," he smiled, the dazzling boyish smile that seemed to light up the night, "It is not seemly for a lady to be out unescorted at this hour. What will your proper Boston neighbors think of the exotic Widow Thomson?"

He laughed easily, a deep chiming laughter, but he didn't move and Samantha was glad he didn't. *Maybe,* she thought, *he wants this moment to stretch into eternity, as I do. We would lie here forever and make love, and the sun would rise and set, and the stars would come out and recede, and still we would lie here and make love again and again.*

Mallory Jones looked at her wistfully for a moment. Then suddenly he patted her on the back, a short brusque pat, and stood up. "You tidy yourself, Samantha, while I go down to the river and get the horses."

They rode to the bridge in silence. Samantha kept waiting for him to say something—anything, a word of reassurance—but he had drawn the inscrutable Oriental mask over his fine features again, and the strange way he looked at her now in the moonlight turned her blood cold.

She did not want to give him up again. She could not. How could he have made such passionate love to her, if she meant nothing to him? She remembered his anxious, worried face when she woke up and found him bending over her and the gentle way he had bathed her bruised forehead and kissed it tenderly. *I will say something, if he doesn't, when we get to the bridge,* she decided. But when they were still a few strides away, he said, "You will be safe from here," and before she could utter a word, Mallory Jones had vanished.

"Mallory, Mallory," Samantha called, but he had disappeared into the night just as he had in China.

Samantha sagged in the saddle, her bosom heaving with sobs. "Don't leave me, Mallory, not again," she whispered, her voice choked with grief.

Snowstar craned his neck around and whinnied sympathetically. "It's just you and me, Snowstar," she sobbed. "It will always be just you and me," and throwing her arms around the sleek white stallion's neck, she rode into Boston.

Nora was at the door with a lighted taper when Samantha cantered up Beacon Hill. "I was about to send for Mr. George to go searching for you, Miss Samantha, that is how worried you made me. Where have you been at this time of night? Look at yourself," she gasped, holding the candle up to Samantha's face, "all grass-stained and tear-stained!"

Samantha tried to turn aside from the telling light, but Nora would have none of it. She was a kind, big-hearted Irish woman who had been tending to wealthy women's needs ever since she was sixteen, but she had never cared a fig for any of them until Samantha arrived at the Potters' house. Nora's generous heart had gone out to the beautiful, sorrowful young widow. Now she would allow no harm to come to the girl, but neither would she take any of Miss Samantha's foolishness.

"My lord in heaven," she cried when the light shone on Samantha's forehead, "you have a lump the size of an apple over your right eye."

"I took a fall, Nora. There is nothing to be concerned about, if you would just bring an ice-bag to my room. I am tired and I would like to get some rest." Samantha was in no mood for remonstrations, no matter how well-intentioned.

"That wild horse will be the death of you yet," Nora scolded. "You know Mr. George doesn't want you riding it alone."

"Nora, it was not Snowstar's fault. Now, if you will excuse me, I am very tired."

Nora, taken back by the curtness of her mistress's tongue, said no more. But as she watched Samantha walk slowly up the broad stairway, she muttered to herself that Mr. George would hear about this accident. She would make sure of that.

CHAPTER THIRTY-FOUR

Mallory Jones to Marry

Concealed by the dark night, Mallory Jones watched Samantha at the bridge. When she called his name, her voice urgent and pleading, his heart leaped in his chest, but he did not allow himself to answer. He watched her slump in the saddle when nothing came back to her except the echo of her cry. He waited for her to ride away, but instead, the wind carried her whispered words to him, "Don't leave me, Mallory, not again," and Snowstar's sympathetic whinny.

He steeled himself against the passion she kindled in him and against the anguish he had felt when he saw her fall. Jones had thought that his love for Samantha was dead—mortally wounded on the island of Pagalu, killed forever in Paris with Jean Levoir.

He had been surprised and dismayed to meet her at the Potters' Christmas party, and disgusted by her kiss. Jane had plied him with questions about the Widow Thomson. But he answered sharply that he did not know the woman, nor did he ever want to know her or hear Jane speak of her again. Yet the passion of her kiss haunted him through the winter and spring.

Mallory Jones lived quietly in a spacious yellow farmhouse in Cambridge with his son, Jonathan, whom he grew to cherish more and more each day. With Houqua's help he had become one of the wealthiest men in America, yet he chose to live simply away from the bustle of Boston. There were many who said he was a recluse and an eccentric. The truth was that tragedy had tempered and quieted him, and now he preferred to keep his own counsel.

At home, Jones still dressed like a Chinese mandarin in his silk robes and slippers. He left the day to day work of Porter & Co. to his associates and spent hours reading and writing in his garden or playing with young Jonathan. Apart from delivering an occasional lecture at Harvard College on the Orient or receiving an occasional Sunday visit from the merchants and sailors who had been his friends in Canton, he saw almost no one but Jane.

She was young and devoted—a kind girl, not striking but pretty enough in a plain way—and he had grown fond of her. He was tired of living alone, but, more important, Jonathan liked her, and his son should have a mother.

Jane did not drive him wild with passion. He treated her circumspectly, not wanting to take advantage of her youth or her affection. When his immense needs were too powerful to deny, he did not take Jane. He rode into Boston and claimed a young Portugese whore for the entire night and often for most of the next day as well. The lusty Marielena was the best in Boston and she boasted that she was Mallory Jones's woman. So enormous were his needs that only she could meet them, she'd say proudly, and this only added to his exotic reputation in the community. But because Jones was so rich and so free with his coins, few criticized him openly. When he came into the Silver Dollar Bar where Marielena danced, everyone fawned on him. His aloofness seemed only to make them try harder to please.

On his first visit to the Silver Dollar, Jones had sat in a dark corner alone, drinking slowly, watching Marielena dance with indifferent eyes. He had only been in Boston a few days. No one knew who he was, and, with his inscrutable Oriental mask drawn over his face, no one was anxious to make his acquaintance.

Abruptly, in the middle of her performance, he had stood up and walked over to the stage. He betrayed no hint of desire, no suggestion of warmth or even interest. He simply dropped a twenty-dollar gold piece in her cleavage. "I want you for the night. Where is your room?" he said, his voice cold and emotionless, his eyes icy.

"One flight up, first door on the right," Marielena said, surprised by the cold stranger but thrilled by his gold piece, which was enough to buy her services for months.

What went on behind those closed doors that night Marielena never said, but from that night on she boasted that he was the richest, most passionate man in America and Mallory Jones became a frequent late night visitor to the notorious Silver Dollar.

After the Potters' Christmas party, Jones had escorted Jane Martin home and then went immediately to the Silver Dollar where, for the first time since he returned to Boston, he became very drunk and boisterous. He demanded that Marielena leave with him in the middle of her dance. The other drinkers gasped and then cheered as he lunged at the woman and ripped the scanty bra from her voluptuous bosom. He kept the girl working for two nights and days.

Yet, for all that, the memory of Samantha's kiss lingered on. Then one day in early spring, when he was riding in the hills, he stopped at an overlook to rest the horse and saw a couple riding in the field below. Their happy laughter floated up to him and he felt the surge of jealous anger rise in his heart.

Every day after that, Mallory Jones rode out to the overlook in the early afternoon and watched for Samantha. Sometimes she would be with George Potter, sometimes she would be alone, and when she was alone, she rode with a wild abandon—the same abandon, he remembered reluctantly, with which she had made love to him. He never made his presence known. He just watched from the distance, and that was how he happened to witness her accident.

He could see it happening even before it occurred and he called to her instinctively, knowing as he shouted that she would never hear him. Spurring his horse sharply, he galloped to her side. The years that had passed between them had only enhanced her beauty. But now she was lying white and motionless. He was sure that she was dead and he took her limp body in his arms and wept.

Mallory Jones wept inconsolably for the woman he loved as he had never loved any other, even the sweet Ming-la. He wept for the woman he would always love, whatever she was, whatever she had done, and as he did Samantha stirred slightly.

Jones's heart skipped joyfully. He rushed to the river, dipping his kerchief in the cool water, and, bringing it back, he laid it across Samantha's forehead. He slipped off her riding jacket and folded it in a pillow for her head. Then he gently wiped her face and neck with the wet cloth and, opening her blouse, he wiped her bosom. The purity of it astonished him as it always had before, but every thought and desire was concentrated in his efforts to awaken her.

When she opened her sea-green eyes and smiled up at him, his joy was immeasurable. She would be well, he knew.

Now, hidden by the darkness, he listened to her heartbroken whisper on the wind, "Don't leave me, Mallory, not again." He wanted to go to her. He wanted to forget everything, to possess her again and forever, and be possessed by her. No woman had ever consumed him with such furious passions of lust and love, of jealousy and hate. Marielena knew how to satisfy his superficial needs. Ming-la had enchanted him with her total submission. Jane comforted him with her devotion. But Samantha enslaved him, made him a captive of her heart. Only little Jonathan could keep him from her.

Her whispered words carried on the wind surprised and confused him. She had left him, after all, for Jean Levoir. She had abandoned their son for the same man. Wrapped in these disturbing thoughts, he rode home.

Mallory Jones sat alone in the garden long into the night. Finally, as the dawn broke, he tiptoed upstairs and slipped into his son's nursery. He stood at the foot of the trundle bed, looking down at the boy for a long time, then he bent over and kissed Jonathan's golden curls.

The following week the engagement of Mallory Jones to Miss Jane Martin was announced in the Boston papers.

CHAPTER THIRTY-FIVE

Little Jonathan Meets His Mother

Mallory Jones's behavior baffled and distressed Samantha. For five days and nights she had gone over and over it in her mind and it was still not clear to her. She kept to herself in her upstairs sitting room and, each time George called, she made Nora say she was indisposed.

For the second time in her life, Samantha had to face the cruel, unbearable truth—Mallory Jones, the man who awakened such devastating passions within her, did not love her and had never loved her. Now he had used her again, coldly, cruelly.

And yet . . . and yet, the face that looked into hers when she came around was not a cold, cruel face. The memory of his concern, his happiness when she awoke was clear in her mind, and the passion of his kisses, the fire of his fingers, the abandon of his love-making were real. Could he be this way with every woman? Samantha could not believe it. He had taught her love—

and lust. She had given into it once, almost twice, almost three times. But it was never like this, never the all-consuming fire he kindled within her.

Now that Mallory Jones had awakened her again, Samantha could never be content with the tame domestic life she would have with George Potter. George—lovable, charming, dear as he was—would never excite those wild passions within her. She could never live a halfway life. She realized now that she had been fooling herself and George all along. With her, it must be all or nothing. A tepid life would stifle her. But how could she tell George and what would she do without his infectious fun and friendship?

Samantha stayed in her upstairs suite all week, hoping against hope that Mallory Jones would call on her. But each day passed and only George visited. Finally when she realized it was heartless of her to put him off any longer, she went down-stairs to greet him.

"Samantha, I have missed you terribly," he said taking her hand and leading her to the sofa. "We have all been beside ourselves with worry. You know I have begged you not to ride Snow-star so fast when you are alone. Perhaps a less spirited mount would be better. Uncle Joseph says he has found the perfect one for you."

Samantha could not believe her ears. "You mean you want me to give up Snowstar?" she asked incredulously. The thought that anyone would suggest such a thing had never even occurred to her.

"But, darling, you could be thrown again, and not get away the next time with just a bruise. I can't ride with you every day."

"George, regardless of what Nora may have told you, it was not Snowstar's fault. It could have happened on any horse. In any case, there is nothing so frightening about taking a tumble once in a while. Now the subject is closed. I won't hear any more talk about taking Snowstar away. He is all I have," Samantha's voice broke suddenly and, unable to control her uneasy emotions, she began to cry.

"Oh, my darling, I did not mean to upset you. Don't cry. Of course you can keep Snowstar if you feel so deeply about him. You can have everything or anything in the world it is within my power to give you. Do I need to tell you that?"

George's words only made Samantha cry the harder. "You are too good for me, George," she sobbed. All the frustration and tension and disappointment she had kept bottled up inside her that week spilled over and she cried on his shoulder.

"Now, now, Samantha, no more tears. I won't mention Snowstar again and neither will Uncle or Aunt. Instead, I'll tell you all the latest gossip. So dry your eyes and perk up your ears, because you will never guess who has announced his engagement."

"Not you, George."

"Oh lord, Samantha, not I. I am still waiting for a word of encouragement," he smiled half-mischievously, half-sadly, and chucked her under the chin. "An even more unlikely candidate for the altar from what I hear from the yokels who frequent the Silver Dollar tavern and sample the joys of the buxom Marielena. Mallory Jones has announced his engagement to Jane Martin."

Samantha blanched. "What did you say?" she gasped faintly.

"Mallory Jones and Jane Martin are going to the altar," he said laughingly. "She will have her hands full from what I hear."

George went on cheerily, oblivious to Samantha's stunned reaction. Her heart was pounding so fast, she was sure he would notice something was wrong. But he rattled on as innocently as if he were reporting the weather.

"They say, the local gossips, that is, that he is marrying her because she is so fond of the child, and now that the boy is getting older he needs a fulltime mother, not just a nursemaid."

"What boy?" Samantha asked, her voice shaky and weak.

"Mallory Jones' son. Surely you heard, Samantha. He brought the child back with him when he returned from China. It was only an infant then—a beautiful child, everyone who has seen him says. But no one knows who the mother is, and no one dares ask. There is something so aloof about Jones, don't you think? Sometimes he seems like the friendliest man you could meet and the next moment he has put a distance between you that you think you can never bridge. So no one to my knowledge has dared ask who the mother is or where she is, although the rumor is that she was an Oriental girl who died before he left China. The child, of course, was illegitimate."

Samantha was in such a state of shock that she could barely comprehend the full meaning of what George was reporting.

"George," she said, interrupting his chatter, "Please forgive me, but I am getting a little dizzy again. I must not be over the fall yet. If you would excuse me, I would like to lie down."

"Certainly, Samantha. How thoughtless of me to tire you out with idle gossip. Do forgive me. May I help you up to your room?"

"No thank you, George, Nora will help me."

"Very well, my dear, but do take care of yourself. You are very precious to me, you know."

"I know, sweet George," she said, patting him fondly on the cheek. But thoughts of Mallory Jones and his son were swimming crazily in her head.

When George was gone, Samantha fled to the solitude of her room, trying to make sense out of all the contradictions. The mother had to be Houqua's daughter, and yet Mallory never told her he had a son, even when he was planting another child in her body.

Why was he marrying now? Why not months before or months later? Why now, when she could still feel his lips burning against hers? How could he be so heartless? How could he make love like that to her one week and marry another woman the next? How could she love a man like that?

And yet she did. She loved him even more fiercely knowing that he would soon be lost to her forever. And the boy . . . the boy. George's words rang in her head like a horrible chorus: "The rumor is that she was an Oriental girl who died before he left China."

Even then as he was caressing her, even when she had gone to his retreat in Macao and he had seemed so happy—so hungry for her lips, for her breasts, for her smooth stomach and long silken thighs and tawny mound that he had covered her body in kisses—even then, hidden somewhere close by, his son was lying, the son of Houqua's daughter, the son of the alabaster bust. No wonder he was so angry when he found her holding it. She was the mother of his son.

Even so, Samantha could not simply let him pass out of her life again. She had to make sense out of all the puzzles. She had to know once—and finally—if she had ever meant anything to him; if she did now. She could not live without ever tasting his desire again.

Recklessly, Samantha decided to go to him, however disastrous the consequences. Without telling Nora or any of the other servants that she was going out, Samantha slipped downstairs and saddled *Snowstar*. She was not at all sure where Mallory Jones lived, only that it was somewhere outside the city in Cambridge. But she had found him once before, she could find him again.

Samantha gave Snowstar his head as they crossed the Charles River to Cambridge and the white stallion flew through the fields. Soon they were farther from the city than she had ever dared to ride before. Blind instinct alone led her. But she was beginning to think it had steered her wrong when she saw two riders in the distance up ahead. She dug her heels sharply into Snowstar's flanks and the stallion shot forward, rapidly closing the gap between them. One rider was a small boy, the other looked to be a groom.

Samantha hoped the man would give her directions. She did not want to ask directly where Mr. Mallory Jones lived. A single woman riding like that would cause too great a scandal.

"Excuse me," she called as she drew along side him, "I seem to have ridden further than I realized and now I am quite hopelessly lost. Could you be kind enough to direct me to Cambridge and tell me if there is any house in the vicinity where I might stop for a drink of water?"

The groom looked at Samantha appraisingly. "You are a far cry from Cambridge, lassie," he said good-naturedly. "There is no home near here except my master's and he doesn't take kindly to strangers at best. Lately he has been in such a frightful temper, I don't dare offer to bring you back with me. Fine lady though you be, you would be safer by far going to the river for a drink. It is just a few miles south of here."

"Thank you for your kindness," Samantha said, "but if you don't mind my asking, who is this terrifying master of yours?"

"He is not really terrifying, ma'am. Usually he is the most charming man you could meet, but lately he is not fit for man or beast."

"And his name?" Samantha pressed.

"Mr. Mallory Jones," the groom said, "the richest man in Massachusetts they say, and this here is his young son."

Although he was only a toddler, the boy sat straight in his saddle and smiled enchantingly at Samantha. Golden curls framed summer blue eyes that she could never mistake. Whoever his mother was, the child was Mallory's son, she thought disconsolately. She had been hoping that he had adopted the boy for some reason and brought him home. But the child's eyes denied her wish.

"Thank you for your help," Samantha said to the groom and turned Snowstar in the direction of the river. But no sooner had he ridden

411

off than Samantha doubled back and, leaving a discreet distance between them, she trailed in their path until they turned into a tree-lined lane.

Now that she was so close to her destination, Samantha began to grow wary. *What if Jane is with him*, she wondered, *or he refuses to see me?* Putting her doubts out of her mind, she tethered Snowstar in the lane and, steeling herself for the encounter ahead, she forced herself to walk to the yellow house. The groom, she calculated, would have gone on to the stables by now and the boy would probably have been dispatched to the nursery. What would she say to Mallory Jones? How would she explain her sudden appearance at his door? Now that she was so close, Samantha wished she had not come. But it was too late to turn back. The house was just a few steps in front of her and there, standing on the front lawn by himself, watching her intently, was the child.

Samantha stopped dead when she saw his clear blue-eyed gaze, so much like his father's, fixed upon her.

"Where is your white horse?" he asked earnestly.

"Tied to a tree at the end of the lane," she answered, uncertain of how to talk to a small boy.

"Mine is eating in the barn," he said.

"And where is your father? Is he at home?"

"He is in the garden," the boy said, "I will show you." He held out his small, soft hand.

"You are a pretty lady," he said smiling up at her, and Samantha noticed something glimmering around his neck.

"What is that you have?" she asked.

"Flowers," he answered innocently, holding up the small enamel disk for her scrutiny.

Samantha did not have to read the inscription on the back. "Where did you get this?" she asked the child weakly.

"I was born with it, Father says." The little boy spoke clearly and brightly for such a young child. "It is pretty like my mother."

"Did your father tell you that?" she asked softly.

"Yes," the boy nodded. The pretty lady was still kneeling beside him and he touched her cheek gently. "Don't you want to see my father?" he asked her solemnly.

Samantha took the child's hand and allowed him to lead her. Why was he wearing the locket she had given to Owino? How did he get it, unless . . . unless? Her son would have been about the same age as this boy. *But he was dead. Aunt Maude said so herself. He was born dead, born dead; the child was born dead.*

The words beat against her brain as the little boy led her into the garden. Mallory Jones was sitting under an oak in his white silk mandarin robe, engrossed in his reading. He did not hear them approach until the child ran to him, pulling Samantha with him. "Father, Father," he called, "see the pretty lady I found."

413

When Mallory Jones saw his precious son standing in front of him holding his mother's hand, a furious rage swept through him. How dare she come here? What right had she to see the boy? His passion for Samantha was swept away by his anger, remembering how she had deserted the boy. *If she has come to take him from me, she will do so over my dead body*, he thought ominously.

"Son," he said gruffly, "Nurse is looking for you. Run inside and find her."

Mallory Jones watched silently until the boy was out of sight. Then he turned to Samantha to warn her never again to so much as lay eyes on the boy. But she was even paler than she had been when she lay in the field. He leaped up and caught her in his arms as she fainted, but there was no tenderness in his touch now. He slapped her sharply across the face to bring her around and shook her roughly.

"Why did you come here?" he demanded fiercely. "What do you want from us?"

"The boy, Mallory. You must tell me. Who is the boy?" Samantha's faint voice was urgent, pleading.

"He is my son, as you well know, although it never meant anything to you until this moment," he answered coldly.

"Mallory, the locket the boy wears . . ."

"Ah, you came for your locket. Very well, I will get it for you and then you can be gone," he said angrily and started toward the house. But Samantha grabbed his arm and clung to it.

"Where did you find it, Mallory? I must know," she begged, desperate now.

"Don't you remember who you gave it to, or do you dispense your favors so freely that you cannot keep track of what you have given to whom?" His tone was as icy as his eyes.

"Mallory," Samantha spoke softly, forcing herself to control her turbulent emotions, "I gave it to a young boy on the island of Pagalu. It is somewhere off the Ivory Coast of Africa on the other side of the Equator. He helped my aunt and me escape."

"That is not all he helped you do, I understand," Jones answered sharply.

"Who are you to judge me so harshly?" she lashed out at him, wanting to hurt him as he had hurt her. "You sent me away bearing your seed in my womb to be shipwrecked and enslaved on a barbaric island. Our child was born after only seven months—born dead." She spat out the words violently as if she were striking him with each syllable. "My shame died with the child and I vowed then I would die too rather than ever again be humiliated by any man."

Mallory Jones stared at Samantha in disbelief. *Her audacity is boundless*, he thought as he replied in a voice brimming with sarcasm, "So now you expect me to believe that our son, whom you named 'My Shame,' was born dead. Who

415

then should I presume is the child you saw to-day? A figment of my imagination?"

Samantha stared at him blankly.

"Enough of your play-acting, Samantha," he shouted angrily. "I don't know what you came here for or what you are trying to accomplish with this little game of yours, but, whatever it is, it won't work. You abandoned our son, a helpless baby, on a barbaric island and ran off to marry Levoir. But he proved more—or less—than you bargained for and now you have come here to take what is mine. You gave him up, Samantha, and you can never have him again. No court of law in the land would give a child to the mother who deserted him."

"Mallory," Samantha screamed hysterically, "our son is dead. He was born dead. Aunt Maude told me so herself." Sobs wracked her body and tears streamed down her tortured face.

Looking at her then, Mallory Jones realized he had misjudged his love. He did not know why she had come to him, he knew only and with utter certainty that she was telling the truth. He took her in his arms and pressed her closely against his broad chest, stroking her shimmering hair until her sobs quieted.

"Samantha," he asked gently, "who do you think the boy's mother is?"

"Houqua's daughter," she whispered.

"Ming-La's child died with her," he paused, "in a fire in Canton. It was more than two years later that I found Jonathan on the island of Pagalu." Mallory Jones voice was low and even.

Samantha looked up at him, her green eyes wide with wonder.

"Sit here with me," he said leading her to a chair under the oak, "and I will tell you the story."

CHAPTER THIRTY-SIX

Passion's Slaves

"In Canton, China," Mallory Jones began, "I met a girl, the most beautiful girl I have ever seen. She stood before me one night, her torn dress and petticoats lying on the floor at her feet, a brilliant flower I had wantonly plucked. I was astonished by the perfection of her form— the exquisite face, the long, slim body, the perfect breasts, the full round buttocks. I wanted to look on her beauty forever."

Samantha blushed to the roots of her lustrous hair and lowered her eyes shyly as he talked.

"It was a terrible time in my life and I treated the flower roughly. Even though I was cruel, the young bud opened in my hands and blossomed into a passion flower, with tempestuous desires as tremendous as my own.

"I took whatever she offered me, which was nothing less than her body and soul, and then I retreated. I dared not commit myself to another woman. I had destroyed one innocent girl in my

420

lifetime. I could not risk destroying her as well. And so I retreated.

"I watched from afar as she was drawn under the spell of another—a man whose character I knew was seriously flawed. Finally, when I heard she was leaving Canton to marry him, I could no longer hold back my violent passion.

"Under the pretext of returning a velvet ribbon, which I had hoped to cherish forever, I entered her boudoir unannounced. She had been living in my villa and many nights I lay on a straw mat in my solitary retreat imagining her drifting gracefully through the airy rooms. I knew, or I thought I knew, the room she would choose for her own. It was a bright, sun-filled corner room next to my own bed chamber where once I would sit writing home to my mother, telling her of the strange, very formal, deeply fascinating world I had come to know better than Boston.

"I would lie on my mat and imagine her filling the rooms with her wit and warmth and her unmatched beauty, and the picture in my mind, coupled with the memory of her passionate embrace, would kindle a tremendous fire in my limbs. I lusted for the taste of her skin and the touch of her hand on my flesh, and I wondered if she were lying in that room I loved so well feeling the same tremendous surge of desire for me. I had never known a more sensual woman."

Samantha's flush deepened to scarlet as he

spoke. Mallory's blunt, sexual talk embarrassed and excited her. He seemed so calm, so cool, and yet his words were a steamy torrent that aroused her as surely as his hands. She loved the words he spoke, words she had never thought she would hear, and yet she was not sure she could listen to them anymore and still control the storm of emotion they raised inside her. She wanted to hear how he had longed for her, lusted for her, tormented himself with desire for her. Yet, at the same time, she wanted to show him what she had felt, still felt, would always feel for him.

Mallory Jones smiled at Samantha and reached for her hand. Kissing the open palm, he said softly, "Where were these pretty fingers, Samantha, when I was lying in my cabin sick with hunger for you? Tell me, darling, where did they stray?"

Samantha sensed an undercurrent of anger, a fine line of metal in his tone. But the touch of his lips and the hint of his tongue on her hand made her unwilling to resist him. She felt that he was manipulating her, teasing her, playing with her, sure now that her passion for him was undiluted by any of his cruelties or misunderstandings.

For the first time she understood that if he knew her body had risen to the touch of other hands, her fingers had embraced the flesh of other men, he would not want her. Ming-la was a virgin to him forever. No other man had ever touched her. She belonged to him alone. She had never looked at another man with desire.

Samantha could not say the same and she realized now that Mallory's jealousy would be as powerful as his desire. If he knew what she had gone through, the lusts she had felt, would his desire for her be as strong as his anger, or would the anger win out and would he abandon her again? Could she take that risk? Could she chance losing him again when she had just found him?

"How many men have these long, lovely fingers strayed to, Samantha? How many have they stroked and lingered over?" His clasp tightened around her hand until his knuckles turned white and through his grip she felt the furious currents of his jealous heart.

"While you were lying in your cabin thinking of me," Samantha answered, her eyes still lowered and her cheeks still flushed, "these fingers you are crushing were following the path yours had taken, hoping to recapture the unfamiliar, unforgettable feelings you stirred."

She looked up at him shyly through her half-raised eyes; a flicker of a wise, knowing smile played at the corners of her mouth. Laughing, a deep, rich, sensual laugh, he stood up and pulled her into his arms.

"You are a vixen, an enchantress, a passionate devil, a wild wench hidden by your fine clothes and aristocratic face."

Still laughing, he picked her up and carried her into the house and up the winding stairs.

423

Evening had descended. The house was dark and quiet. The child and his nurse were sleeping.

Mallory lit a taper on the table beside his wide teak bed. The candlelight glowed warmly across the comfortable room and lighted Samantha's eager eyes. Boldly, deliberately, she started to undress.

Samantha stood in the center of the room as she had in Macao, but now she was a different woman, proud of her body and of the beauty she possessed to give to her love. Mallory sat on the edge of the bed, mesmerized by her beauty and her boldness, and watched with mounting desire as Samantha slowly, provocatively undressed. First her riding jacket dropped to the floor, then her cravat, boots, blouse, breeches, until she stood willowy and breathtaking in nothing but her lacy undergarments.

She reached up and unpinned her hair. The tawny locks fell loosely around her face and shoulders. She raised the chemise over her breasts. Naked now, except for a single garment, she paused and smiled tantalizingly at him, then slowly she drew down her panties and stepped out of them. Tossing her hair back behind her shoulders, she stood revealed before him, allowing him to savor the fullness of her beauty, to feast his eyes on her gentle curves. Slowly, shamelessly, she walked toward him and, cupping her breasts in her hands, she offered them to him.

At the first stroke of his cool tongue, her nipples rose like tiny swords. He ran his hands along the smooth curve of her hip until he reached her secret mouth.

"Is this where your lovely fingers strayed?" he asked wickedly. "Let's see how deep their trail goes."

Samantha trembled with desire as his fingers explored her hidden recesses, her fragrant, dewy cave, and then she could wait no longer, and she opened his mandarin robe. His chest was bare underneath it, as it had been the first time in Macao. They lay naked, their bare bodies undulating against each other.

"What do you want, Samantha?" he asked her again, kissing her lips and her neck and her eyes and her hair. "Tell me, my beautiful blossom, my passion flower, what do you want from me?"

"I want you," she whispered, "I want you to make love to me and never stop, and I want to make love to you and never stop."

She raised her hips up to meet the thrust of his huge passion and he penetrated her, driving deeper and deeper, until she groaned and clutched his firm, muscular buttocks. Her nails dug into his demanding flesh and they were lost in the wildness of their love, abandoned to an ecstasy Samantha knew she could never live without again or forsake or relinquish, whatever the future brought.

They lay together spent yet exhilarated. Sweet exhaustion swept over them and they clung to each other, their bodies still entwined, still tingling from the thrill of their union.

"I was such a fool to ever let you go, my love," Mallory Jones said, his low voice caressing her warmly. "Can you ever forgive the violence of my passion for you, the cruelty and abuse I made you suffer? I could not offer myself to you in China. It frightened me. It was still too soon after Ming-la. I could not offer myself to anyone else. Yet I could not refuse the intensity of your passion. Oh, my darling, was there ever a woman whose desire burned as hotly as yours?"

"You consumed me, my love," Samantha whispered sensually, "consume me again," and her hands began to move hungrily along his body and her breasts pressed invitingly against his.

Mallory Jones took her in his arms again. "When I watched you leave China," he said, "I realized too late how much I love you, and I made up my mind to follow you to the ends of the earth if I had to. To kill the treacherous Levoir and plead for your hand, beg you to marry me. And so, after fifteen years, I left Canton to find you."

He paused, breathing deeply for a moment and then went on: "Instead, I found our son, abandoned. You were gone in a tall ship across the sea to Paris, I was told. You can imagine what I thought. I never wanted to set eyes on you again and I came back to Boston with the boy. I had almost succeeded in putting you out of my mind completely, when I found you in Paris."

At the memory of that debauched scene, he

pressed her so tightly in his arms Samantha thought he would crush her.

"Thank God, you remember little of that nightmare. I cannot bear to remember it either, although it is etched forever in my mind," he murmured. "But I knew that you had gone freely to Levoir and so I returned to Boston, more determined than ever to erase you from my mind forever.

"I almost succeeded," he smiled, "until we met again at the Potters' Christmas party. I treated you terribly again, Samantha, I know. In part I think it was because you were even more ravishing than I remembered. When you kissed me, after all that had come between us, your mouth seemed to mock my love. I think at that moment I hated you, and yet, ever since, I have been haunted by you. The taste of your kiss lingered on, tempting me like a taunt which I could neither forget nor respond to."

"And now?" Samantha asked, her eager, loving eyes searching his face for the answer she longed to hear.

She felt his body slacken in her arms. "I don't know, Samantha," he said, anguish clouding his extraordinary eyes. He pulled away from her embrace and sat on the side of the bed, his head buried in his hands.

"Oh, God, I don't know," he cried aloud as if he was calling on the heavens to free him from his torment, to give him the assurance that he needed.

Samantha lay motionless on the bed, shocked by his response. "Is it your fiancée?" she asked, biting her lip and fighting to hold back her tears.

"No, no Samantha" he squeezed her leg reassuringly, "there is no woman in the world who could keep me from you. Jane is a fine girl and I know she cares for me. But she is young. She has not felt the torrents of passion yet and she will, in time, love again—and more wisely, I hope."

"Then what is it, Mallory?" Samantha pleaded. "You love me. I know you love me. You must tell me, darling, you can't just walk out of my life again."

Mallory Jones pulled on his dressing gown and paced the floor furiously, his blue eyes shining wildly, his face distraught.

"How do I know, Samantha, how do I know it is me?" he cried. "You call out in your passion, you seem to hunger for me, your desire is as savage as my own. It thrills me. I cannot refuse it. I cannot turn away from it." He bent over her and raised her up in his arms, clutching her violently. "But I don't want it," he swore. "I don't want it, if you are like this with other men."

He let her go and she dropped softly into the pillows. Samantha lay, looking up at her love, her eyes deep wells of tears, her thick hair spread over the pillows.

"I love you, Mallory Jones," she said clearly,

flatly. There was no passion or pleading in her voice. "I have always loved you. Is it wrong that you drive me wild with desire? I can't help myself," she said. "Do you wish that I could?" She reached up and drew him to her and their lips merged and mingled in a long, loving kiss.

"Samantha," Mallory said, his voice husky with emotion, "are you sure it is me you love and not love itself?"

"I have never loved anyone but you," she murmured softly, "I have never belonged to anyone but you."

Mallory Jones's eyes pierced her soul. "Never lie to me, Samantha," he said in a low, ominous tone. He held her gaze for a long, searching moment, then he said, "There was a boy on Pagalu, a young boy who cared for Jonathan. He said the child's mother had a beauty mark right . . ." he pulled the sheet down not roughly, but reluctantly, "right there." He pointed to the dark circle on her white belly. "There is only one way he could have known that," he said, turning away and staring into the dark night. "And then there was Levoir, and your husband, and George Potter—I saw how his lips replaced my own at Christmas—and I don't know how many more.

"How can I believe you have never belonged to anyone but me? I have to know. I have to know the truth."

Samantha looked at the man she loved, his

429

tormented face now silhouetted against the window. If she told him the truth, the whole truth, she would lose him. If she lied to him, he would know it.

"Yes, Mallory," she confessed, "I have known other men. Some have forced themselves on me, as you well know. Others I have chosen. But there is only one whom I have loved. The same one I love tonight, now and forever. Isn't that enough for you? My heart, my soul, my body? What more can I give you?"

"Your memories, Samantha. I don't want you to remember anyone but me."

"I don't."

"I cannot bear to think of you giving yourself to anyone else. Any other hands touching you, caressing you. Any other man pleasing you. Don't you understand? I must know the truth no matter how awful it is, or the questions, the doubts, will stand between us forever. Tell me, Samantha, each man that touched you—what he did, what you did, what you felt. Don't try to spare me. No truth could be worse than my imaginings."

In spite of her unquenchable love, Mallory's persistent questioning angered Samantha. After all, he was the one who had initiated her so brutally and she did not demand to be told about the women he had known—had loved.

"Very well," she responded coldly, "I will tell you, although it is not a very pretty story. I became a woman one moonlit night on the side

430

of a hill in Macao, China, by a man who took me brutally by force, and again . . . "

Mallory winced as if she had struck him. "I deserve that, darling, and worse," he said contritely. "You are right. I have no right to ask you these things and you have no need to tell me. It is just that I love you so much, I am overcome with selfishness. I don't want to share you. I cannot bear to think that you have felt this passion, surrendered yourself with such abandon to anyone else."

"I haven't, I couldn't," Samantha said. "Only you waken the lusty beast that slumbers in my bosom. But I will tell you whatever you want to know as best I can."

The intuition that has protected every woman since Eve told Samantha what memories to confess and what memories to omit as she related to Mallory Jones her daring, dangerous odyssey from China to Boston. When she was finished, she lay back quietly in the pillows and waited for his response.

The sun was beginning to rise over the horizon and his summer blue eyes were shining with tears. Without a word, he drew back the sheet and exposed the full beauty that so many men had tried to possess. His eyes embraced her creamy flesh for a long time and then, turning her over tenderly, his mouth covered the flesh of her full round cheeks where the lashes of the fat man had struck.

Wherever her body had been touched by

431

another, he banished the memory with his mouth until she knew only his burning lips. Then Mallory Jones parted her tawny forest and claimed Samantha for his own.

EPILOGUE

The marriage of Samantha Shaw Thomson and Mallory Porter Jones was the talk of Boston. The bride, radiant in a fluid buttercup silk gown, was escorted to the altar by Joseph Potter and an intimate, jubilant champagne celebration at the Potters' gracious home followed the ceremony.

George Potter had returned to London the previous week to take over his father's firm. But he stole his kiss from the bride-to-be before he left. George's pleasure in seeing Samantha glow with joy at last outweighed his own disappointment. He had always put her happiness above his own, and even now he did not fail her.

Down at the Silver Dollar, Marielena was boasting that the groom would be back the day after his wedding night. But when Mallory Jones took Samantha into their marriage bed, he knew he had found the answer to his every desire.

His brilliant eyes were glowing with love and

anticipation as he rose enormously over her. "Home, at last, Mrs. Jones," he murmured happily.

"Yes, Mr. Jones," Samantha smiled wickedly, opening her creamy thighs wide, "and the home fires are burning."

Special Preview!

PASSION'S PROUD CAPTIVE
by Melissa Hepburne

*The following pages are excerpts edited from the first chapters of this new novel scheduled for publication in July, 1978.**

Jennifer struggled wildly to break free from the grip of the two sweating, smelly sailors as they dragged her down the ship's narrow passageway toward the ladder to the upper deck. She did manage for a moment to break away, after kicking the bearded one in the shin. But there was nowhere to escape to. Desperately, she ran back down the passageway a few paces, but then they had her again and the bearded one twisted her arm viciously behind her back. "You filthy Colonial slut," he sneered, as he marched her forward.

He would have beaten her mercilessly, Jennifer thought through her agony and despair, but for the fact that the ship's captain was still standing at the far end of the passageway, stern-faced, hands at his hips, supervising her transport to the upper deck. The punishment she would suffer, she knew, would be at the Captain's pleasure, not that of a lowly seaman.

She had gone too far this time, she was sure. She should never have slapped the Captain. But what else could she have done? The long-faced, rough-skinned mariner had come into her tiny cabin and, this time, had not stopped at the lewd overtures he made toward her, but had become physical. He had come up to her and without any warning put his cupped hands to her breasts, over her clothes, and squeezed them gently.

She had slapped him stingingly, instinctively, without thinking, and that was when he had yelled for the two sailors to come into the room. "To the deck with her!" he ordered in a rage. "Bind her to the mast!"

Captain Trevor stopped directly in front of Jennifer, who had to crane her neck back painfully against the mast to see him. A tense hush fell over the ship as the Captain reached down with a crop he was carrying in his hand to the hem of her frilly, high-necked brown dress. Slowly he raised the hem of her dress, and the petticoats beneath, up to above her knees. A sharp exhaling of breath and an appreciative murmur emanated from the crowd, along with several low whistles. The seamen's eyes were wide, their attention rapt.

The Captain, looking at his audience, grinned sardonically. He stuck his hand in under the hem of the dress and then let it fall back down into place, so that his hand was inside her dress, hidden from view.

For a long moment there was no movement, no sound, no change in Jennifer's expression. Then suddenly she let out all her breath and yelped in horrified surprise, her mouth remaining wide open. The Captain's hand was still invisible from view.

The sight lasted but a fraction of a second, and then the hem of the dress was quickly dropped and his hand removed. Jennifer was panting for breath and sobbing unrestrainedly, in burning shame and humiliation. She had never been touched by any man before. She had never been exposed to a man's eyes. And now, to be laid bare and abused like *this*, before a horde of filthy, drooling beasts.

Jennifer felt strips of leather against her skin, as the First Mate placed his cat-o'-nine tails above her naked white backside, letting the strips of raw leather dangle down so that they touched her in intimate places.

The Captain came around in front of her and moved forward quickly, so that the crotch of his britches brushed against Jennifer's lips before she could jerk her head away. There was a hard, roll-shaped swelling behind the britches. He squatted down to face her at eye level and said with sneering superiority, "Does the representative of the Colonies care to submit now . . . or later?"

437

Jennifer looked at the mob of lusting seamen, staring feverishly at her degradation and nakedness. No, she thought through her terror and agony and humiliation, she could have done nothing differently. She had done what she had to do. And now she would take what Providence had in store for her. She hawked up all the saliva in her parched throat and spit it into the Captain's face.

"*Aaarrr!*" he roared, reeling backward, jerking his sleeve up to wipe his face. "Flail the bitch!" he shrieked. "Whip her skinless!"

A shout of approval rose from the seamen. The First Mate raised his whip high, the leather straps swishing up in the air, and then, laughing maniacally, he jerked it violently downward.

But the whip leathers did not slash forward. They seemed caught on something. The First Mate turned in startled puzzlement and saw that a strong-featured, blond-haired man had come up behind him and grasped hold of the whiplashes. A look of utter disbelief registered on the First Mate's face as the blond man smashed the heel of the drawn sword he was holding in his other hand into the center of the Mate's forehead, knocking him down unconscious.

An angry roar went up from the surprised seamen and they surged forward. But instantly a black-haired man with a scar on his cheek sprang forward with a dagger that he jerked against the Captain's throat. "Have them hold!" he ordered.

"You'll be hanged for this, you pirate!" the Captain yelled at the black-haired man.

At this, the blond man, who was just finishing cutting the lashes from Jennifer and helping her to her feet, said in a heavy French accent, "Excuse me, *mon Captain,* but if you please, thees eez no pirate. He eez Lancelot Savage, a captain in ze Americain Navy."

*　*　*

Jennifer had never known anyone like Savage. His brooding, intense manner . . . the flashes of charming boyishness that sometimes surfaced through his ruthless masculinity . . . the dashing heroic way he had rescued her . . . all these things struck an emotional chord in her. She felt a powerful feeling of deep affection for him. But she felt anger, too, at the way he refused to give any sign of feeling similarly toward her.

Did he have any deeper feelings for her at all, she wondered. Yesterday she had caught him in an unguarded moment, gazing at her with a look of strong affection and caring. Then when she casually asked what plans he had for his future now that his wound was almost healed, he answered in an unexpectedly harsh, stern voice, "My future involves my men and my ship, and a war, and a *damn* good chance of getting killed. Let's not pretend it's otherwise. It wouldn't be fair to y—" He broke off the sentence, unfinished.

As she was remembering this now, Jennifer suddenly heard a loud crashing sound. She jerked upright in the bed, her body tense. Something heavy had been thrown against the wall in Silas's room, as if in frustration. She heard footsteps upon the wooden floor. She saw a hint of movement at her doorway, and looking there, she gasped and jerked the blanket up to her chin.

Savage stood in the doorway, illuminated by the yellow glow from the fireplace. His lean, powerful body was stark naked. He stood rigidly with his legs braced apart, hands down at his sides closed into fists. His handsome face, which at times could look so boyish, now looked gauntly masculine and menacing, his cheeks sunken, lips pressed together in a hard, unyielding line. It was the face of a jungle animal that knew only one law: the urgency of its own need.

Jennifer was crying uncontrollably, trying to curse him through her tears and sobs. She clutched the rumpled blanket from the base of the bed and pulled it over her, her legs curled up to her chin as she lay on her side. "You bastard," she sobbed. "Oh, you bastard!"

He said nothing. His expression was that of a man who has done what he set out to do, but was not at all happy about it. He turned and left the room.

She lay awake all the rest of the night, huddled in her bed with the blanket wrapped tightly around her, still trembling from the violent sensations that had wracked her body. The sensations had been unlike anything she had ever experienced. She had not known such feelings were possible.

Her mind wanted to dwell on the feelings, to recall in intimate detail the things that lean, muscular animal had done to her body to make her feel this way . . . but she forced herself to turn away from such thoughts. At the

439

back of her mind she knew there was grave danger in admitting to herself the way she felt. It went against all she had been raised to think of as right and proper.

She must fight the memory of what tonight's brutal, degrading rape had made her feel. Even so, she knew that the true way she felt about it would always be with her, at the back of her mind, threatening to come out. Something powerful had been awakened within her and she would always have to be on guard against it. She would resist the feelings with all her might, hold them down in the deep recesses of her soul, no matter what it took!

* * *

Without warning the Governor went behind her, bent down, and stuck his hands under the hem of her pink dress and petticoats. He rose quickly and grasped her buttocks tightly through the thin cloth of her underdrawers. Jennifer yelped in shock and tried to turn, but he was clutching her too tightly. Finally, she managed to jerk around and step away from him, her eyes wide in horrified outrage, her mouth open. She raised her hand to slap him—but then hesitated in midmotion, her hand just inches from his face.

The Governor smiled maliciously at her hesitation. "You do have an idea what this is all about then, don't you?"

She slapped him. Then she rushed for the giant double doors, only to find them locked. She turned back to face him, breathless and fearful, her palms and back pressed against the doors. "You can't do this," she said under her breath. "Even a Governor can't rape a citizen—"

He laughed an evil, sneering laugh. "Rape?" he scoffed. "That will hardly be necessary." He went over to the windows overlooking the courtyard and drew aside the brown velvet curtains. Jennifer looked out and now saw the source of the thumping sounds emanating from the courtyard. Lancelot Savage was down on the ground, his hands manacled, being beaten by two large, burly guards. His expression as each new blow landed on his body was one of pure agony.

Jennifer screamed in shock and revulsion, then covered her mouth with her fist. "Make them stop!" she cried. The Governor did not budge. She said it again, this time with pleading in her voice. "Make them stop!"

The Governor smiled. He came forward and put his hands on her breasts, over the thin bodice of her dress.

440

Jennifer started to pull away from him, but the sight of Savage being beaten to death in the courtyard below made her stop. She forced herself to remain motionless, her face wincing in torment.

The Governor smiled even more maliciously. As Jennifer stood there, he pushed her shawl off onto the floor, then unlaced the front of her dress slowly, as if time meant nothing to him. Then he jerked down the bodice and the white chemise beneath it. He pulled the bodice and chemise down to just below her breasts. Her full young bosom stood nakedly exposed, rising and falling with her quickened, fearful breathing. The Governor looked her right in the eye, smiling as he put his hands to her breasts and began squeezing and kneading them. He pinched her nipples, hard. She tried, but could not stifle the groan that came to her lips. Still she did not pull away from him.

In keeping with his end of the unstated agreement, the Governor now went over to the window, opened it, and yelled down to the guards below. "Cease that barbarism, you heathen scum! This is a civilized age. Prisoners are not beaten . . ." he closed the window and pulled the drapes shut again, then turned back to Jennifer. ". . . Only hanged," he concluded.

Jennifer now stood with her arms crossed in front of her, a hand on each shoulder. The Governor slowly walked around her, looking at her appreciatively. "You will be my mistress," he said, "for a period of one year. In return, I will pardon your pirate from the gallows. And when the year you spend with me is over, I will let him go free."

Jennifer said nothing. Tears welled up in her eyes and streamed down her cheeks. She pressed her arms tighter against her breasts, as if that somehow protected them.

"Come, come," demanded the Governor harshly. "I haven't all day. Do you accept my conditions or do you not? I'd really as soon hang the bugger anyway."

Jennifer's eyes showed her agony. She could not make herself speak. Slowly, with deep anguish, she nodded her head.

"Excellent," said the Governor. He grasped her dress and chemise and jerked them down past her hips to her knees. His hands went to her petticoats and pulled them down also to around her knees.

She could not just stand still and take it! It was impossible! When his hands reached for her underdrawers, she lost control and shoved them away. She tried to scratch his face. He grasped her wrist. She swung at him with her other hand, nails bared, and he grasped that, too, then pushed her backward until her buttocks and shoulder blades slammed up against the wall.

"A spirited one, eh?" he said, grinning cruelly, his face almost touching hers. "Fine, fight me if you can. It'll only make your degradation all the sweeter when I finally break you. And break you I will! I'll have you cringing and broken long before your year is through!"

* * *

At the mercy of a man she despises, Jennifer makes a supreme sacrifice and becomes a prisoner of lust. It was but the beginning of unspeakable humiliations that she would endure. Her beautiful, voluptuous body would excite many others, driving them to acts of unbridled passion . . . shattering her very innocence . . . igniting fires she would struggle desperately to control . . . reducing her to a hopeless captive of her own unquenchable hungers—until love set her soul free!